T0114178

# HUNTER'S GOLD

*by* Barrie Harmsworth

Trafford
PUBLISHING™

Order this book online at www.trafford.com
or email orders@trafford.com

Most Trafford titles are also available at major online book retailers.

Note for Librarians: A cataloguing record for this book is available from Library
and Archives Canada at www.collectionscanada.ca/amicus/index-e.html

Printed in the United States of America.

ISBN: 978-1-4251-1627-9 (sc)


*Trafford rev. 04/29/2011*

 www.trafford.com

**North America & international**
toll-free: 1 888 232 4444 (USA & Canada)
phone: 250 383 6864 ♦ fax: 812 355 4082

## Chapter One

# Off to England

Myna birds screeched in the lone green tree under which squatted a flock of little Arab boys. They waited on the sandy bank until a barge loaded with timber drew level. Ignoring the threat from the propellers of the tugboat, with yells and shouts of excitement they surged into the water like otters. Wearing nothing else but loose, white, cotton boxer shorts, when they reached the barge, they clung to it and were dragged through the water.

Some of the braver ones climbed on board despite the angry protestations of the crew who tried to chase them off. Running around the deck, their wet, brown lithe bodies shimmering like fish in the bright sunlight, their white shorts, almost translucent, revealed their strong buttocks. With more shouts and yells, they dived from the barge, some even somersaulting in the air before hitting the water. Finally, the barge surged towards the sea and the crowd of young Arabs swam back to the sandy beach.

Exuberantly pushing and shoving each other, they ran up the bank towards an old building sitting back from the Creek. Under an ancient tap connected to a rusted iron water tank, they washed. Under its feeble flow, they fought to clean off the salt water. Overhead, the seagulls wheeled and cried against the bright blue sky.

On the opposite bank sat the old coral limestone buildings of Shindaga. They were neglected and rundown. Around them were groups of Arabs in shabby *dishdashas*. Several large, wooden-hulled dhows lying on their sides were being worked on by a mixed crew of Indian and Arab tradesmen.

A bell sounded and the young Arabs idled towards the school building, picking up their *dishdashas* from the rocks where before they'd slung them as they raced for the Creek waters. Lethargically, they pulled them over their heads and wandered into the classroom.

They slumped into the dilapidated wooden chairs behind the old school desks. Above them, punkawallah fans hanging from the ceiling slowly rotated in silence. In front of the class, a small elderly Indian with greying hair and dressed in a black suit mumbled in English the words of Robert Louis Stevenson's *Treasure Island* as he read from the book cupped in his hands. Most of the class understood very little, and some began to drop off to sleep in the warm, humid atmosphere.

Only one young Arab at the front sat alert and attentive. Although he did not understand every word, he could pick up the story. English and mathematics were his favorite subjects and he was by far the best in his class. Since he showed interest in the subjects, the old teacher often stayed behind and coached him. In six months time there would be an exam for the English Curriculum School Certificate and he would probably be the only one who stood a chance of passing.

Closing the book, the teacher faced the class. "Who is the pirate that becomes the friend of Jim?" As expected, only one hand went up, "Yes, Ali Essa?" The response was quick and nearly accurate. "Long Jones Silver, sir." Smiling, the teacher nodded. "Long John Silver, that is correct. Well done." From behind him came hisses and threats from the rest of the class. Ali Essa Al Ghofran ignored them.

He was slightly older and physically much bigger than most of them. His father was a trader, as was his grandfather, who had made and lost a small fortune in pearls. Now the family lived in a small rundown compound not far from the school. Ali Essa's uncle was captain of a large trading dhow and he'd already taught Ali Essa how to fight and use a knife. Few of the boys in the class would have been willing to take him on.

Not that he was a physical person. On the contrary, Ali Essa made friends with everyone. Patient to a fault, he often withstood physical assault by some of his protagonists rather than fight back.

Nobody was surprised when only Ali Essa passed the exams. Not only did he pass but he also received distinctions in English and mathematics. Reading was his favorite pastime and he'd read the books his teacher had bought from England and America. Books like *Huckleberry Finn* and Robert Louis Stevenson's other famous book, *Kidnapped,* had really taken his fancy. Algebra was his first love in mathematics; solving neat equations was really satisfying to him.

When not at school, he would help his father in his store on the Creek. Occasionally, a ship's captain or another trader would come with a complicated English contract or document. With pride, Ali Essa's father would get his son to translate, refusing money for the service and basking in the pride of their adulation of his son's prowess.

Raj Kumar, his teacher, sat in front of Ali Essa's father in the store. "Saif, your boy is very intelligent and a good student. I know you would want him to work for you in your business, but without being…how shall I say…without being rude—you are a good man and will understand—he will be wasted."

Ali Saif eyed the old teacher carefully. You could never be too sure. Raj Kumar was an Indian, even though he had lived in Dubai since he was a young boy. "Raj Kumar, I believe you may be right. Allah has blessed my son with the brains I have never had. Pray go on."

Making himself comfortable on the stool in front of Saif's rather untidy desk in the shop on the Creek, the Indian elaborated. "The boy should study for his Higher School Diploma. He can come back to school and I will personally teach him." Curious, Saif eyed him even more carefully. "And?"

Sensing his distrust, the teacher tried to reassure him. "You are wrong Saif. I do not want money. All my life I have taught boys who will be nothing more then fishermen. This is a rare chance. Ali Essa is a rare student."

Again Saif wasn't too sure. It was true what the teacher had said. Most boys would only be fishermen or perhaps traders. None of them cared for a proper education. "Tammam, Raj Kumar. But I will pay. Nobody need give me charity, but you must teach my boy well."

For the following term, Ali Essa sat with the new intake of first-year students. At first, he was self-conscious but gradually, as Raj Kumar took more interest in him, he forgot the others. Whenever the old teacher had to leave the class, he invariably left Ali Essa in charge. That was when he began to realize what a difficult and unsatisfying task the old man had in front of him with each intake.

For his examinations, he had to go to the British High Commission and sit with the small gaggle of British expatriate children who were also taking the Diploma exams. Shy at first, he was encouraged by being able to speak English with them.

It wasn't as difficult as he'd thought. Sweating with fear and nerves, each day he ploughed through the exam papers. Almost with a sigh of relief, he picked up the algebra paper. At least this was more like his world. Slightly amazed, he watched the majority of the small clump of candidates leave after five minutes. Putting his head down, some one hour later when the time was up, he was confident he'd finished all the questions.

Upon receiving the results, Ali Essa's father celebrated. He bought a lamb in the market that was slaughtered and cooked along with a huge rice dish. All the neighbors were invited and Raj Kumar was the guest of honor. Never in the history of the Ghofran family had any son achieved such academic standards.

During the festivities, Saif approached Raj Kumar. "Thank you, Raj Kumar. It has filled our family with great pride, but what will my son do now?" The teacher took the trader's hand. "I thought you would ask me that, Saif. He could become a teacher, but although I do not regret my chosen profession, I would not wish it on Ali Essa. I have a friend, one Britisher who is in charge of the police force. With your permission, I will introduce Ali Essa to him."

Taken aback, Saif looked worried. "What? My son become a policeman?" Raj Kumar tightened his grip on the father's hand.

"A police officer." Saif stood looking at the teacher. "Meaning?" Smiling, the other man tried to sooth him. "A highly respected man, well-trained and looking after the welfare of our community. Maybe answering directly to the Sheik."

Saif was silent for a moment. His brushes with the local force that had taken over from the Oman Trucial Scouts were not pleasant. Mind you, he had been breaking the law. How would he tell his brother, who had been caught by the Indian Customs when he was smuggling gold and had spent five years in Bombay prison? That was another thing! Looking around, he saw the others. Most would not amount to anything and Dubai was beginning to grow. A police officer. Regular good salary, respect and power. Maybe answering to the Sheik. Why not? "Yes, Raj Kumar. Please speak to your friend."

It was a week later. The old teacher sat upright in front of the British adviser's desk.

"Thank you, Raj. Yes, his results look very encouraging, and your report of his character is even more so."

Sipping his tea, the old teacher smiled. "Thank you, Jack. He is a rare boy. Studious, patient and, as you can see, tall and healthy." The British adviser nodded his head in agreement. "Very good. I'll run it past the Sheik. Best to check. Maybe some family or political agenda I'm not aware of. Otherwise, yes. Bring him back in a week's time."

Ali Essa's father was speechless. He'd never seen his son dressed in anything else but a *dishdasha*, but now, here in front of him, stood his son in a police cadet's uniform. So splendid he looked! The whole family trooped in to see him, and the women were abuzz with excitement.

After he'd been accepted, Ali Essa was taken off to training camp for three months of solid training to get him fit and disciplined. Run by a British ex-sergeant major from the Trucial Scouts, it was tough. Almost too tough. Of the thirty boys who'd joined, only twenty were left, and several of those didn't look like they'd last. Surprisingly, Ali Essa didn't find the discipline all that difficult. It was as if he was used to being pushed and shoved around.

On one occasion, though, it was nearly too much. In the desert, in forty-five degrees centigrade heat, they'd marched till they dropped. Five minutes later, they were back on their feet again. Wanting to give up, in his mind he could hear Raj Kumar's advice: "It's all for a purpose, Ali Essa. Don't falter or quit. It's all for a purpose." Just when he thought he could not go on, the camp appeared over the top of the horizon. Only nine of them had made it; he was the first.

Each day Ali Essa would report to the assigned police station where he'd been to carry out his duties and learn. Those who proved to be the best five out of the twenty whom were left would go to England for further training. Ali Essa badly wanted to be one of those.

Some month's later; he was entering by the back door of the old Bur Dubai station. As he stepped in the door, he was confronted by a skirmish between five policemen and two huge Pakistanis. Suddenly, the bigger of the two wrenched a pistol from one of the policemen's holster and without hesitation shot the man. The other four policemen froze.

Nodding to his accomplice, the armed Pakistani held the four at bay while the other prisoner picked up a rifle. Keeping guard on their captives, the two of them backed cautiously towards the door where Ali Essa stood half-hidden. When the bigger man was close enough, Ali Essa leaped on him with a shout. Flinging his arms around the man, with all his strength he forced the escapee's arms down to his side.

A loud shot rang out, followed by a scream. The force of Ali Essa's attack had caused the man to shoot himself in the foot. Wailing in agony, he doubled over then fell to the ground, taking Ali Essa with him. Startled, the other criminal dropped the rifle and raised his hands in surrender. In a flash, the four policemen leaped at them.

Disentangling himself, Ali Essa struggled to his feet and leaned, gasping for breath, against the wall. Straining hard, he could not stop himself from trembling all over with delayed shock and fear. On the floor, the big Pakistani continued to yell and writhe in pain. As he did, blood splattered all over the walls and the policemen, who finally, subdued both of them and unceremoniously dragged them, handcuffed, into a cell.

That night, Ali Essa, his father, his uncle and friends were seated around the *majlis*. For fear of his father's disapproval, Ali Essa had not told him of the incident at the station. While they sat, the servant entered and announced that Abdul Rashid was at the gate.

"Show him in. Show him in immediately. Why have you left him at the gate? *Yallah!*"

Smiling broadly, Abdul Rashid strode into the room. In traditional greeting, he moved around and shook the hands of each member of the group as they rose to meet him. Known to them all, he was the head of the Sheik's private guard.

With well-accustomed grace, he sat by Ali Essa. "So you are the one." Saif's father stiffened with concern. "The one what, Abdul Rashid?"

The visitor's gaze was serene as he looked at the worried father. "Let your son speak, Saif. There is no reason for you to be upset." Ali Essa hung his head slightly. "Are you talking about today at the police station?"

Instantly, all eyes turned to the young man. "What happened? Tell us!" As in all small towns, they were hungry for news and gossip. Babbling with their questions, the noise became unbearable. Raising his hand, Abdul Rashid silenced them.

Softly at first, Ali Essa told of his adventure at the station. Only when he got to the part about the shooting did he let his emotions rise.

"Allah be praised, my son! You could have been killed. What foolishness, why?" Saif's emotions now ran high.

"It is my job, father." With that, the *majlis*, including Abdul Rashid, sighed and muttered their approval. Tears of pride welled in Saif's eyes.

"Tomorrow night, Saif, the Sheik has asked that you and the boy join him in his *majlis*. About nine o'clock, no?" Both men nodded. "Good, I'll tell him to expect you both."

Saif entered the *majlis* followed by his son who was in his uniform, and when he saw the Sheik, stood to attention and saluted smartly.

Immediately, the Sheik rose to greet them. Not a tall man, but still imposing. The rest of the *majlis*—about thirty men— remained seated on cushions and watched silently.

After the greeting, the Sheik bade Ali Essa to sit next to him. Alongside him was an Englishman dressed in a neat, lightweight safari jacket. It was the same man who had interviewed him for the job. Speaking in Arabic, his mother tongue, the Sheik addressed the Englishman. "Well, Jack, are you happy with your choice? This is the man. Ali Essa."

The Englishman laughed. "Yes, Your Highness, I made an excellent choice." Looking at him sideways, the Sheik grinned wryly. "This time, Jack, but not always." Again the Englishman laughed. It was obvious the Englishman was very fluent in the local dialect.

"Such courage cannot go without reward." The Sheik turned towards Ali Essa. "What is your rank now?" Looking him straight in the eye, the young man responded briskly, "Cadet, *seedi.*"

Stroking his beard, the Sheik turned back to the Englishman. "Cadet. Is there a higher rank than that, Jack?" Shrugging his shoulders, the Englishman looked a bit puzzled. "I suppose we could make him senior cadet." The Sheik looked pleased. "Very good, very good. Also, Ali Essa, I want you to live near my palace. I need brave people around me. Ghaffar!"

At the shout of his name, a small Indian man turned his attention to the Sheik. "Ghaffar, there is a plot of land near the South Gate. Arrange to have it gifted to this young man." The little Indian raised his eyebrows in surprise. "Yes, Sheik. All of it?" For an instant the Sheik looked mildly annoyed. "Why not? One day he will have a family! Yes, all of it!"

Once again, turning to the Englishman, he spoke in a loud voice. "Oh, and Jack, have you decided which cadets are going to England for training?" It was Jack's turn to look a bit startled. "Not yet, Your Highness." A twinkle appeared in the Sheik's eye. "Well, we have at least one now, don't we?" With a loud laugh that was so infectious the whole *majlis* joined in, the Englishman agreed. "Definitely, Your Highness, definitely!"

Raising his hand, the Sheik silenced the *majlis*. "This is Ali Essa Ghofran and his father, Saif. They will always be welcome in this *majlis*. The whole *majlis* chorused as one, "Allah be praised."

At this, the majority of them returned to the original conversations they were having with their neighbors. A warm wind blew in the scent of roasted lamb and spicy byriani rice. It signaled the arrival of several servants carrying plates and trays of food. The Sheik beckoned Ali Essa to start eating, and the son, following the old traditions, offered the first plate to his father.

Several hours later, the father and his son walked across to their old truck parked in the soft sand under the stars. Driving home along the bumpy track, they rode in silence. It was only when they reached home and the servant met them with the lantern that Ali Essa saw that his father had been crying. Stepping from the truck, Ali Essa took his father's hand. Immediately, his father hugged him. "I am so proud of you, my son. Allah has thrice blessed me. I am the father of a hero. But now you must leave us and go to England." Tears welled in Ali Essa's eyes. "I will be back, father. I will be back."

# Chapter Two

# England

Through the window of the plane as it landed, Ali Essa saw his first glimpse of England. Beyond the dark green grass was a soggy collection of buildings under a grey, cloudy sky. Carrying his large personal bag and followed by his four compatriots, all in police cadet uniforms, he strode up the access way into the labyrinth of corridors that was Heathrow air terminal. At the top, they were met by a uniformed police officer and a policeman who snapped to attention and saluted them as they arrived. Taking their passports, the welcoming party guided them through to Immigration Control. Ali Essa was amazed by the swarming, colorful crowd. Sikhs in turbans, Pakistanis in pajamas, Africans in bright dresses, Chinese in uniforms, and many other nationalities queued in a long snaking file. Hurrying through the VIP reception, they quickly found themselves and their luggage in a police minibus driving through the heavy traffic on their way to their barracks.

"So how do you like England so far?" Puzzled, Ali Essa couldn't understand the officer's accent. "Sorry, I didn't understand you." More slowly, the friendly policeman repeated his remark. "England…how do you like England so far?"

Beaming, this time Ali Essa had understood. "Very nice, very, nice. Okay. England is okay." Instantly his colleagues asked him in Arabic what was said. Ali Essa replied to them in English, "The officer asked how we like England. Now we are here, we must speak

English." Nodding, the officer agreed and turned to them, smiling. "He is right. You are here to learn English."

Lodged in their barracks, they unpacked and settled in. Life in the training facilities was hard but interesting. Amazingly, the first six months passed rapidly. It was only as the daylight started to shrink and the nights got longer did Ali Essa and his fellow cadets start to miss their bright, sunny Dubai.

Their holiday back in Dubai seemed too short and then they were back in England. Soon it was late spring and Ali Essa was pleasantly surprised how bright and green all the countryside had become in his absence. Six months more of the course and he would be back home. While he liked many aspects of his life in England, he missed his family and his culture.

On leave he'd met up with his cousin Humaid, a son of one of his father's sisters. She had married a wealthy local landowner and they had a family flat in north London close to Swiss Cottage. Humaid lived in it while he was studying at an English polytechnic. Exchanging phone numbers, they'd promised to meet. Normally, Ali Essa only socialized with his four colleagues. Together, they'd go to the cinema or a restaurant or simply wander the shopping malls. Although his English had improved, the others' command of the language had mainly stayed the same and when out they relied heavily on Ali Essa to translate.

Having settled back in, he rang Humaid, who immediately invited him around on the weekend. Dress in casual clothes, he caught a taxi to the Swiss Cottage address. Initially he'd thought of taking the others, but as it was family it would be better if he went alone for the first time.

Ringing the bell, he stood a little apprehensive, waiting for it to open. Perhaps he should have dressed more formally. He needn't have worried. Humaid opened the door wearing a T-shirt and jeans. Grasping him by his hand, he pulled him in. "Welcome, cousin, welcome. *Tayhl*. Come in."

At the entrance of the main lounge, Ali Essa was left speechless. Decorated in sumptuous furnishings, it was extremely large. In the centre there was a beautiful table over which a chandelier twinkled.

Scattered carelessly over its polished top were paper trays of pizza and other junk food surrounded by bottles of whisky.

Milling around the table and lounging in vast expensive chairs was a crowd of young Arab men. In a far corner, seated at another table, was a group of young men playing cards. Cigarette smoke created a haze that stung his eyes. Mixing with the Arabs were a number of white girls dressed in highly revealing outfits. Baulking for a moment, he hesitated to go in.

"*Yallah*, Ali Essa. *Yallah*. Introduce yourself." With a shout, Humaid called out that this was his cousin Ali Essa and he was to be made welcome. Confused, Ali Essa wandered around the Arabs introducing himself. Stopping at the card table, he watched as six intense young men gambled feverishly. Finally he found a space and sat down.

Shortly later, a girl with long brown hair and carrying two glasses and a bottle of whisky joined him.

"You're new, ain't you?" Ali Essa could hardly speak. Without warning, she sat next to him. Her red dress was so revealing at the top that he could see the full outline of her breasts and nipples. Shaking his head, he tried to tell her to go. Ignoring his waving hand, she offered him a glass. "Whisky?" The young man's eyes opened in horror. "No, no, I don't drink!" Again the girl ignored his protestations. "Go on. Don't let me drink alone." Pouring a drink, she put it in his hand.

Sipping it out of courtesy, the acrid liquid burned his lips and mouth. Involuntarily, he spat it out.

"Oy! Mind me dress! You want something with it? Dry ginger, that'll be better. Mind you, it's bloody Black Label. Seems a shame."

When she rose to get the dry ginger soft drink, he tried to escape but there were no other spare chairs. Returning, she wiggled down beside him. "There you go. You'll like that." In an attempt to get rid of the girl, he again politely sipped the mixed drink. It did actually taste better. Despite himself, he found that out of nervousness he had drunk all the contents of the glass. The girl poured him another.

Feeling more comfortable, he took the glass. As she handed it to him, he noticed that one breast had completely eased itself from her dress and her skirt was riding so high that he could clearly see her panties. Scared, he looked around, but no one seemed to notice and several of the others were already pawing some of the girls who laughed and giggled.

As she handed him his drink, the girl leaned over him and his face almost touched her bare breast. Breathing in his ear, she whispered, "My name is Jean. What's yours?" Hardly able to breath, he stuttered, "Ali. Ali Essa." Suddenly there was a hand on his crotch. Unaware, he'd been aroused by the sight of her breast and its hard nipple.

"Ooh, you are a big boy, Ali, a really big boy, and I think you like me." Almost hypnotized, he carelessly swallowed the second whisky. He was losing control. Trying to stand, he felt himself overcome by a warm feeling. Instead of leaving, as was his intention, he let the girl lead him into a nearby bedroom.

Feebly protesting, he was undressed by the girl who just as quickly removed all of her clothes. On the bed, he felt her mouth on his and then her head moved down his body. This was *haram*. This was bad. He tried to get up, but the whisky and the girl had him in their grips. A soft, warm mouth closed over his erection and he tried to push the girl away. Nature now dominated his whole body, and without warning he reached a quick climax. Just before he did, the girl pulled away and his body fluid jetted over his naked body.

"Oy, careful. Jesus, I thought you Arabs were stayers. I don't do that. I don't do blow jobs!" Pushing the girl from him, Ali Essa felt utterly ashamed, dirty and sick. Rushing to the bathroom, he grabbed a towel and had started to wipe himself when he threw up and only just managed to land the contents in the toilet bowl. His mind was foggy and unclear.

After washing himself, he staggered back into the empty bedroom, dressed and hurriedly made for the door. Back in the main room, his head was swimming. Vaguely he caught sight of the brunette, who was now talking to another Arab. Seeing him, they started laughing. She was dressed in only a bra and panties. Surrounding them were half-naked white women and Arab men.

At the front door, he flung himself out into the street. It was raining and that helped clear his mind. Grabbing a taxi, he headed straight back to the barracks and his room, avoiding meeting any of the others. Once in the safety of his room, he undressed and stood in the shower. It was almost an hour before he emerged.

He climbed into bed, covered his head with the sheet and shuddered in the disgust and horror of himself. The next morning, he awoke with a terrible headache. This, he convinced himself, was punishment for the previous night and he refused himself any relief from pain relievers. The headache lasted all day. He never rang his cousin again.

Towards the end of their year in England, they were each assigned to a division for a week as experienced. Ali Essa was astounded by the variety of tasks and operations carried out each day. Come the end of term, they again sat for exams and, as usual, he passed with distinction. Almost as quickly the seasons changed from spring and summer to autumn, the time of the year he'd first arrived.

When he left after the graduation parade, at which he was honored for his success, Heathrow Airport appeared much the same as when he'd arrived a year ago—crowded with the earth's mixture of people. He and his colleagues said goodbye to their escort then struggled through the formalities to reach their plane. As it taxied down the rain- sodden runway, Ali Essa took his last look at England, where the trees were already starting to lose their leaves.

## Chapter Three

# Home at Last

Early the next morning, he stepped off the plane into the warm, fresh air of Dubai. His family was there to greet him, along with several police officers and a couple of old friends. It was so good to be back in the sunshine with the blue skies at last. He was due a few days leave before he was to report for duty so he relaxed in his traditional clothes behind the counter of his father's shop on the Creek. Each meeting with an old customer was a pleasure to be savored as they came, sat, drank tea and told tales.

Too soon, he was reporting back into police headquarters. On his first day back, he sat with the four others in front of the assistant chief of police. After congratulating them on their graduations, he outlined their futures. Each of them was to spend time in the various departments to gain experience and from time to time they would be moved to another. Hoping he would be allocated to criminal investigations, Ali Essa's face showed his disappointment when he was given Traffic.

"Don't worry, Ali Essa, you'll be given a different department in the future. You won't be in Traffic forever." Eighteen months in traffic seemed like forever.

Having just finished duty on the second day of his appointment, he was called back for an emergency, a serious collision on the Abu Dhabi-Dubai highway. Although it was eight o'clock in the evening, he leaped into the patrol car and the driver sped from the station. With the siren blaring and lights flashing, they traveled at breakneck speed through the evening traffic.

At the scene, he forced his way through a crowd of onlookers held at bay by a lone motorcycle patrolman. Taking control, Ali Essa forced the crowd further back then walked around the mangled wreck of a four-wheel drive that had rolled several times. Such horror he couldn't imagine. The severed head of the driver lay on the sand, tongue lolling out, in a pool of blood. Under the bonnet of the upturned vehicle lay the remains of his crushed body. Hanging out of a side window of the screwed-up metal cab was the lifeless figure of the passenger, bloodied and smashed almost beyond recognition. Both were young Arab men. With difficulty, he thrust his head into the cabin of the four-wheel drive. The smell of whisky overpowered him. The smell was very familiar to him, one he'd never forget. Reeling back, he ran to the patrol car to radio for assistance, but already another patrol car, followed by an ambulance, was arriving.

Two ambulance men ran towards the crash. Ali Essa had a quick conversation with the newly arrived patrolmen, and as they went to inspect the smash he turned his back on them and violently vomited onto the ground.

Not that every night was like that, but there were enough of them. The first night he'd not slept at all and too often he had sleepless nights. Several times he went to the doctor complaining of his sleeplessness and subsequent headaches. So many wasted lives. On occasion, it was up to him to break the news to the parents.

Finally, he decided he could take no more. Seeking an interview with the deputy chief, he threatened to resign if he wasn't moved.

"Ali Essa, what would happen if we all resigned? There are men who have been there for many years. You think they are insensitive? Pray to Allah for them and for yourself. Someone must do this job." Ashamed, Ali Essa left and continued working in Traffic. To his great relief, he was transferred six months later.

Transferred to Headquarters! Within a week, he was almost wishing he were back in Traffic. Paper, paper and more paper; checking administrative documents, leave schedules, pay schedules, licenses, traffic fines, petty cash vouchers and myriad other pieces of paper; week after week of what seemed to him to be mind-numbing procedures. Then, on to court duties that were almost as boring, except for the occasional sensational case. Most were petty crimes of theft, burglary, returned cheques and paper fraud. After two years of this, he was ready to be transferred to the moon if necessary. Anywhere to get out.

Unexpectedly and to his relief, it was the ports. At least that department had a bit of color and pace to it. Occasionally, he'd escort the Coast Guard to run down smugglers bringing in illegals. That could be dangerous. On one trip, the smuggler reacted by throwing the cargo of struggling human beings overboard then opened up on the Coast Guard vessel with a machine gun. Pulling his pistol from his holster, he returned fire in anger for the first time in his life, to no avail. The smuggler disappeared at high speed into the darkness while they were preoccupied trying to save the screaming, jettisoned and drowning cargo.

At other times he was involved in capturing illegals when they landed. For the most part, they were a pathetic lot; most had been cheated by unfeeling crooks that took their money and left them stranded. Occasionally, one or two were so depressed and desperate they tried to take their lives in the lockup holding cells.

As much as he felt sympathy for them, it was impossible to show compassion. He'd tried it once and rued the day. Within minutes, dozens more were grabbing at him and pleading for the help he couldn't give them. Any sign of humanity was taken as a sign of weakness to be exploited by these creatures that were almost beyond God's help.

Otherwise, it was drunken sailors. There were the odd times when one of them would fall into the harbour and drown. The mixture of seafarers, adventurers, drunks and desperados made his day go in a flash. Almost to his surprise, his two years were up and he was transferred, at long last, to the Criminal Department. Further cause for celebration was that he'd also been promoted to Captain.

Celebrating his transfer and his promotion, he joined his family at a feast on a Friday after prayer. While he ate and chatted, his father approached him with a man he knew but whose name he could not recall.

"Ali Essa, meet Moh'd Khalfan Al Marri, an old friend." Standing, the young man took the newcomer's hand. "Welcome, Moh'd. Welcome." After the greeting, Moh'd Khalfan looked expectantly at Ali Essa's father and then at him. Appearing slightly agitated, Ali Essa's father turned to him. "Come to the *majlis*, son, Moh'd Khalfan and I have something to discuss with you." Curious, Ali Essa followed the two into the *majlis* where his father closed and locked the door.

Concerned, Ali Essa looked at Moh'd Khalfan and wondered what trouble he was in that he needed his help. It would be hard to give as a police officer and now a senior one. It wasn't possible to bend the law, not even for a friend of one's father. To his surprise, it wasn't for the law they wanted him; they wanted *him*!

"Ali Essa, my son, I've been thinking that it is time you were settled down. Moh'd Khalfan has a daughter he is willing to let you meet." Almost choking, Ali Essa dropped to a cushion.

*Marriage*. He'd not given it a thought. Police duties almost filled his every waking hour. Not entirely, though. Occasionally, he'd go on a picnic with his family but also, at the insistence of the Sheik, he'd built a wall around his property and constructed a small house on it. He doubted if it would be suitable for a bride. Marriage. Allah, help him!

Taking his silence as agreement, the two older men began to make arrangements. It was the start of a cultural piece of machinery that once started, not even divine intervention itself could stop. Certainly it would have been beyond Ali Essa's capabilities to prevent it, especially when the women found out. Within three months, he was the guest of honor at his own wedding!

True to tradition, he barely knew his bride and he only really got to know her on their honeymoon. Two weeks in Singapore was not only a holiday but also a revelation. Concerned that on the first night he'd fail, he also feared that the incident in London years earlier would have somehow affected him. Both concerns were groundless.

By the end of the honeymoon, both he and his wife knew each other intimately and the memory of Swiss Cottage had slipped deep into the past. Nine months later, his wife presented him with a son of whom he was immensely proud. So was his father and, in particular, his father-in-law, who surprised them with a gift of his own: a new and much larger house on their property.

After their honeymoon, Ali Essa had been too busy to even think about a house and they'd lived in the family compound. It was only at the last moment that he'd found out that his wife and father in law had built an elegant two-storey villa on the land. Delighted, he, his wife and newborn son moved in. There was another surprise a week later: a houseful of furniture sent by the Sheik! Not be outdone, the Police Department had their own surprise—a promotion to Major!

## Chapter Four

# Leaving Home

It was dark, very dark. Mike lay in his room wide-awake. Fear raced through his mind and his heart pounded. Last week was his seventeenth birthday. It was Saturday night and he was scared. Fear nearly overcame his loathing and hatred but not quite. Tonight was the night. No more. He would not put up with it anymore!

Lying in his underpants with the sheet up to his neck, he heard the clock ticking in the room. *Ticktock, ticktock.* It seemed so loud it hurt his ears. His heart was beating faster and louder than the clock. It was that time—not that he knew exactly what time it would happen, but it would; it always did.

With his ears strained he listened for the dreaded footsteps and the sound of the key in the door. Faintly, ever so faintly, he heard the singing then the thumping footsteps. Then there was the bang as the front door of the house opened and crashed closed. Heavy footsteps tramped up the stairs, past his room and on to his mother's bedroom.

The crack under his door lit up as a light outside flashed on. His mother's voice, at first soft, began to whine in fear. There was the drunken loud voice of his father shattering the peace. Loud shouting was the prelude to what would happen next. A slap, then a heavier slap followed by his mother crying and begging.

"Stop it! Stop it! Stop it, now!" Both his parents turned and stared at the slight skinny frame of a young man in his underpants silhouetted in the doorway.

"Don't you hit my mother again!" His voice was thin and shrill.

"What the fuck!" His father loomed over him, naked to the waist, ugly beer gut hanging out over his trousers, whisky breath like a sour fog around his head. "What the fuck!"

Struggling not to show his fear, Mike snarled, "Don't you hit my mother, you bastard!"

The big man sucked in his breath and lurched closer, hovering with menace over the teenager.

"What're you talking about, you scrawny little fucker?"

Shaking from head to toe, Mike stood his ground, tears of anger and frustration starting to well in his eyes.

"Don't hit, Bill. Don't hit him." His mother's voice was high-pitched in anguish and terror. "Don't hit him!"

The ugly drunken face turned toward the woman. "Get the fuck away, you useless bitch. Fuck off!"

A big paw reached out and gripped the boy's neck. "Time you went to bed! Now fuck off!" Lifting him off the ground by his neck, his father threw him halfway out into the corridor. Like a cornered cat, the boy sprung back onto his feet and hurled himself in anger at the big bulk of the man. Tears of rage scorched his cheeks as his fists bounced off the gut like it was made of solid rubber.

With a laugh, the big man pushed him off, then with one casual swipe with the back of his hand smacked him into the wall.

Stars swam in his head as he slumped, nose bleeding, half-unconscious to the floor. A sickening stench brought him to his feet. Wild emotion had caused him to lose control of his bowel and he'd dirtied his underpants.

"Ah, fuck off! Jesus, the little fucker's shit himself! Get out! You stink. Get out!"

Embarrassed beyond belief, hating his puniness, despising his father, he scurried from the room straight to the bathroom. In disgust he flushed his underpants down the toilet, cleaned himself and ran back to his room.

All was silent in the house, his drunken father having fallen into an alcoholic slumber. Unable to sleep, he lay awake till dawn, his head full of bitterness. With the sunrise he drifted off into a short, fitful sleep.

As it crept through the curtains, the wan winter's sun awoke him. It was Sunday morning. Staying in bed, he brooded for a while, rose, showered and then looked in the mirror. Both eyes were black and his nose was swollen and red. Maybe it was broken; it seemed crooked. With tears welling in his eyes again, he dressed and pulled an old suitcase from the wardrobe. At random, he threw some clothes into it. He could only think of one thing: to leave home!

After he'd packed, he eased his way with caution down the stairs to the kitchen. It was silent. His mother was slumped at the empty table in the half-light. Dressed in an old torn candlewick dressing gown she, too, had a black eye and a swollen cheek. A cigarette burned idly between her fingers, its wispy smoke wafting towards the ceiling.

As her son entered, she took a deep draw on it then blew a large cloud of smoke upward into the air. With the instinct of a heavy smoker, she flicked the ash into a dirty ashtray on the table without taking her eyes off her son. Without a word, he went to the stained worktop next to the sink, filled the kettle and stiffly waited for it to boil. Making coffee for himself, he walked with his head down to the table. Clumsily he sat down at the table opposite his mother, who looked down at the brown drops that he'd spilt on the cloth without uttering a word.

"I'm leaving. I'm not staying." He tried not to cry and gave a deep sniff. His father's snoring could be heard even downstairs. It made the whole house shake. His mother flicked the ash off her cigarette then took another draw that was feebler than the first.

"Not his fault, son. Not his fault. He had a terrible time when he was little."

His mother's voice was weak and grated. Mike's eyes were mean as he stared at his mother.

"Aw, give over, Mum. That's a load of crap. He's just a pisshead and a mean fucker."

The woman's shoulders slumped with resignation and she shook her head. Her straggly, mouse-grey and brown hair flopped over her forehead, making her look even sadder.

Mike sat in silence, and then drank his coffee. Not another word passed between them. When he'd finished, he rose and climbed back up the stairs to his room. He edged like a cat carefully into his parents' bedroom. On the bed stretched the half-naked body of his father. Face contorted even in sleep, he lay on his back and with every harsh breath the fat gut rose and fell above the grey, stained underpants that sagged below his waist. Mike tiptoed around the bed to the chair where his father's coat had been tossed over its back. With one deft move he slid the wallet from a pocket.

He backed out of the room quivering with fear. There was no break in the snoring as he hurried to his room. In his room the shaking stopped and without any hesitation, he knelt on the old suitcase forcing it shut, grabbed his jacket and headed back downstairs. At the kitchen door he stopped for a moment, looked at his mother and whispered, "Goodbye, Mum." She glanced up, a small tear starting to trickle down her cheek. "Goodbye, son. Goodbye."

He opened the door, shook his head then made off down the path. "Fuck him, fuck him. I hate the bastard." Tears began to run down his face and his mumbled words were lost in the thick collar of his jacket.

It was a cold but sunny winter's morning. The wind was bitter, and distant clouds threatened rain. Though he wanted to look back, he didn't and without slackening his stride, he headed off down the road towards the town centre.

## Chapter Five

# The Pub

On Sunday little happened in town. A few people dotted the street, and a runner in an Adidas tracksuit passed him, stirring up the leaves and scraps of paper on the pavement in his wake. Far off, the garish orange neon billboard of a McDonald's beckoned. Despite his dark mood, he was drawn like a bug to its bright interior.

Ignoring the stares of the several couples already seated at tables, he ordered a cheeseburger and Coke. After he had paid for them, he sat down and lay open his father's wallet on the table. Gnawing with disinterest on the fast-food, he counted the money with one finger. Sixty pounds. Not much with which to start life, but enough to get his father roaring with anger. For sure when he woke up, his father would come looking for him, mean as an angry bear.

As he swallowed the burger, his throat hurt where it had been bruised by the powerful, strong fingers of his drunken father. It made him hate and fear his father even more.

"Bastard," he snarled as he stood up to leave the fast-food restaurant. One of the diners looked up in surprise. Outside he wandered toward the centre of town and ended up at a bus station. With a mind still full of hatred and anguish, he bought a ticket and boarded the bus. Soon he was miles away from his hometown.

The bus ride was monotonous, stopping innumerable times before it arrived at the next town centre. By now the blue sky had gone and a drizzly rain had replaced the sunshine. Grey, wet and dismal, the weather matched his mood.

Alone, not knowing what to do next, he walked down the street and entered the doorway of a welcoming pub. There were several empty tables and, putting down his suitcase, he plunked into a worn leather seat at one of them. Looking around, he saw a clutch of faces, all of whom ignored him. On the wall was a TV set playing "Match of the Day." Although it didn't interest him, he watched it for over an hour as one game after another started and ended. When the show had finished, he went to the bar and ordered a diet Coke. Back at the table, he stared at the bubbles rising in the dark-brown liquid. He had no idea what he was going to do or where he was going to go.

The pub shut and he made his way out into the cold, gloomy afternoon. Still the rain drizzled down and soaked his head, then dribbled over his forehead to the tip of his nose. Although his nose and throat still hurt, the burning anger had cooled down and he felt gutted. The rain trickled down his cheeks, masking his tears of loneliness and fear. With nothing better to do, he ambled down an empty street. There was an open café and he went in, sat at a table and ordered a sandwich with a cup of coffee.

Worms of sorrow made their way through his mind. He wanted to flee back home to his room and the security it offered against the world, but it was impossible. Home to what? That fat drunken bastard who called himself his father and beat his mother every time he came home pissed! Several years ago his elder sister had been driven out. She had left home wild-eyed and distraught. He knew why. He'd heard her muffled cries late in the night as his father had entered her room. Bastard! He wished he would die a miserable death. Cancer maybe, but that would be too quick.

Outside the café, the streetlights flickering in the rain shimmered in the cold puddles that had formed on the dark road. He left the café, lugging his suitcase with him. Again he went into another pub. This one was livelier. At the bar, a group of young men with short hair were singing out of tune to a juke box. With hunched shoulders he tried to become invisible as he slipped behind a table into a seat in the corner. A young girl in a white blouse, short blue skirt and carrying a tray asked him what he wanted. Despite the temptation to take a chance and order something stronger, he stuck to a diet Coke. Returning, the girl smiled and placed it on the table.

The night dragged on until the pub closed. Dejected, Mike left and wandered onto the street. He had nowhere to go and he slumped against the damp, cold wall. In the distance he saw the bus station. It was where he would spend that night, the next and the next.

During the day he wandered the city centre, after changing into whatever clean clothes he had in the public toilet and ate at McDonald's. Each day was the same. The nights got lonelier. One afternoon he found himself dragging his heels along the canal. His mood was morose as he walked the towpath watching the cold muddy water make oily patterns as it swirled past the locks.

The dark water drew him like a magnet. That's where he should be, in the canal, his life ended. There was nothing left in his life, just an empty sadness, and he was so lonely. He took one step closer, tears welling in his eyes, and dropped his suitcase on the ground. A chill of fear gripped his heart as he stood balanced on the edge of the steep bank. One step, just one step, and all his problems would be over.

"Hey! Get back!" The shout disoriented him. He turned, went to step back, slipped, then suddenly he was in the freezing cold water. He gasped with the cold and the shock and then clawed at the bank. There was a foothold and he worked his way along to a slimy ladder then hauled himself up.

"I warned you! Stay back next time." From the opposite bank, an old man had shouted his concern and was now limping off. Mike stood on the bank shaking with cold and fright. The icy water dripped from his clothes. Sodden, he picked up his suitcase. Sullen and embarrassed he dawdled back into town.

That night as he sat alone and forlorn in the pub, the same group of young men bounced in through the doorway. With the money he'd stolen from his father running out, he sipped on a diet Coke. One of the young men caught his eye.

"Hey, man, get you. Come over here." Mike looked closer at the owner of the voice. Tall, slightly muscular, short hair, he had welcoming eyes. Although he felt shy and uncomfortable, he abandoned his suitcase and slouched over.

That's how he ended up in the Army. This merry group proffered him one beer after another and the night became vague. All he could recall was being violently ill as he was helped from the pub.

Next morning he awoke with a pounding head in a strange bed in some unknown barracks. Later he was in front of an overly-enthusiastic recruiting officer. Cajoled into lying about his age, he signed up. With a desperate need for company and an even more desperate need to eat as the stolen money had run out, he allowed himself to be carried away by the bluster and attention. Given an advance, he went back into town for his suitcase.

Next day, after having forged his father's signature on the recruitment forms, he was on his way to boot camp. After all, at least his country might need him. He knew for sure nobody else did, particularly his father.

# Chapter Six

# The Army

It was hell on wheels. Even worse. Nothing like he'd expected. He was shaven, bullied, shouted at and confused.

"*Sergeant* to you, boy! Not fucking 'Sir!' I wasn't born some silver-spooned bloody arsehole. *See these stripes? I earned them. Sergeant*, do you hear? *Sergeant!*" Standing over him, the brute of a man struck fear into his heart.

"Yes, sir. I'm sorry, sergeant, sir." Inches from his face, Mike could feel the man's hot breath on his cheek.

"Are you fucking deaf? Or just bloody stupid! *Sergeant! Sergeant!*" Mike's ears rang as the fierce uniformed man yelled at full throat in his face. Home would have been better than this. At least then he could leave the house and go down the park and kick a ball or something. Here he was trapped, nowhere to go.

During the night he lay with his face in the pillow to muffle his sobs. He wished he'd stayed in the canal and was dead. Now his life was almost too cruel to bear. If he'd known how to kill himself he would have. Worst of all, he was lonely. He missed his mother, his friends and his room. God, he was lonely.

In this state, on one of these days, he was in the toilet when from the next cubicle he heard a choking sob. He tried ignoring it but there was a second and a third. It disturbed him and he banged on the wall.

"Shut up, for fuck sake. Shut up so I can shit in peace." There was a brief silence. "Sorry, sorry. I'm very sorry." Then there was a scrambling noise and the toilet flushed. In anger, he too flushed and emerged pulling up his trousers. A figure was just leaving.

"Hey, stop! Wait! For fuck sake, wait!" There must have been a sympathetic tone in Mike's shout and the other young soldier hesitated and turned around. Mike recognized him as one of the new recruits from the next barrack.

Mike caught up with him. Bigger than Mike, he was also better built. His face was red with embarrassment and shame. He seemed almost too young to be in the Army.

"Name's Mike. What's yours?" With his hand out he waited for it to be gripped by the man opposite him. When it was, Mike grimaced with pain as it was shaken up and down. "Mick. Mick. I'm Irish. They keep takin' the mickey out of me." For the first time in weeks, Mike's face cracked into a grin. "Jesus Christ, you really are Irish, Mick!" Leaving the latrine, they headed for the canteen. Over coffee and cigarettes they poured out their troubles and woes. Both at first were tentative but the conversation flowed like they were friends. Within a week they were, and the Army didn't seem quite so bad.

## Chapter Seven

# Mike Gets Promoted

"Am I hurting you, soldier?" The sergeant's face was one breath away from Mick's nose.

"Uh, no, *sir!*"

Going bright red with indignation, the drill sergeant drew himself to full height. Confused, Mick started to shake with the effort of trying not to laugh.

"Yes, I don't know si...*sergeant!*" Full of menace, the sergeant loomed in the face of the trembling soldier. "I asked you a question, soldier! *Am I fucking hurting you?*"

Mick was baffled and could only mumble an answer. Barely audible, it further enraged the Sergeant.

"Are you fucking deaf? Answer me!" Straightening up, the youth drew in his breath.

"*No, Sergeant!*" Glaring at the recruit, the fierce drill sergeant's response was harsh.

"Well, you should be! I'm standing on your hair. Get a haircut and you're on a charge!"

Turning to the corporal, who was escorting him through the ranks of the early- morning parade, he barked, "Get his number. Tomorrow morning, 0600 hours on the square. Thirty-minute drill!"

After scribbling in a notebook, the corporal then snapped to attention. "*Yes, sergeant!*" Mike struggled to hide the same nervous laughter in his eyes as the inspecting sergeant approached, but to no avail.

"Well, soldier, you find this funny?" Squaring his shoulders, Mike replied loudly, "No, *Sergeant, no!*" The sergeant's eye had a malicious glint. "Then you can join Elvis Presley here on the square tomorrow. He needs company and you look like a fun lad. *Name, soldier?*"

Under his breath Mike cursed. "Hunter, *Sergeant.*" Stepping on, the sergeant growled to the corporal, "You get that, corporal?" The corporal scribbled again. "Yes, *Sergeant.*" Marching down the ranks, the sergeant's voice carried over the ranks. "Corporal, have we any more Elvis Presleys or Benny Hills in the section?" One pace behind him, the corporal flashed a faint grin then snapped back, "No, Sergeant!"

The sergeant glowered, stopped and glanced back. "Well, we'd better fucking well not have. Two are enough!" Catching up, the corporal acknowledged the man's comment. "Yes, Sergeant, yes!"

The grey fog covered the parade ground as the two of them marched in battle kit to the steps where the corporal waited. With clipboard in hand, he briefly inspected them as they stood to attention in front of him.

"Quick march!" The two of them strode out across the square ground that was bathed in a dim, sulfurous light as the sun began to break through the fog. "Left turn! Right turn! Halt! Quick march!" For over half an hour the pair wheeled and marched to the bark of the duty corporal until they left the parade ground, sweating and exhausted despite the cold. As they passed their tormentor, he whispered venomously at them, "You bastards have me up this early again and you'll do it all at fucking double time. Do you hear me?" Disappearing towards their barracks, they chorused, "Yes, Corporal," then vanished into the fog.

Struggle as he may, Irish Mick could not avoid being punished. He showed a singular aptitude for being caught for some misdemeanor. Morning after morning he drilled at double time to the furious commands of the frustrated section corporal.

Mike had learned his lesson. It didn't take much to stay out of trouble. Besides, he was starting to like what he was doing. Every evening he dismantled his rifle, cleaned it, then reassembled it. With care he spit polished his boots and brassed his buckles. Whenever he had a chance, he read the books on army regulations and procedures that had been issued to him. Sitting attentively in class, he absorbed like a sponge the lectures on infantry minor tactics and guerrilla warfare.

Six months later, they sat for exams and to his delight he passed them all with distinction. Over the months, with regular meals and exercise, he'd grown and put on weight. The physical training instructor had taken a liking to him and encouraged him to work out and box. A year later, he was in the regimental boxing team and celebrating his real eighteenth birthday. His gift from the Army was to be paraded in front of the commanding officer and given his first stripe. Lance Corporal Michael Hunter proudly returned to the barracks. It was off down to the local pub that night where he got very drunk and first met Carol.

Carol didn't really like Army types, but there was something about this one that was different. Not that much different, though, as he passed out on her shoulder. Still, she felt sorry for him, as he looked so young. She helped him to her car then drove him back to the barracks. Fortunately, the guard at the gate was Irish Mick, who smiled as he looked in the car. Waving them on, he laughed as Mike woke from his comatose state and tried to salute. Arriving at the barracks, Mike tipsily thanked her then wobbled off to his quarters.

## Chapter Eight

# Mike Marries Carol

Sitting in the commanding officer's office, Mike listened half-heartedly as the lieutenant droned on. He'd only contacted his mother a couple of times after leaving home. The last time was a few weeks ago. Now this. Ironic, really. He who lives by the sword dies by the sword, but in his father's case it was by the bottle. Hit by a bus as he drunkenly staggered onto the road after leaving the pub.

Mike was angry. Too quick, really. After what he'd done, he deserved to die a more painful death. After reading him his mother's telegram, the lieutenant was trying mistakenly to console him. All he wanted was to get out and down to the pub just to celebrate the bastard's death.

Since his first disastrous meeting with Carol, he'd made it up and was now taking her out on a regular basis. Several weekends ago he'd met her parents, and while the mother was a bit of a prude, the old man wasn't too bad. He'd been in the Army during the war and took to the young soldier. Before he'd received the news in the telegram, he had made arrangements to stay with them for an overnight leave. Bugger it. Trust his old man to fuck things even after he was dead.

The church was nearly empty. It was a cold, grey day. Both his mother's and his hair lay dank over their foreheads from the drizzly rain. Bareheaded, they'd followed the hearse with its coffin down the crunchy, stained, marble pebble track to the church in the middle of the cemetery. Mike felt for his mum for the first time.

Probably, before the beatings, long ago, she must have loved his father. Perhaps the way he now felt about Carol. People change. Maybe his father had had a difficult childhood.

Coughing into her hand to stifle the noise, his mother sobbed gently. There was no sorrow in Mike's heart. He resented having to spend a weekend away from his girlfriend because his father had gotten pissed and blundered into the path of a council bus.

Any sympathy he may have had drained from him long ago. Instead he felt his father had gotten better than he deserved. Standing sullenly alongside his mother as she sniveled her way through the priest's meandering, banal sermon annoyed him even more. By the time the priest had finished, all he felt was anger

After they had watched his father's coffin disappear into the curtains of the crematorium, he and his mum went back to her flat. Only a few mourners had come to the funeral, mostly the pub crowd. Obviously his old man had pissed off most people he knew.

There were ham sandwiches and pale ale in bottles, not cans. Mike's sister hadn't come, even though he'd finally gotten a message through to her. She was staying in the outskirts of London in some sort of a commune. Probably on drugs. Sad about his sister. From what he could remember, she was quite pretty. Dirty bastard, his old man. For what he did to his sister he should burn in hell.

On the train travelling back to his barracks, Mike got the morose thoughts of the funeral out of his mind and back onto Carol. Last time they'd been out together he'd gotten most her clothes off in the car. Just the memory of it caused his trousers to tighten around the crotch. He slouched back in the seat and the train's motion rocked him to sleep. A couple of hours later, he was back in the barracks. So much for his father's funeral.

"Hunter! Right flank. *Move!*" Crouched over his weapon, Mike scurried through the half-light and mud to take up a position in a small clump of trees. Dropping onto his stomach, he swept the full field of view through the sights of his service rifle. Infantry minor tactics, exercises out in the open—Mike loved them. Just like the real thing, except there were no bullets. If there had been, he'd have enjoyed it even more. There were plenty of thunder flashes and explosives, but no real rounds. With a grin, Mike reflected on the first time that he'd tried to fire his rifle. It was on the range and despite the instructor's advice, he'd closed his eyes as he lay on the ground, pointed the rifle somewhere near the target and pulled the trigger. The pain was electric. Slamming back into his shoulder from the recoil, the rifle taught him a lesson he'd never forget. From that day on he gripped it tightly to his shoulder. After several attempts, he finally opened his eyes as well. To his surprise and that of the somewhat hard-bitten range instructor, his aim improved dramatically. Eventually he would become one of the best shots in the regiment. In the end, he'd made the interservice rifle shoot team as a reserve.

Carol's parents had decided to go to Cornwall for Easter. They were staying at her brother's place. He had a butcher's shop in the high street with a three-bedroom flat above it. Married, they hadn't had kids. Cornwall for Easter was not Carol's idea of fun.

"Well, you can stay here," her mother whined, "but stay out of trouble." The young girl glared at the older woman. "I'm nineteen, Mum!" Shrugging her shoulders, her mother continued to complain. "Trouble doesn't respect age. Look at your father." Looking at her father, she saw him wince, then, when her mother's back was turned, break into a grin and wink at her. She wondered what her father had done in the past. As he left the room he whispered in her ear, "Don't do anything I wouldn't do," then disappeared.

There wasn't much else to do on a Good Friday night, so Carol and Mike sat on the couch in front of the TV. With a beer in his hand and a white wine in hers, they munched away at takeout Chinese. Thank god the Chinese weren't Christians or they would have starved. Mike threw a couple more logs on the fire and they snuggled closer, watching but not watching David Frost on the screen. Another beer and another wine found them locked in a passionate embrace. There was no resistance as Mike slid onto the soft floor rug in front of the hearth with Carol in his arms. Within minutes they were both naked. Mike marveled at Carol's soft white skin and her firm round breasts. Hard pink nipples rose and fell as he planted kiss after kiss on her lips then moved sensuously down to her breasts. As nature had intended, his rigid penis slipped unopposed into her warm body. Both of them writhed and moaned in the thrill of their lovemaking. Without warning, Mike climaxed and collapsed exhausted into Carol's arms. All weekend their lovemaking continued—in the bath, in the bedroom, in the kitchen and, if they could have, on the ceiling.

When Carol's parents walked through the door, Mike saw by the look in her father's eyes that he could tell. Her mother just gabbled on about Cornwall, the weather, the price of meat and whatever rubbish came to mind. The old man, though, he knew, Mike could tell. When it was time for him to leave, there was no warmth in Carol's father's goodbye. He knew.

Weekends came and went. Mike made steady progress in the Army. Three weeks after Easter he was promoted to Corporal. On weekdays he studied at night school for his general certificate exams in English, Math and Geography. Every weekend he would be with Carol and they would make love whenever they could. Neither of them had had any other lovers in their lives before, and when Carol became pregnant it was a surprise to both of them.

It was also a shock to Carol's mother, and her father was fit to kill. Mike had misjudged the old man; he wasn't as nice as he had thought. "Of course you are going to marry my daughter." Not that Mike was opposed to the idea. It was the threatening tone in Carol's father's manner that made him almost rebel. Still, this was no joke. It was reality; there was no choice. So, just before his twentieth birthday, Mike got married.

Mike and his bride enjoyed their wedding. Church bells rang and Carol looked radiant and beautiful in white, while he looked handsome and resplendent in his dress uniform. His mother cried and, to his surprise, his sister came. Looking haggard with shadows under her eyes, she, too, cried as the couple left the church. Captain Neville, his platoon leader, was the master of ceremonies at the wedding breakfast and gave a light- hearted and amusing wedding speech. Several of his Army mates became very drunk, dancing and singing all evening till finally even Carol's father lightened up.

Around midnight, Mike and Carol disappeared to a bridal suite in a nearby hotel. They were too exhausted to make love that night, but they made up for it the next day, not getting out of bed before dinnertime.

Carol lived at home for awhile while Mike lived in barracks during the week. It was awkward on weekends when he stayed at her parents' house. Their bedroom was next to the parents' and their lovemaking was restrained and subdued as a result. As Carol's pregnancy became more than obvious, she left her job. Fortunately, at the same time, married quarters became available and she moved into the Army barracks.

# Chapter Nine

# They Have a Daughter

Mike lay in the freezing snow, the cold seeping through his thermals. For three hours he'd been on the run. To be captured now would be the end of his current ambitions. He had to survive the night. This was the final test. Put forward by his commanding officer for the Special Armed Services, he had a chance to make something of himself.

The cold stretched his willpower to the limit. Then faintly, with his ears strained, he heard the soft crunching of snow underfoot. He tensed and lowered himself even further into the snow bank. Like a cat ready to spring, his eyes widened as he watched for any movement. Into his peripheral vision came the sight of one of the enemy, ever so cautiously seeking him out. Silently, he repositioned himself behind a fallen trunk.

Ghostlike, the figure of the other soldier moved into his range. Swift as a hawk, Mike had the man pinned to the ground with a knife at his throat.

"Captured, soldier. You're dead!" Grunting, the man gave up. Mike wrenched the weapon from the captured man's grasp then deftly tied his hands behind his back.

"Eh! You're not going to leave me here, are you?"

Back on his feet, Mike looked down. "Yes." The response was flat, without emotion. In the half-light, fear could be seen in the captive's eyes.

"I could fucking freeze!"

Smiling grimly, Mike started to move off. "Just keep moving and you'll be all right."

Trying to struggle from his bonds, Mike's captive snarled back, "Smart fucker, you just tied me up!"

There was little sympathy to be had from Mike. "Stiff, use your imagination." Without another word, Mike slipped into the night. Shortly after, he could hear his victim yelling frantically for help.

"Corporal Hunter."

Standing rigidly to attention, Mike replied, "Sir."

Staring up at him, the officer continued. "Corporal Hunter, you went beyond what was required. That soldier could have frozen to death."

Unblinking, Mike stared back.

"Sir?"

Shaking his head, the officer looked back down at his file. "Forget it. Congratulations! You're in."

Saluting briskly, Mike stepped back, wheeled about and marched smartly from the office. Jubilantly he returned to the mess where the others were waiting. The look on his face told it all and they whistled and shouted their approval. To cap it all, he was given an envelope by the duty clerk. He'd passed his exams. In a few more years he'd be eligible for Sergeant. Life couldn't be better.

"Corporal Hunter, SAS. Sounds good." Grabbing his wife, he danced around the kitchen. "Although I liked private," he whispered as he kissed her behind the ear. "Well, I like *your* privates."

Laughing, his wife pushed him away. "They're out of bounds, soldier. Stand easy. You'll have to wait."

Mike tried to grab her again. It wasn't easy. Nine months pregnant and it was almost impossible for him to get his arms around her.

In stark contrast as she'd swelled, he'd slimmed. Carol was roly-poly while he was like a racing greyhound—all muscle and sinew. "Come on, Carol. Champagne. There's one bottle in the fridge."

She shook her head. "No, Mike, it's for the baby."

Grinning, he accepted. "Alright, alright, I'll stick to beer!" Opening the door, he reached in and took out a can of Heineken, flicked open the top and swallowed half its contents.

Carol pulled a face. "Slow, soldier, slow. You might be needed tonight."

Drinking slightly slower, Mike looked at her carefully. "That close?" She nodded. "That close."

After dinner, they watched a little TV then headed for bed. Kissing his wife on the forehead, Mike tried to playfully carry her upstairs to their bedroom. "Careful, Mike. I'm almost due!"

Still trying, Mike laughed. "I'm just helping. Perhaps I'll stir it along."

Carol slapped his hand away. "Don't you dare!" Struggling up the stairs, Mike towed his wife behind him. In the room, they both fell on the bed laughing. Mike kissed his wife in excitement. Quickly they undressed and slipped beneath the sheets. Several minutes later, Carol gave a sharp cry of pain. "Mike! The baby's coming. Oh, my God, it's coming!"

Mike strode back and forth. "Mr. Hunter?"

Immediately Mike jerked around.

"Doctor?"

In front of him stood a man in a white gown with his hand extended. "Congratulations, it's a daughter and they are both well." Gripping the doctor's hand, Mike shook it vigorously and smiled. The doctor winced in pain at his tight grip and pulled his hand free.

Rubbing it for a moment, he stared at the excited young man. "You can see them both now."

In keeping with tradition, his wife looked tired and sleepy but somehow radiant. In keeping with the same tradition, his newborn baby was asleep and wrinkled like a prune. She wasn't prune-like when twelve weeks later she screamed the church down at her christening. Elizabeth. Neither of them really liked the name, but it was the only one they could both agree on. Still, it was a nice christening, and when they got home they drank the champagne. It was good to be a family.

## Chapter Ten

# Mike In the SAS

At last Mike felt his life was really worthwhile. In the SAS he was a serious soldier. Before, the Army seemed like just a job that anybody who was prepared to wear a uniform could do. This was different. Day after day, he learned how to professionally kill people—unlike before, when he fired his rifle randomly at some target, not really caring whether he hit it. Only caring that in any war the enemy would be as bad a shot as most of his side. No, this was the real thing, often hand-to-hand. Unarmed combat, swift movements with a knife or just his bare hands, all aimed at one goal: to kill and kill effectively.

Mike learned how to abseil, parachute jump, leap from a moving vehicle, set booby traps and move with speed and stealth. He continued with his studies and became proficient in German. Along with his fellow soldiers, he'd become tough, resolved and steely hard in his outlook. Strength and fitness were mandatory. Moving away to barracks in another camp when he'd joined the SAS, he only saw Carol and Elizabeth on the weekends.

Carol had grown big and cuddly. Having little or nothing else to do but look after Elizabeth, she'd filled in her time watching TV and eating. Even at home, Mike was on a knife's edge. Every morning while he was on leave during the weekends, he did his hundred pushups and sit-ups. Watching him from the corner of her eye, Carol was impressed by his sleek and well-proportioned body. What didn't impress her were his mood changes.

Since the baby, even though they only saw each other on alternate weekends depending on his roster duty, Mike was not interested in making love. Carol couldn't work it out. She longed for the feel of his body engulfing her, penetrating her, but it never happened. In Mike's mind she was now his daughter's mother. It didn't seem right to have sex with the mother of his daughter. Instead, he exercised more so that he fell quickly into an exhausted sleep while his wife lay beside him, sleepless, a bit angry but more confused.

Twelve months after he'd been in the SAS, he was transferred to Germany as part of a NATO force exercise. They fought imaginary battles against a serious enough threat from the communist world. Isolated from his family, Mike gradually slipped into the life of a bachelor, reluctant at first but soon enough to become the real thing. After their first major exercise, he and several in his section found themselves with local leave. After a brief debate, Mike succumbed to the suggestion they go to nearby Hamburg. Interested in improving his German, he packed a bag and led the way.

Three hours later, they were in their hotel rooms in the centre of the city. That evening, they voted to go to the Reeperbahn.

"No, not there!" Mike's protests were howled down. "Yes, yes, yes!" Except for Mike, the vote had been unanimous. After ringing his wife and lying about going to the cinema, he leapt into a cab with the others and headed downtown to the dockland nightspot of worldwide notoriety. Laughing and shouting, they hit the streets of Europe's sleaziest night venue.

They stopped briefly in one of the nightclubs where they listened to some English rock group from Liverpool. Unkempt and pimply, they were singing a raunchy Chuck Berry song. The lead singer was called John somebody. They moved on to the next club where they drank pints of strong German lager and watched lithe young girls strip on the bar. From that bar they went to another, then another.

Later that evening, Mike found himself in bed with a Danish girl who claimed she was eighteen. What did it matter? He was drunk and England was a long ways away.

On their way back to camp, Mike was moody and quiet. His friends kept teasing him and he felt bad. He'd actually enjoyed himself, but now his guilt was biting hard. Carol was his daughter's mother! What had he done? Putting up with the taunts for longer than he could bear, he finally snarled, "Fuck off," then stared blankly out the train window. The Danish girl had been pretty good and he hated himself for liking her.

# Chapter Eleven

# Australia

During his absence, Carol had badgered the camp adjutant until he'd found her married quarters where Mike was stationed. She never told him in her letters or the occasional phone call. On his return, he was more than surprised to find himself in with Carol and his daughter. To add to his delight, he found that he'd finally been promoted to Sergeant, arguably at a very young age, but in these circumstances, who was arguing?

Several nights after his return they celebrated his promotion with a party. More than a little concerned about what his fellow soldiers might blurt out about Germany, he kept them under constant surveillance whenever they neared Carol. He needn't have worried; they were paragons of virtue in that respect, although one or two of them got fairly drunk. Early in the evening, Mike played the proud father and paraded his daughter around in his arms, but it wasn't long before both he and she tired of it and her mother trooped her off to bed. Within a couple of weeks, their lives had settled down and their relationship had stabilized, although not to Carol's real liking. Despite this, she found herself enjoying her life. In the wake of his overseas appointment, Mike devoted himself to the Army. During the day he worked as hard as he could and at night he studied. Taking both military and civil courses, his nights were full of either lectures or course work. On the other hand, Carol busied herself with Eliza (not Lizzie or Liz, as Mike hated it.) Breakfast, then play school, then Army wives' club, then tending her family's needs and TV at night.

By bedtime, both of them would feign exhaustion, slump from the bathroom to the bedroom and out of habit quickly fall asleep, avoiding as much physical contact as possible. On occasion, Mike contemplated moving into separate rooms or back to barracks, but this routine was too comfortable to be broken for the want of something intangible.

After several more years of study, he and his wife celebrated his passing exams in English, German, Math, Chemistry and Geography. That night they arranged a babysitter and dined out at a fine restaurant. Feeling he'd finally achieved something in life, he had a sense of pride in himself that he'd never felt before. Walking towards the restaurant, Mike caught sight of their reflections in a shop window. Looking taller than he was, his suit hung off his sparse but muscular frame while Carol, who had started to lose weight by going to the Army wives club fitness club, shone by his side. With her hair now long and blonde, she wore an expensive and well-cut dress with a low front showing her white, ample figure.

"Not bad, not bad," Mike whispered, taking his wife's hand as they entered the restaurant. Seated at the best table, they enjoyed a candlelight dinner with champagne. No expense was spared. Heading home in the taxi, Mike put his arm around Carol, and by the time they reached the house, they were kissing passionately.

Paying off the babysitter, Mike hurried to the bedroom, but Carol wasn't there. She was in Eliza's room. "I think she's running a bit of a temperature. I hope she's not coming down with the flu. It's all around the playground." The feeling was gone. Brushing his teeth in silence, Mike slipped moodily into bed as his wife continued to fuss with their child. By the time Carol came to bed he was sound asleep.

Four years! It had taken four years of bloody hard study for him to be standing where he was that evening. Surrounded by a number of other candidates, he waited until he was called.

"Sergeant Hunter. Congratulations, you are no longer a sergeant. You are dismissed, Warrant Officer Hunter."

Warrant Officer. Mike couldn't believe it. Saluting, he crisply turned and marched back to his seat. Carol and Eliza beamed with pride as the rest of the gathering applauded. In his smart ceremonial blues, Mike looked the part of an SAS field officer. After the formal ceremony, his family happily endured the photo session and then it was off to the bun fight and beer.

Shouldering his responsibility, Mike had kept his drinking to a minimum, but when they returned home, Carol produced a bottle of Moet and Chardon champagne. Even Eliza was allowed one glass. Giggling, Mike carried his seven-year-old daughter to bed. By the time he'd said goodnight and reached his own bedroom, Carol was already in bed.

Try as he might, he couldn't make it with his wife. The barrier was too wide. In silence they rolled over to look at opposite walls, and within minutes both were asleep.

Warrant Officer Mike Hunter moved into the role of trainer and instructor with ease and aplomb. It meant a lot of travel. He'd specialized in guerrilla warfare and unarmed combat. Heavily in demand, the work was arduous but rewarding. Travelling around the country, he would occasionally meet a woman whose interests were not too far distant from his own. At first he enjoyed their company with a good wine and a fine restaurant, but as time went on, more and more liaisons ended up in his private room in the officers' quarters of the regiment where he was working.

It no longer affected his conscience. After all, he reasoned, he was a good provider. Neither drinking heavily nor gambling, he saved his money and was giving Carol a good home and Eliza public school education. They had nearly saved enough to put a deposit on a house down South. Nobody in Mike's family had even been south, let alone thought of buying an expensive house in that area!

"Mike, it's beautiful. Can we afford it?" Putting his arm around Carol and his daughter, Mike laughed. "Nothing is too good for the two most beautiful women in the world." Having recently been promoted, Mike decided to buy the house in the South. No more Army life for his wife and child. He would live in the barracks when on duty, but off duty it would be home to a normal life. For his family, it was to be a civilian life in a proper house.

Leaning forward in the chair, Mike stared into the face of his commanding officer.

"Where, sir?"

Staring straight back, the man in an immaculately pressed uniform replied with a strong tone, "Australia, WO Hunter. Australia. We have a request for a specialist instructor from the AMF. Vietnam is a lot closer to Australia than here, and it may not be long before they are sucked into the war. HQ has sent the request to me. I believe you are the best choice."

Silent for a moment, Mike spoke up.

"My wife, sir?"

"You can go as married accommodation. Army style, of course."

Wincing, Mike confronted his wife's anguish.

"No! No! No! Mike I am not going to live in Army Quarters again, even in Australia. *Especially* in bloody Australia! What about Eliza? Doesn't she count? She's not going to become a boot camp kid again. No! No! Go, by all means. Go to Australia, but without us!"

In silence Mike and his wife lay awake in their expensive bedroom for most of the night. They greeted each other courteously in the morning, but nothing could hide the sliver of ice between them. Carol was determined to stay, and equally, Mike was determined to go. There was no common ground. Within an hour of arriving on duty, Mike had accepted his appointment in the AMF on unaccompanied status.

# Chapter Twelve

# Swanbourne Barracks

From his window seat, Mike watched the clouds effortlessly drift by—strange, white puffy shapes that looked like islands in a sky-blue sea. It seemed impossible they could fly through them when they appeared so solid. Landing at Bombay, he disembarked and wandered through the transit lounge. Through the window of the plane he'd seen little slum dwellings filled with people. When the approaching plane flew overhead, the peasants barely lifted their heads. Totally oblivious to the landing plane, they carried on their day-to-day tasks.

Inside the transit lounge, he looked through the glass to the immigration counters. Stern, brown-faced officers in dark green uniforms with yellow braiding scrutinized each and every passport. From time to time they would throw a passport on the counter with an obvious show of contempt. The seemingly offensive booklet would slide off onto the floor where its confused owner would grovel around, pick it up, then scurry off to somewhere beyond his vision. A myriad of cleaning men and women worked in a desultory manner around the aging, grey concrete structure. The men wore singlets and wraparound cotton skirts folded up, baring their hairy, knobby knees while the women, scraggy and worn, had brightly colored, tight-fitting tops showing bare waists, below which hung even more brightly coloured saris. All around, the place teemed with people, making the oppressive heat and humidity seem even hotter.

Seated in the passenger lounge, Mike stared from his near stupor as a waiter in a tired, threadbare dinner jacket dropped an even more worn out menu on the table. For safety's sake, he chose a cheese sandwich and coffee. Pale white and crustless, the bread curled up around a miserable slice of cheese as the whole concoction lay on a slightly dirty plate. Almost as bad was the sickly sweet, milky coffee that was lukewarm in a cracked cup that sat in a ring of spilled dregs on the saucer.

Glad to be back on the plane, he tried to sleep as it continued its apparently endless journey to Australia. Although he stayed on the aircraft in Singapore, when he went to the door he could feel the damp, hot air with its musty odor sweep into the cabin. There was a primitive jungle smell as the new passengers came onboard. Bags and bodies were pushed and prodded, and then the plane shuddered, rolled forward, picked up speed and lifted off.

Again he endeavored to sleep in his seat as the flight headed down its final leg of his long destination. Eventually he arrived at its end.

In contrast to the previous two stops, as he stepped from the plane at Tullamarine airport, the air was crisp and clean. It was summer and they had landed in Melbourne in the early morning. Bidding goodbye to the airhostess who had been kind to almost flirty from Singapore; he headed for Immigration and Customs.

"Gidday, mate. Stayin' long?" Taken aback, Mike could hardly understand what was being said to him. He knew it was English but the thick, heavy accent made it almost unintelligible.

"Good morning. Yes, thank you," was the best he could muster in his confusion. Outside, an Army driver awaited him, handed him his papers and then headed off to the outskirts of the city. Driving through the traffic, he was amazed at the orderliness and openness of the surroundings. But the tiredness and jetlag tugged at his eyelids, and he quickly slipped off to sleep. Arriving at the modest hotel, he registered then made for his room. After an almost too brief sleep, he was back out to the airport next morning.

Six hours later, he stepped off the plane into the bright afternoon sunshine of Western Australia. He'd been travelling for nearly two days. Crossing the tarmac, he looked around and was surprised to see only one more international aircraft on the apron. The sun beat down on his uniform, causing him to start to sweat. It was too hot. Almost instantly, flies surrounded his face.

Irritated, he pulled his bags off the trolley that was parked by the path leading from the tarmac and made his way to the low, two-storey terminal building. Passing through the glass exit door, he headed for the main entrance. On his right were a garden complete with blackboys and a small pond that contained a live black swan paddling to and fro. Outside, an Army car and driver waited. After he had thrown a quick salute, he threw his bags into the back seat then followed them.

When the car drove off, he was surprised to see almost everybody around wearing little else but T-shirts, shorts and rubber thongs, women and children included.

"What a hell of a place," he muttered to himself. Later, as he sweltered in the not air-conditioned vehicle, he understood why, and wished that he, too, could strip down to the same garb. Still plagued by jet lag, he looked at his watch as the car entered the barracks. "Thirty-seven hours. Bloody thirty-seven hours. I hope it's worth it," he grunted.

Slightly turning towards him, the driver responded, "Sir, is there something?" "No, soldier. Carry on." Mike shook his head, trying to clear away the tiredness. It wouldn't go away.

"Warrant Officer Hunter, welcome to the 3rd Regiment SAS."

Sitting down, Mike removed his cap.

"Thank you, sir." Opposite him sat the company commander Major Morrison. Feeling better after nearly fourteen hours of undisturbed sleep, Mike had reported for duty.

"Hunter, you don't mind if I call you Mike?" Mike smiled. "No, sir." The Australian informality was legendary and he liked it.

"Mike, your reputation precedes you. We asked for the best and we seemed to have gotten it. Youngest WO in the Corp. Well done. We hope you bring us luck. We'll need some. It will come as no surprise to you that this regiment is very likely going to be sent to Vietnam. Not a popular war in this country. We've already established the protocol. You can go along as an advisor, if that is acceptable."

Acceptable! Acceptable? Wasn't that what he'd trained for? To fight in a real war? Without a moment's hesitation, he replied, "Yes, sir!"

That night, Mike wrote to Carol and Eliza. He didn't mention Vietnam. No point in scaring them unless it happened. Instead, he told her about the Camp, the bright sunshine (so bright it burned your skin within minutes), the strange kookaburras that woke him by laughing every morning from the treetops and the occasional goanna on the doorstep flicking out its blue tongue. He wrote about the casual, friendly people that seemed so different from those back in England.

Though he enjoyed it, the informality took a little getting used to. Immediately the uniforms were off, it was "Hey, pom" or "pommie bastard" or more commonly "sport" but mostly "mate." Totally different to what he was used to in the regiment back home. Speak like that to a higher rank and you'd be charged with insubordination, in uniform or out of it! On the other hand, they were still very disciplined and tough.

What surprised him was their almost instinctive habit of covering each other and backing up as they trained for battle. Perhaps it was the culture. Back home, each soldier almost acted as an individual; here they were individuals, but they knew where each other was.

Training was hard. At first it was the heat. The others were used to it, but he found it almost too much. Thankfully, after several weeks, although still warm, it had cooled down enough for him to handle it. Each morning they would rise at sunup and run for ten miles. On the odd occasion they returned by the beach in front of the barracks. In the cool morning air, it would be fresh with the tang of seaweed. Standing on the edge of the crisp white sand, ankle deep in the water as the waves swept in, fishermen stood with long beach rods angling for a feed of fish for breakfast.

By a quirk of the weird laws of the land, it was also a nudist beach. In the warmer weather, they would find themselves accompanied from time to time by slim, tanned naked women and men who laughed and teased them as they headed back to the barracks. *Strange country. Bloody strange,* thought Mike as he struggled, gasping, over the last sand hill and finally back to the showers.

Come Saturday nights, they would head for the local hotel. Inside was a sprawl of a bar with a bandstand in one corner. One of the more popular rock bands would be giving it hell and the place would be packed. Next door was a betting shop with welcoming doors and sprinkled with sad-looking punters. Occasionally, Mike would try a bet but he never won.

More often he'd have better luck with the fresh-faced, lively local girls. On a good night, one of them would end up in the backseat the old car he'd bought, drinking beer. He would park it in the sand hills near the barracks. If the night was warm and his luck was really good, they'd strip off all their clothes and bathe in the chilly Indian Ocean. Once or twice he would manage to make love with them, but come the early morning they'd want to be off and gone.

Not long after he arrived, he received a letter forwarded to him from his old regiment. At first he couldn't recognize the handwriting, but then as he read it, he realized it was from his sister. She'd tried to contact him. His mother had died. Now his sister had moved north to somewhere near Edinburgh. There was no return address on the envelope or the letter.

Mike walked outside into the night. In the southern hemisphere the sky was so clear. You could almost touch the stars. Maybe his mother was up there somewhere. It was a foolish thought; he didn't believe those things. But she'd deserved a better life. For a while he stood motionless, then, wiping away the small tear that had snuck down his check, he went back inside.

## Chapter Thirteen

# Vietnam

Three months after his arrival, Mike received a letter from Carol. Why had he forgotten Eliza's birthday? Shit! So he had. How could he? Seven or eight, he couldn't even remember. Saddened, he put the letter down and sat for a while with his head in his hands. What was happening? Although he'd never had a proper family life when he was young, he thought he could make this work for him. It was falling apart. That night he got seriously pissed in the mess, waking up next morning in the backseat of his car, the hot autumn sun still burning through the window, searing his face.

Struggling through the day with a killer hangover, later that night he sat with the others in the lounge watching TV. Without giving it much thought, he joined in as they hissed and booed the scenes of anti-war protesters marching in the main streets of the city. When police mounted on horseback appeared on the screen and rode them down, they jumped to their feet and cheered. It could be touch and go if he ever reached Vietnam. Australia's policy of conscription was souring public opinion and building up pressure to quit their plans to go to war. He may never make it. Luck was with him. The week after, they received their orders.

Shaking with fear, Mike cautiously moved through the thick jungle clutching his weapon. Somewhere, it was waiting for him. He knew; he could feel it. They'd told him it could smell poms, and although he thought it was ridiculous, now he wasn't so sure. Try as he may, the senseless fear would not go away. Within hours of the regiment landing at the jungle training centre in Queensland, there had been warnings.

"Jeez, mate, look out for bloody taipans. Seriously, they're bloody dangerous. Rear up on you, they will. When they strike, they go for your balls. Savage them, they will, and they're more poisonous than a fucking cobra. No anti-venom."

Later at the briefing, the training officer had given a similar warning about this extremely dangerous reptile. Since he'd been here he had begun to wonder what he was doing there. What a hell of a country! You couldn't swim or you'd be stung to death by some bloody little jellyfish or be eaten by a shark. Go to the toilet and some red back spider would bite you on the bum. And now this fucking snake that was out to get him. His balls would be savaged by a vicious, poisonous killer snake. He'd nearly had enough! The sooner he got to Vietnam, the better.

It was his last weekend before he left Australia. After writing to Carol, he'd jumped into a taxi with the others. That's nearly all he could remember. Sunlight now cruelly levered his eyelids open. Moving his head carefully up from the pillow, he was jolted awake as his hand touched naked flesh alongside him. With his eyes fully open, he realized he was in a strange flat. Almost too scared to look, he peeped at the figure lying beside him. With a sigh of relief, he saw it was a girl.

"Hi, I'm Jan. Bet you don't remember me." Embarrassed, Mike nodded his head. Kneeling up beside him, her long black hair hung down over her bare shoulders. Sun- tanned all over, her figure was almost boyish. Almost, but enough of it wasn't and she looked fine. Dark nipples rose stiffly from her small breasts as she leaned towards him.

"You were good last night but you don't remember, do you?" Again Mike stayed silent, his head starting to hurt slightly. Laughing, the girl threw her head back. Despite his head, Mike found himself warming to this naked sprite of a girl.

"It's those Bundies. Get you every time if you're not used to them." Vaguely he recalled the hotel bar. Bundies...yes, that's what they were called. A lethal mixture of local rum and Coke served by the jug! Four jugs had been ordered as they sat down in the heaving bar with its loud rock band. Within minutes, they'd been surrounded by girls. Legend had it Brisbane was famous for its girls, and there were lots of them that night. They were everywhere!

Leaping from the bed, the girl's pretty bare bum disappeared behind a screen of dangling beads that tinkled as she passed through. Promptly, she reappeared with a cigarette in her smiling mouth and winked at him.

"Sex makes you hungry. Want some breakfast?"

Eating in silence, they sat looking at each other. He'd pulled on a pair of shorts she'd given him, but she was still naked. Finishing breakfast, they showered together. Before they reached the bedroom, she pulled him to her. By now his head had cleared.

"You've a beautiful body," she sighed, her hands moving all over him. In one smooth movement, he lifted her small frame up to him and with ease slid into her. Groaning in ecstasy, she wrapped her legs around his hips.

Minutes later, they collapsed exhausted onto the bed. For a while they lay there, motionless. "I have to go." The girl didn't open her eyes. "I know."

Mike continued, "I'm leaving for Vietnam." Her eyes stayed closed. "I know." There was silence for a moment. "I'll write you." Opening her eyes, the girl sighed deeply then kissed his cheek. "No you won't. You're married." Startled, he sat up abruptly. "How did you know?" With a coy smile she handed him his wallet, open at the picture of Carol and Eliza.

"Goodbye, Warrant Officer Mike Hunter. Look after yourself. Please don't die."

Wordlessly, Mike rose from the bed, dressed and without turning back, quietly opened the door and left. Outside he caught a cab back to the barracks.

Effortlessly, the Qantas airliner lifted off from the strip, circled Brisbane town then headed north. Initially it was quiet in the cabin as the soldiers contemplated their leaving home, but soon enough the regimental comradeship washed over them and the atmosphere was filled with loud chatter and bright laughter.

Standing astride his kit bag as it lay on the tarmac, Mike looked around. Hot and humid, the air was mixed with the smell of burned fuel as transport planes, helicopters and fighter jets came and went. Typically Army, they waited in the sweltering sun as their papers were processed. American jeeps drove back and forth between parked aircraft. Almost invisible, drab-colored local Vietnamese shuffled around sweeping and cleaning.

Saigon. He'd arrived at the war front.

# Chapter Fourteen

# The Vietcong

Almost deafened by the slapping of the huge rotors in the air, Mike huddled along with twenty others in the belly of the large Chinook helicopter. Packed in around his section were their kitbags and weapons. Following behind them were two other choppers of the same ilk carrying the rest of the regiment and their equipment.

Apparently, the Americans were more than willing to transport them to the Aussie base. Australia was the only other western nation willing to join the Yanks in what would end up as a useless fight. The Americans didn't like being alone on the world stage.

High above the green Vietnamese jungle, the helicopters flew unmolested, the skies being dominated by the U.S. Air force. They were flying south to a base further into the jungle close to the Cambodian border. Less than an hour later, the big flying machines changed the note of their engines and gradually descended from the clouds onto a clearing in the dark-green canopy of trees. Mike emerged from the body of the aircraft into a substantially different world. All around him was military activity. Another row of the big Chinooks were parked side-by-side, while on the other side of them about forty smaller Bell "Hueys" squatted, surrounded by men in jungle fatigues. Some, stripped to the waist, worked feverishly on repairing and maintaining them while others stood lolling around on guard, their weapons hanging from their shoulders or stacked nearby.

The heat and humidity hit him like a slap in the face. In no short time he was dripping with sweat, his entire uniform of jungle battle fatigues soaked and sticking to his body. Around the base, the area had been stripped of foliage and only the brown dust of what had been the forest floor remained.

Just after the third and last Chinook landed, they were ferried off to the base camp in battle-scarred, beat-up Army Land Rovers. Without any preliminaries, the regiment was ushered into a large tent where a podium, on which a sad-looking microphone lay waiting. Moments after they were all seated, a Major in fatigues stepped up to the lectern. Holding up his hand as the men began to rise, he spoke briskly into the microphone.

"Welcome to base camp. Shortly you will be taken to the front. This is active service. The way you conduct yourself will reflect on the Australian Military Forces and our spirit of ANZAC. Your country expects the best from you and I'm sure you'll give it all you've got. Thank you. Stand easy."

As soon as he stepped down, a sergeant promptly gave them their standing orders. They were to move out within the hour. The choppers to move them forward would be ready shortly.

"What a load of fucking shit!" Mike's attention was instantly drawn to the soldier alongside him. "Say again, soldier." Scowling, the young man stared at Mike. "What a load of crap. I've been conscripted and I hate this fucking Army. And you can stick your Anzacs up your arse!" Calmly, Mike tried to defuse the situation. "Is that all, soldier?"

Turning on his heel, the angry youth spat back, "Get stuffed," then stormed off. Shaking his head, Mike contemplated disciplining the recalcitrant warrior, but in the end thought better of it. This was the Australian army and they did things differently.

This time there was only eight of them to a chopper. Lighter and more maneuverable than the big Chinooks, it skimmed over the treetops followed by ten others. Alert at the open doorway was a machine gunner scanning the ground below for any suspicious movements. In the clearings between the jungles, the peasants worked in the paddy fields alongside lumbering buffalo. Weaving back and forth, the choppers avoided the obvious path that would bring them in contact with the hidden Vietcong. Mike's group sat in silence; the noise preventing any light conversation even if they'd wanted it.

Scurrying under the still whirling blades, Mike and the rest of the section headed for headquarters on foot. Going in the opposite direction were several jeeps loaded with the wounded. Behind them was one more stacked with full body bags. Mike took a sharp intake of breath. They were now into reality. Serious war, where soldiers got wounded or even worse, killed.

Without ceremony, they were shown their accommodation in the camouflaged tents, then ordered back for a briefing. They were to patrol the perimeter lines until further orders. Despite himself, after the commander had finished, he asked his one and only burning question.

"Are there any taipans, sir?" Slightly bemused, the captain was taken aback. "What, Warrant Officer?" Not sure, Mike looked around. All the faces were deadpan. "Taipans, sir. Snakes." The round of subdued laughter caused Mike to realize his error.

"Warrant Officer, taipans are the least of your problem. If there had ever been any they would have been eaten by the Vietcong ages ago." Another round of slightly louder laughter greeted the commander's comments and Mike blushed mildly in discomfort.

"Any more questions?" The captain looked pointedly at Mike. Silence was the answer. "All dismissed, then. Good luck."

By now, all pretence at being a British Army advisor on guerrilla tactics had been dropped. Warrant Officer Mike Hunter was in action with a submachine gun in his hands, safety catch off and alert to enemy contact.

Leaving the perimeter in the very early morning, his patrol would work their way around the edge of the base zone until first light when they would slip back through the barbwire and machine gun posts to the protection of the base.

Some ten days after his arrival, Mike was lying on his camp bed in the tent. A head thrust itself through the flap and the owner breathlessly blurted out the message. "WO Hunter, sir, CO's tent at the double!"

On entering the CO's tent Mike threw a quick salute. Without looking up, Captain Wright spoke briskly. "Hunter, take eight men in a chopper to Alpha six. Appears there's an ambush. Bring back what you can. Dismissed. Move it!"

Crouching in the low flying chopper, Mike's squad was tense as it swooped down over the jungle cover into a crudely hacked landing zone. With bullets whistling through the fuselage like angry bees, the pilot swayed the chopper back and forth as it hovered slightly above the ground. They waited until it slowed enough, then Mike's men leaped for their lives and scrambled for cover.

Clutching a heavy machine gun that he'd swapped for his lighter weapon, Mike dropped to a crouch, fired from the hip and sprayed the foreground left and right with bullets. Following, his men spread out as the chopper hovered to a safer height.

Yelling orders, Mike led his men, screaming in defiance, at a run through the thick grass and low scrub. They closed on the soldiers that were pinned down. Their arrival swung the odds and the Vietcong rapidly retreated.

Mike followed fast on their heels, firing now in sharp bursts from the shoulder. A black shadow darted from cover. Mike aimed and fired. With a scream the figure dropped to the ground. In his side vision he saw another, swung and fired again.

One of the men had a flamethrower working. With it roaring he moved into the brush, flames spewing like a dragon. Covering him, two other soldiers sprinted into position firing from the hip with semiautomatics.

A few minutes later, Mike called a halt. The enemy had disappeared. Moving over to where he'd seen his two targets, he found nothing but a large patch of blood and gore. To avoid giving any information, the Vietcong rarely left their wounded behind. If they did, they made sure they were dead. Mike called the chopper in. His hands were shaking. He was gasping for breath as he helped load on the two badly wounded, groaning men. One of them screamed in agony. There was only enough room for half of the ambushed patrol. Minutes later, a second chopper picked up the rest of the patrol. Mike grunted and shoved a dead body on board before scrambling on as the chopper lifted off.

Mike reported in after he'd washed some of the blood and muck off his fatigues. His CO shook his hand. "Bloody well done, Hunter. Pity there wasn't a few captured fucking Cong. You did fine. I'm writing you into my report."

Exhausted, Mike collapsed on his camp cot. As night fell he was still reliving the rescue and thinking of what he might have done differently. The adrenaline still hadn't settled down and he couldn't sleep. Wearing only his jungle fatigue trousers, he lay restlessly under his mosquito net. In spite of the CO's comments on taipans, he still had his suspicions and always tucked himself well inside the net. Alongside him lay his submachine gun and a belt with a long commando knife tucked in its sheath.

Around midnight he dropped off to sleep. A shrill whistle awoke him with a start. He rolled off his bed, snatched up the submachine gun and buckled on his knife belt. In a low crouching position he left his tent.

Outside, the bright moonlight lit the camp like it was day. The Cong shouldn't have been attacking during this time of the month, but they were, and as the whistles stopped, a mocking, high-pitched Asian whine came over a loudspeaker.

"Aussie soldier going to die. Aussie soldier going to die tonight."

Then it became more personal. "Private Glen Smith, you going to make widow" and similar were broadcast in a singsong Asian accent. Bloody Vietcong.

During the day, the gooks hung around the camp working in mess, cleaning and cooking. At night they slipped away to become the enemy. What a fucking war!

Then it was Mike's turn, and his hair stood on edge.

"Warrant Officer Hunter. You Engleesh soldier. Aussies not like you. Go before you die." Christ, they even had his name. Keeping low, he headed for the nearest foxhole. Just in time. As he dived in, the first mortar round thumped into the base.

The rounds rained with huge thumps, causing havoc in the compound. Machine gunfire opened up. It seemed the enemy had magically conjured up the clouds that rolled across the moon, plunging everything in darkness. Blackened figures swarmed through the night. All was filled with screams and gunfire.

With his knife in one hand and his weapon in the other, Mike left the foxhole and in a crouching run headed back towards his tent. A shadow caught his vision. Before he could fire off his submachine gun, a rifle came up. Mike hurled himself through the dark as a burst of gunfire flamed out. He plunged his knife into a black, pajama-clad body as an excruciating pain seared through his leg, halting his progress. The bullet tore through the muscle, shattering bone and crippling him. In agony, he forced the knife deeper. His attacker gave out a high-pitched scream into his ear. It ended when, unconscious, he slumped over the twitching body that twitched once more before its death, which went unnoticed.

Faint voices with Australian accents stirred him. In a fog of semiconsciousness, he realized the action was over. He tried to drag himself to his feet. Around him, the ground was a slippery mess of blood and mud. Fine rain was sprinkling down. Sliding off the still body, he froze in horror.

Even with the dim light he could make out the small oriental face that was now exposed. The rain washed away the tears from open, sightless eyes. A stain of blood trickled from the open mouth. It was the face of a young girl. He'd killed a young girl. Shocked and in agony, he threw up into the mud, then collapsed back into the filthy mixture, gasping for breath. Sobbing, he tried to crawl from the fearful corpse.

Through the dark night a torch flashed. "Over here. Here's another one!" Two young medics lurched over with a stretcher. A face drifted over Mike's. "Don't worry mate. We've got you."

Mike, gasping in pain, tried to direct them to the body next to him. Ignoring his gestures, they rolled him onto the stretcher. The pain was too much and he passed out again.

# Chapter Fifteen

# Melbourne

Flapping over the treetops, the helicopter began to hover then landed alongside the military camp hospital. Mike lay drugged and nearly comatose strapped to a stretcher lashed to the outside of the landing frame. Above him an empty blue sky hung motionless. Immediately when they landed, waiting nurses and orderlies quickly transferred the wounded to the backs of jeeps.

Faint from the loss of blood, Mike vaguely remembered being bandaged by the paramedics and the warm feeling of a massive shot of pain-killing morphine. Within minutes of landing, he was on the operating table and the blood-spattered surgeon swiftly repaired the life-threatening torn artery.

Stitched up with his leg in a plaster cast, he was bundled off to the recovery area. The nurses hurriedly hooked him to a fresh plasma pack then rushed back to rescue and repair the queue of other waiting wounded. From time to time the nurses would grunt or, in desperation, sob as one of the wounded died in their care.

Several days later, the surgeon, on his rounds, stopped at the side of Mike's bed.

"Not good, Warrant Officer. Not good. Your leg's in bad shape. Don't know if we can save it. Your war's over. We're flying you out tomorrow."

After he'd left, Mike waited stoically until he was alone. Unable to roll over, he lay there with tears rolling down his cheeks. A cripple. He didn't want to end up a cripple. He preferred to die.

Aboard the airliner heading for Australia, Mike put on a brave face and chatted cheerily to the cabin crew. Recovered except for his leg, he was allowed a beer or two. It helped while he was awake, but when he dozed off the young Asian girl's tortured face as she died haunted him. Like a terrible nightmare, it refused to leave him and danced in his mind until he awoke, denying him precious sleep.

Touching down on the landing strip, the pilot gently braked on the wet tarmac then cruised the plane to a halt in front of the terminal building. Mike waited until most of the others had left, then, with the help of one of the girl cabin crew, limped painfully down the aisle to the exit. Below, at the foot of the stairs, waited a khaki-colored army ambulance that was dull and sodden from the grey drizzly rain.

Aided by two more of the cabin crew, he negotiated the steps to the bottom. As he entered the vehicle, he looked back to see two of the pretty hostesses standing in the exit of the plane. Waving to them, he was pleased to see them laugh and wave back.

Riding in the ambulance, Mike gazed out of the darkened window that made the dull day even duller. Melbourne on a wet May day didn't have a lot going for it. People scurried along the streets, huddled against the cold wind and driving rain. It was midday but the streetlights still burned, trying weakly to add their little strength to the dimness of the gloom. The only warmth was in the shop windows filled with bright merchandise glowing under the mini spotlights.

When the ambulance drew to a halt, he was transferred to a ward where he was stripped of his uniform, dressed in a gown and then examined by a doctor and a surgeon.

"Miserable day, eh, soldier?" Turning, Mike looked at the young nurse standing in front of him holding his hospital pajamas. "In more ways than one. Thanks." Taking his pajamas, he waited for the nurse to depart. "Put them on, soldier. Don't worry, I've seen it all before."

Smiling a wicked smile, he dropped his gown and stood naked as she handed them to him. Taking them slowly, he quipped, "Then you'll be a good judge."

With a smile lighting up her face, she looked down.

"Four out of ten." Then she laughed.

"Wait till after the operation." Again she laughed. "That's what they all say!" Mike was still laughing after she left. It was the first time in months he'd felt almost human.

Above him, the ceiling swirled and swayed back and forth, the motion finally making him sick. Half dazed, he rolled to one side of the bed and was sick in the bucket by his bed. A cool hand supported his forehead as a soft voice tried to comfort him.

"Take it easy, soldier. Take it easy." Slumping back on the pillow, he tried to focus. A pretty face swam in and out of focus. Abruptly he fell asleep again.

Awake some time later, he was confused but at least the ceiling had stopped moving. Standing over him were two doctors, and a little behind them was the nurse.

"How do you feel, soldier? It was a long operation. Six hours. We had to screw and pin your leg. For a while it was touch and go to see if we could save you from being a cripple. But we think it'll be alright. Hurt a bit for a while, and you'll have a limp. Better than the alternative."

Relieved, Mike gasped, "Thanks. I'm thirsty…can I have water?" Nodding the first doctor turned to the nurse. "Of course. Nurse, water please." The pretty face came back into focus as he shakily reached out for the glass.

With practiced tender care, the nurse guided it to his mouth and he drank it down, slopping drops of it on the bed. Tired beyond belief, he slipped back into a deep sleep.

"This breakfast looks like it's already been eaten." After two days on a drip feed, it was time to try solid food.

"It has been, soldier." Mike scowled. "It's *Mike*."

"You're an officer." A frown crossed his face. "Call me Warrant Officer Mike." Not smiling the nurse looked at him. "Yes, WO Mike."

Glancing sideways at the nurse, Mike found her too pretty to be angry with. "Your name?" Not fazed, she looked him straight in the eye. "Nurse Nelson." Now he was getting peeved. "Cut the formal crap." With a faint smile she leaned over to his ear. "Valerie," she whispered. "Call me Val." It was his time to smile. "Okay, nurse Val."

He munched on the soft porridge that was his first meal after his operation. It was disgusting. Now he felt fully recovered from the effects of the operation and a shadow of a beard was appearing on his face. Painkillers stopped him from too much of an ache in the leg that was supported in a frame at the end of his bed.

When he had finished, he handed the plate to the nurse. "More please, sir." Val laughed. "The operation hasn't damaged your sense of humor."

Grimacing, he nodded his head in the direction of his plaster-covered leg. "Hasn't done much for my sex life."

The nurse shook her head then touched his head with her fingertips. "Time, soldier. Give it time." Mike looked into her eyes and winked, "And opportunity!"

Two weeks later, he was on his feet. It hurt like hell. In agony, he followed the exercises given him by the physiotherapist.

"You like watching me in pain, don't you." Grinning, the male physiotherapist urged him on.

"More than you can believe, mate. Keep going." Sweating with the pain, Mike pushed his toes back and forth. "Shit that hurts." Shrugging, the physio sat back. "No pain, no gain, soldier."

"Warrant officer," Mike grunted. The physio shrugged again. "Sorry."

When the painkillers began to wear off, the dreams started. Often he awoke cursing and shouting, sweat pouring from his brow. During the day he thought of Carol and Eliza, both of whom he'd not seen for over eighteen months. Carol he didn't miss, but he felt bad about his daughter. Whenever he could, he tried to talk to Val. It seemed to him that whenever she could she tried to talk to him. He wanted to talk about the Army, the girl he killed, and the fight he could no longer fight. Five weeks after the operation, he was back in quarters awaiting a decision about his future.

Reluctant at first, finally Val agreed to go out to dinner with him. Opposite her, he gazed at her dark brown eyes and dark brown hair.

"Italian. You've got Italian blood and it shows. You're beautiful."
She looked down, then back at him with a smile. "Maybe you're a
good soldier, but you're a lousy judge. My parents are Scottish, both
of them." Feigning shock, Mike looked stunned. "Really? No!"

She smiled again. "Really, yes."

After another glass of red wine they slipped comfortably into the
warmth of their own company as the bustle of the restaurant moved
around them. In the background a piano player tinkled out soft
versions of Beatles tunes. Outside, a cold winter's night drove heavy
rain onto the window, leaving little room for the cold darkness to
slip though.

All around them, handsome people crowded the tables filled with
bottles of wine that surrounded a candle or two. Waiters scurried
back and forth carrying food and empty plates. Mike and Val's
conversation slowed to a halt as they sat staring into each other's
eyes. When they left the restaurant, they threw themselves into the
backseat of a taxi and hugged each other close as it sped through the
black night back to Val's flat.

Gently Mike's finger traced a sensual circle around the erect
naked nipple of Val's breast. Grabbing his hand, she rolled on top of
him and kissed him. Soft morning light crept through the window.
The rain had finally stopped.

"I know you're married." Mike lay motionless as she spoke. "I've
known since you arrived. It was on your hospital card. Dependants,
next of kin. You'll go back to them, of course." Mike stayed silent.
"I don't want to be a home breaker. You're tempting, very tempting,
and I'm more than a little in love with you." Tears ran from her
cheeks and dripped onto his shoulder.

"Me, too, Val. Me, too. I love you." Val sobbed slightly. "Go,
Mike. Go to back to your family." He held her tight, tears now
welling in his eyes.

## Chapter Sixteen

# Home

Despite his limp, Mike walked at a brisk pace down the long corridors of Heathrow airport. Wearing his uniform with its decorations didn't worry him on his home turf. In Melbourne it had been different. The Vietnam War had become very unpopular. There his uniform just invited trouble. Aussies could be friendly but they could also be bloody mean.

"We've enough troubles fighting this fucking war without some pommie bastard out here to fuck it for us." The taunts would ring in his ears as he left the bar that was full of tough men in working clothes. One-on-one, he would have been able to take them, but as a bunch they'd have ripped him limb from limb.

Leaving Val was hard, very hard. It was her resolve in the end, not his. He wanted to stay. She was right; he had to get back to his family. He had decided that if it didn't work out he would go back.

After passing through Customs, he looked around. In the crowd was a face he recognized. But standing next to Carol was a young girl he didn't. Pushing through the crowd, he made his way to his wife. Excitedly, the young girl ran to him and slung her arms around his neck.

"Daddy, daddy, you're home! Daddy, daddy!" Mike hugged her to him, smiled broadly at Carol and kissed his daughter on the cheek. Then, lowering her down, he gathered up his wife, hugged her and kissed her briefly. "It's good to be home." Looking relieved, Carol smiled. "It's good to have you back, Mike."

The next day Mike reported back to his old regiment. In front of the Adjutant he felt tense and uncomfortable.

"I've had enough, sir. I've had enough." Across the desk from him, the lieutenant looked Mike up and down. Tempting as it was, he didn't call him a coward. The haunted look in Mike's eyes told him there was a story behind the man. It wasn't just a simple case of a lack of courage.

Mike had anguished over his decision night after night. All the rational arguments that it wasn't his fault, that the enemy used children, particularly in this case, didn't work. War was war, he knew that, but it couldn't erase the memory of his knifing someone not much older than his daughter to death. Even though she would have killed him, he could not escape this guilty feeling.

"We can offer you an administrative posting. With your injury, active service would not be practical. On the other hand, you can take a pensionable retirement on the grounds of disability. There is a retraining scheme. You'd be entitled to that and a small pension."

With a small sigh of relief, Mike spoke in a low voice. "Thank you, sir." Picking up his pen and starting to write, the officer didn't look up. "Dismissed, Warrant Officer. Speak to the clerk on the way out. He'll arrange everything." For the final time, Mike stood to attention and saluted. His time in the Army had come to an end.

That night, Mike found himself going through the motions. In bed, despite long weeks without a female companion, he found the effort to make love to Carol beyond him. Feigning tiredness, he lay back and pretended to go to sleep. Although she had put on weight, his wife wasn't unattractive. It was just that he couldn't get excited. The fire had gone out. Perhaps they had started too young, or maybe he shouldn't have had those affairs. The memory of Val was still fresh in his mind. No, it wasn't really that. He was different and so was she. They didn't interest each other.

"Welding. I think I'd like to do welding." After several hours of brooding over the technical college curriculum, Mike decided on a course in welding, mainly because he couldn't stand the thought of the others that were on offer. At least welding had a bit of a manly air about it; he would be dealing with hot steel.

The entrance clerk nodded then ticked the form, and two days later Mike presented himself in class. With a slightly red face, Mike glanced around. He was the oldest by at least ten years and he felt a bit stupid. But once the lectures had started, he felt a little more at ease.

Amazingly, he knew a lot more about the subject than he had first thought. Being around weapons helped him understand the need for care and attention to detail. With his older mind, the principles were easier to grasp. Soon he stood out and became a role model for the younger students. It wasn't long before his lecturer used him as an example. "Watch Mr. Hunter," he'd admonish. "That's the correct technique. Careful, don't rush. A good tradesman finishes the job once."

If only he had the same skills at home. Life with Carol was deteriorating. Every day was tenser than the one before. He began to dislike then hate the bedroom. Worse still, the nightmare of Vietnam plagued him from time to time and he would awaken with a cry, sweating and clutching the bedclothes. That would awaken Carol. Next morning she would complain impatiently about a lack of sleep and advise him to see a doctor.

Six months after starting his course, Mike opted to go on and do a welding supervisor course. Another twelve months, but the Army would pay. Advancing rapidly to the top of his class, he joined the first ten in the class on a factory visit to Redpath, Dorman and Long.

"Fixed up for when you've finished?" He was opposite the works engineer at lunch. Mike shook his head.

"Well, RDL have a number of big new contracts and we're expecting another out in the Middle East. Stay in touch. We could do with a good supervisor."

Immediately after his course was finished, Mike started with RDL. Fortunate, really, as his first project was in Aberdeen on a North Sea rig. Good money, good experience and a good distance from his wife. He missed his daughter, but Carol…that was different. It was getting very difficult. Every second weekend he'd go home. Every other weekend, he'd end up with some local girl in Aberdeen. Life was getting very complicated. But at least the nightmares had stopped.

# Chapter Seventeen

# Dubai

Rain sloshed down as Mike made his way through RDL's main fabrication yard. Huge cranes lifted massive steel sections that were guided by highly experienced supervisors on to other equally large steel structures. In the gloomy day, the bright blue flashes of the electric welding sparkled all around him. Heavy drops splattered onto his white hardhat and ran down the curve of his donkey jacket that was pulled tight over his shoulders. Without the day-to-day exercise he had in the Army, he'd started to put on weight, but working on the rig had kept him fit enough. He was good at his job and the management had told him so in his pay packet.

Apprehensively, he pushed open the door to the main office. Instantly the whole world changed. Across the natural stone tiled floor stood a highly polished inlaid veneer desk behind which sat a highly polished receptionist. All around the wall, hung in expensive frames, were pictures of the company's previous projects. Bridges, steel towers, water reservoirs, Queens Award to Industry and finally, in pride of place, a portrait of the Queen herself.

Removing his hardhat and dripping water as he walked, he stepped up to the desk. "I'm here to see John James." Barely acknowledging his presence, the woman's voice was as cold as the weather.

"Mr. James in Projects?" Humbled, Mike muttered in reply, "I think so." With a dismissive wave of her hand, the ice maiden continued in her previous tone.

"Through the door on the right and up the stairs. Speak to the receptionist. She'll know where he is." Then, without another word or glance, she resumed her work. Self- consciously, Mike backed away and followed her directions.

Down the long corridor he passed rooms that were full of drawing boards with industrious young men hunched over them. Walking tentatively, he reached the stairs and at the top of them found the receptionist. This time his reception was in total contrast to his previous.

"Can I help you?" While a little on the heavy side, the slightly older women had a bright, warm and appealing smile. "Mr. James, senior project engineer?"

Mike was clutching his hardhat in front of him, almost as if he needed protection.

"Oh, John. Of course. Down the hallway, second door on the left. I just saw him go in with a cup of coffee." Grateful for the kind words, Mike smiled broadly. "Thanks. Thank you very much."

James was a tall man. Mike could see that even as he sat at his desk. "Sit down, Hunter. Want a cup of coffee? Tea?" Mike shrugged his shoulders and took a chair. "Coffee's fine."

When he stood, the man was taller than Mike had realized. He left briskly then returned moments later with a mug of steaming coffee. "Use my sugar and cream if you like."

Taken aback by the informality, Mike shook his head. "Black's fine."

Lowering himself into his seat, the tall man placed his hands on the desk. "Won't beat about the bush, Mike. Don't mind if I call you Mike?" Again a bit surprised, Mike shook his head.

"No, Mr. James." A broad smile crossed his boss's face. "John will do." With a shrug, Mike returned the smile. "Okay, John."

Settling back, John went on. "Mike, maybe you're aware of the big project going through the shop. Dock gates for Dubai Dry Docks. One of our biggest to date."

Mike nodded and murmured, "Yes."

Leaning slightly forward, James' voice became a little more conspiratorial. "Well, we've got problems on site. Frank Turnbull, our project engineer, is, well, not all there."

Taking more interest, Mike sat upright. "Not there, John? He's returned to the U.K.?"

James shook his head. "Well, not exactly. We don't know where he is. Some story about him clearing off to Bangkok with a girl. Probably the heat and the alcohol. At any rate, we're in the shit." Mike's eyebrows went up. "Thought you couldn't drink out there?" The big man on the other side of the table smiled wryly. "It's almost compulsory!" Mike's eyebrows went up. "Really!"

James shrugged and continued. "Whole point is we want you to go out as a replacement. Difficult at such short notice, I know. Trouble is the main contractor is Costains and their manager is a tough nut and he's causing hell. Threatening damages and holding our payments. We have to move quickly. You're ex-Army; you should be able to handle it."

A bit shocked, Mike stammered, "But I'm not an engineer!"

Not fazed, John waved off his protest. "Don't worry. If you get into technical difficulties, I'll fly out." Still somewhat shocked, Mike was concerned. "Let you know in the morning?"

Looking pleased as if Mike had already accepted, James stood up, reached over the desk and shook his hand. "Good man, good man."

In silence, Mike ate his meal while listening to his daughter and wife chatter about the day's activities. There was little left in common between him and his wife. With his good salary, now they could well afford their new house and Carol spent her days busily rearranging it while Elizabeth was at school.

With RDL he had been away on sites up and down the country. The work was absorbing and he loved his job. He would often stay overnight in hotels, where he'd meet the occasional woman who shared the bed with him. None of them were serious and they'd part in the mornings.

Mike had been surprised how easy it was. When he was young he was scared of girls. Maybe it was his dreadful home life. Now that was gone. His mother had taken ill years ago and was in a home. Every now and then he'd visit her. There wasn't much left of his family; he never saw his sister.

Carefully putting his knife and fork on the plate, he sat back and caught his wife's eye. He poured a glass of wine for himself and then one for Carol. Looking down, he spoke in a low voice. "I'm leaving."

Carol remained silent, partly because she'd expected it to come someday.

"It's not another woman. I'm leaving for Dubai."

Carol broke her silence. "Where the hell?"

More confidently, Mike spoke a little louder. "Dubai. New job out in the Arabian Gulf." Not convinced, his wife looked sideways at him. "Never heard of it. Sure it's not another woman?" Throwing his head back, Mike roared so loud with laughter that his daughter dropped he knife and fork in fright.

"Another woman! Out there I doubt if you'd find a white woman for a hundred miles. No, don't be bloody stupid. It's for RDL. Their new project. The site engineer's buggered off to God-knows-where and they want me out there straight away. Bachelor status, but the money's good. No tax! Leave every six months. Couple of years and I'll have this house paid for."

A small voice interrupted. "You're going away, Daddy?" Looking at his daughter's sad eyes, Mike felt the proverbial lump in his throat.

"Not for good, Elizabeth. Just for a while. I'm going to make a lot of money and we'll be rich!" A wan smile crossed his daughter's face. "Can I have a pony when we're rich?"

It was Mike's turn to smile. "No problem. You can have two!" Carol scowled at him. Shrugging her shoulders, she stood up and gathered up the plates. Walking past Mike, she whispered harshly, "I still think it's another woman."

The following week Mike got on the plane.

PRITHI

## Chapter Eighteen

# The Ski Trip

It was the centre of the airport departure lounge. An incongruous group of young teenagers milled around a similar number of chattering adults. In contrast with the other passengers, they were dressed in winter ski outfits despite the heat. For the British private schools, it was the Easter holidays and the lucky youngsters were off to Austria for the school's annual ski trip. Students of Dubai College, they were mostly the children of British expatriates.

One of the taller ones was a young Indian girl. Although only fifteen, she had the appearance of a much older girl. Her long, dark hair swung freely around her shoulders, swirling above the thick collar of her ski jacket. Flashing back and forth, her almond eyes sparkled with expectation. Tight denim jeans showed off her long legs as they swept down from beneath the brightly colored jacket into fur-lined snow boots.

The rest of the group was dressed in similar fashion, and as they jostled and joked with each other, their parents organized tickets, passports and luggage. Several teachers stood around, trying from time to time to urge their students to quieten down. Apart from a couple of parents, they would be the chaperones on the trip.

Most of the parents were dressed casually in jeans and T-shirts, but the Indian girl's parents stood apart, stiffly dressed and more formal. Her father was in a dark business suit and wore a traditional turban while her mother wore an expensive silk, western-style sari and dripped with dull but real golden jewellery of the expensive kind.

Finally the time to depart had come. The children hugged and kissed their parents, some of the girls crying with excitement and emotion. The boys showed their emotion by pushing and shoving each other around. Kissing her mother, the Indian girl then reached up and put her arms around her father's neck.

A partner with a local Arab, her father half-owned a trading company and had a lot of money with a British bank. With his influence he'd managed to get his daughter Prithi accepted by the Board of Governors; otherwise, she would have had to go to one of the Indian high schools. Growing up with her friends at the college, Prithi hardly noticed she was Indian, and to hear her speak, there was no difference between her and her classmates with U.K. backgrounds.

At ten thousand metres, the jetliner cruised north towards Europe. Next to her best friend Lisa, Prithi could hardly contain herself. Outside the oval window they could see the puffy white clouds drift by.

"White or red, miss?"

Prithi looked up. The air hostess was offering her wine to go with the meal that had just been placed in front of her. Swiftly glancing around, she noticed that none of the teachers or chaperones was watching.

"White, please." Lisa giggled as the stewardess poured both of them a glass of wine. Having never tasted it before, Prithi took a careful sip. "Oh, it's like vinegar! I don't like it." Reaching over, her young neighbor took her glass. "I do!" With that, Lisa scoffed it down. Within minutes, she'd finished her own as well and was becoming noisier and gigglier. Scared they'd get caught, Prithi refused when the airhostess returned offering more.

Almost imperceptibly, the plane landed at Munich. Lisa was asleep and it took some effort by Prithi to wake her. Two wines and she was anybody's. Wearily, the group shuffled half asleep through Immigration. It was here that Prithi learned she wasn't the same as the rest. While she stood in a long queue, the others with their British passports passed through quickly. After what seemed an eternity to her, she emerged, embarrassed for having kept the others waiting for so long.

"Don't worry, Prithi. We understand."

If she'd had a weapon, she'd have killed that teacher on the spot. Aboard the coach, they all soon fell asleep in the warmth until they were roughly awakened by the cries of one of the teachers.

"Look! Snow! Look!" Excitedly they sat up and rubbed the misty windows. All around them the world was white. Silently, the coach pulled in at Ischgl, the tiny village forty kilometres out of the main city of Innsbruck. Travel worn, they filed into the hotel chalet, registered and wearily headed for their rooms.

Prithi shared one with Lisa. They had the rest of the day to recover and then next day it would be out on the learner's slope. Once they'd unpacked, they ran outside in the snow to join the others. Slipping and sliding, some made snowballs; others shrieked as they were hit by them. After lunch, they trudged in a ragged group through the picturesque village. Upon returning, they ate then went to their rooms. Chattering like birds, Lisa and Prithi snuggled down in their beds and were asleep instantly, not stirring till next morning.

On the slope, the ski instructor greeted them. Young lean and very good looking, he was from Belgium. His name was Franz. Unable to hold their feet when they put on the skis, they slipped and slid then fell about in the snow. Whenever Prithi fell, Franz was immediately by her side to pick her up.

"You are beautiful. You will be a great skier." By the second day, Prithi, along with the rest of them, could ski in a modest fashion. In spite of this, she would deliberately fall over just to have Franz pick her up and speak to her in an accent that was as thick as the taste of chocolate.

Soon they were all skiing further and further down the slope. With six days left to go, they all felt like they were going to be champions. Franz was an excellent instructor, and all the woman teachers and chaperones were in love with him. So was Prithi.

On day five, she skied out of sight of the others and fell over. As usual, Franz was quickly on the scene. Pulling her to her feet, he whispered softly in her ear.

"Prithi, you are so beautiful. My heart is lost to you. *Je t'aime, vraiment.* So beautiful. I must come to you. What is your room number?" The young girl could hardly stand. Franz's voice washed over her like a mystical sea in which she was drowning. Out of control she replied, "Thirty-two." Then the rest of the group was upon them. Prithi could not believe what she'd said. What if he came? Lisa was there. She would be safe; the door would be locked.

Dreaming, she thought she was suffocating and then she awoke. A hand softly covered her mouth as an accented voice whispered her name. "Prithi, Prithi, don't be afraid. It is me, Franz." Momentarily terrified, she froze, then carefully opened her eyes.

It was Franz, bathed in the soft, pale blue moonlight that shone through a gap in the curtains. He stood there like a vision, dressed only in a T-shirt and jeans. Without another word, he stripped naked and suddenly his soft, white body was alongside hers under the covers. Kissing her, his hands were all over her. Momentarily still terrified, she lay rigid then melted like butter into warm milk. Vaguely she felt her nightclothes being removed. Franz's kisses were burning all over her body, which responded with a life of its own. Then he was on top of her and there was a sharp burning pain between her legs. Her mind protested, but her young body took over. Franz kissed her and whispered in her ear in a foreign language that only served to excite her more. Breathing heavily, her hips rose to meet his thrusts, and then in one wonderful moment she was transported. Biting his neck, she stopped herself from crying out in ecstasy. Then quickly she dropped back off to sleep.

Awakening with the dawn's soft light, she thought she had been dreaming. In shock, she realized she was naked. Pulling back the bed covers, she saw the dark stain of blood mixed with the remains of her lovemaking. Frightened, she dragged the sheet from the bed and put it under the shower. Still naked, she was surprised by Lisa.

"What's up, Prithi?" Startled, the young girl grabbed a towel to cover her body. "Oh, I guess it's my period. I have these problems." Yawning and stretching, the other girl laughed. "Join the clan. Mine are a bloody nuisance. I never know. Have you any pads?" Prithi looked embarrassed. "No, I forgot." Lisa disappeared and returned with a small packet. "Here, take one of mine. Leave the sheets. The maids will take care. It happens all the time. Don't be long in the shower. I want one."

As soon as Lisa had gone, Prithi checked her body for marks of last night's fantasy. Thankfully, there weren't any. She still couldn't believe it had happened. Standing under the shower, she tried to come to grips with reality. What a dream!

On the slope, Franz immediately skied to her side. "My darling, you are a dream. *Je t'adore, ma cherie. Je t'adore.*" Again, Prithi felt like she was about to fall down and melt into the snow. All day she skied, but her mind was far away.

That night he came to her bed again. This time there was no fear, no pain and she had to smother her face in his shoulder and bite his neck to stifle the cries of her lovemaking. Her only fear was that Lisa would awaken, but to her great relief, her friend snored like a bull in the bunk above her bed.

The next night Franz did not come. In the morning her body felt like it had been tortured and she could not think straight. When he skied to her side, she grabbed his hand. "Where were you? Why didn't you come?"

Taken aback by the panic in her voice, Franz put his arm around her waist and skied a little distance with her. Somewhat reassured, he could feel the tenseness in her relax a little.

"*Ma cherie*, be calm, I must go see my mother. She is old and she is ill. Do not worry. I will come tonight." Glancing around to see if they were alone, he kissed her quickly on the lips then held her gloved hands in his. "*Je t'adore.*"

For the next two nights Franz kept his promise. Out on the ski slopes Prithi struggled not to touch him or hold him. The desire to hug and kiss him was almost overwhelming. Then, without her realizing, it was their last night. After he made love to her, she clung to him. "Please don't go. I'll die. I love you. Please stay. Please." Her breathless whisper had a note of fear in it. Franz kissed her then eased himself from under the covers. "*Au revoir, ma cherie. Je t'adorerai toujours.*" Hot tears scalded her cheeks and she sobbed herself to sleep.

While others slept, Prithi twisted and turned in the coach seat. Inside she felt hollow, empty and so alone. She was afraid. Franz was gone forever. What would she do? By the time they reached the airport, she had to run to the toilet where she was violently ill.

On the plane, she wished it would crash and she would die. Lisa chattered and laughed beside her. An overwhelming desire to kill her crept over Prithi. Thank God she fell asleep after several sneaked glasses of wine. Finally, the plane landed in Dubai. Now she really wished she were dead.

# Chapter Nineteen

# Prithi's Mother

Back at the college, the rest of the students who had been on the ski trip were full of their adventure. Prithi remained silent, almost sullen. Gradually, Franz began to drift from her thoughts and she stopped crying herself to sleep. For the first few nights she went through hell as her body craved and longed for his touch and her mind raced from confused and anguished dreams. Finally, after about four weeks, she had almost recovered her humor, but now there was something else to worry about.

It was something more serious than she'd ever faced in her life. Even though she may have miscounted the days, she was at least fifteen of them past having her period. Trying to put the thought out of her mind, she ignored it. About two weeks later, she started to feel ill after breakfast and had to rush to the bathroom to throw up. Nobody in the house noticed any change. The terror was starting to build in her young mind.

A week later, as she crossed the open square of the college, she collapsed in a faint. Students gathered around as the nurse was called and came running to help her. In the cool of the nurse's room she recovered, but not before the nurse had telephoned her mother. Arriving at the school in a mild panic, her mother insisted that she go to the doctor for a check-up.

It was the last thing Prithi wanted. Protesting in vain, the next morning she and her mother entered the doctor's office. At her mother's demand, they saw the only woman doctor in the office.

She was an American married to one of the other doctors. The examination was thorough. One look at the doctor's face confirmed Prithi's fears. "You're pregnant. Do you know who the father is?" Prithi started to sob.

Putting her arm around her, the doctor led her out to where her mother was waiting. "Your daughter's perfectly healthy." Prithi's mother gave the doctor a sharp look. "So why did she faint?" For the moment the doctor remained silent. "I think she'd like to tell you." Suddenly her mother was sitting upright in her seat. "No, you tell me now!"

Slightly shocked by the aggressive tone, the doctor shot back. "Your daughter's pregnant." With that, Prithi ran for the car. Settling her bill, her mother strode after her. Opening the car doors with the central locking key, both mother and daughter clambered in. Immediately after the doors closed, Prithi's mother swung around in rage to face her daughter. Without a moment's hesitation, she drew her arm back then smacked her daughter viciously across the face.

"*Tu nalay ah, besharam*! It is better that you died. What shame! Such shame on your family!" Burying her face in her hands, Prithi wept all the way to the house. Reaching the front door, her mother thrust her in with a harsh push to the back. "Go to your room and stay there till your father comes!"

Alone in her room, Prithi threw herself facedown on the bed, sobbing loudly. Sometime later, her crying subsided and she sat up. All she wanted was to die. If only there was some way. Lowering herself from the bed, she went to the bathroom and searched thought the cupboards. There was nothing. Maybe she could smash the mirror and slash her wrists with the glass. Grimacing at the thought of all that blood, she went and sat back on the bed.

Not long afterwards, her father burst into the room followed by her still angry mother. "Prithi, you shame this house! I should put you out of the house on the street where you deserve to be. Who is the father? I will kill him! Some local Arab? I'll have the police on to him. I'm not without influence!"

Her father's voice had almost reached fever pitch. Red-faced and breathing heavily, she thought for one moment he was going to have a heart attack. All she could do was sit wide-eyed in fear, shaking her head. Abruptly, he finished his tirade then turned and stormed out of the room, her mother following.

"You will stay in your room. I'll send you roti and water, you… you," words almost failed her, "you slut!" Screeching, her mother also disappeared, slamming the door as she left. Soon after, a plate of dry bread and a jug of water were thrust into the room.

Dejectedly, the young Indian girl chewed at her meal, bathed and then, turning out the light, crept into bed. Vaguely in the night she heard more shouting, then a slap of a hand upon flesh followed by louder voices and perhaps even a scream of pain. In her dreams, Franz slipped in and out of her mind. Clasping the pillow, she called out his name. Snow fell around them, then it was light and she was back in her bedroom, all alone. It was morning.

Abruptly, the door swung open. "Get dressed. Not your school uniform. Your sari. We are going to Sharjah." Mechanically, Prithi dressed. Dejectedly, she descended the stairs and entered the dining room where she ate a little cereal in silence. Why Sharjah, she wondered?

## Chapter Twenty

# Her Father Dies

Still in an angry mood, her mother sped and swerved through the early morning traffic. Prithi sat sullenly in the front seat. Silently, she watched her mother take her frustrations out on the Mercedes Benz and traffic. Neither seemed to mind or care.

Screeching to a halt, her mother leaped from the car, slammed the door and stormed around to the other side. "Get out. Come with me." Struggling to keep up with her mother, Prithi followed her into an old, two-storey building. Fleetingly, she caught sight of a tarnished nameplate on the doorway to the ground floor. "Sharjah Modern Medical Clinic."

It didn't look like it. The reception room was empty of patients at that hour of the morning, and a fat Indian woman receptionist raised her head and stared blankly at them from behind an old stained desk.

"Doctor Krishnan is not in yet." The tone was rude and abrupt.

Prithi's mother's was equal to it. "He will be soon!"

Recoiling from the snarled response, the fat woman lowered her eyes and studied her diary.

Not long afterwards, a nurse appeared. "Dr. Krishnan will see you now, Mrs. Singh." As her mother dragged her to her feet, Prithi saw the receptionist look up in amazement. Beaming, Dr. Krishnan stood and welcomed them in.

"Ah, Mrs. Singh, a delight. Your husband spoke to me last night. Ah, this is your daughter. Lovely girl. Abdominal pains, I believe.

86

Do sit." Plunking herself down in front of the wide desk, her mother opened her purse, extracted a brown envelope and wordlessly placed it in the centre of the desktop. Opening it, the doctor glanced inside and nodded. "Right, then. Shall we examine your daughter? Please…Prithi, I believe…this way."

Helping her remove her clothes, the nurse gave her a dressing gown that did up at the back. Nervously, she lay on an examination bed waiting for the doctor. He arrived and his cold hands spread her legs. Then the examination was over. Leaving her where she lay, he spoke to her mother who'd just entered the room.

"As I thought, Mrs. Singh. An ovarian cyst. Common in young girls. A minor operation. It can be done today if you like."

With a nod of her head, her mother stared harshly at Prithi. A chill of fear went through her. What next? Unceremoniously, the nurse escorted her into what appeared to be an operating room. Dr. Krishnan appeared and offered soothing words as he prepared an injection. Not knowing what to expect, Prithi was horrified as the nurse rolled her over onto her front and the needle went into her back. The next moment she was on her back again with her legs spread. Aghast, she saw the doctor with some sort of instrument in his hand. At that moment she fainted.

Awakening, she was in another room with a drip in her arm. "Ah, Prithi, how do you feel? Slight complication. More bleeding than we expected. You'll stay overnight, but tomorrow morning you'll be well enough to go home." Fearfully, a whisper came from her throat. "Where's my mother?" Dr. Krishnan stood and headed for the door. "Don't worry; she'll be back in the morning." Mechanically, she took the glass of water offered her by the nurse. The sedative it contained had an immediate effect and she dropped off to sleep.

Painfully, she climbed the stairs to her room. At the same time, her mother disappeared into her bedroom. When she entered her room, she saw a strange house girl preparing her bed. Lying on her bed, she closed her eyes. She felt her body was not her own but some dirty appendage she had to live with.

Gruffly, her mother came through the door. "It's not over. You are not to leave this house without my permission. There will be no socializing. Do you understand?" Almost uncaring, she stared at her mother.

"Mother, where's Babu?" Snorting with disgust, her mother's eyes flared. "So it was him!" Prithi looked amazed. "Was what?" Her mother's face was distorted with anger and some satisfaction at her discovery. "The father!" Too stunned to speak, Prithi sat shaking her head. "Your father dealt with him. He's back in India a sorry person." Unable to believe what she was hearing, Prithi just closed her eyes and let her head sink into her knees.

Waiting till her mother had left; she rolled over onto the pillow and cried angrily into its softness. Hating her parents, she vowed never to let them into her life again. The houseboy! How could they think it was the houseboy?

Back at the college, only a few noticed how much she had changed. Rarely did she speak, she never agreed to go out, and finally she was isolated by her peer group. Instead she studied. Every exam result was a distinction. Disregarding her appearance, she let her hair grow long and disheveled and put on weight from endless eating. A year later, she was a girl with no friends but excellent reports.

When the form head unexpectedly entered the class and went straight to the Math teacher, all eyes were raised. "Prithi, please go with Mr. Jones." Apprehensively, Prithi rose and followed the form head. Outside, he gently took her arm and silently walked with her to the headmaster's office. Inside were the headmaster and the nurse. "Prithi, a driver is coming to take you home." Curiously, she looked around. "I'm sorry, Prithi," The headmaster moved closer and took her arm. "Please sit. It's bad news. Your father's had a serious heart attack. You must go home immediately."

The news did not sink in immediately. Prithi sat in the backseat of the car and looked out the window. When they reached her home, expensive vehicles, parked untidily, surrounded the entrance. Still not feeling any emotion, she entered the front door. Instantly she was met by the gaze of her mother's friends who muttered words of sympathy. Rising, one of them led her by the arm into the living room.

Sitting almost engulfed by more friends, her mother sat weeping. Barely looking up, she continued to put her head in her hands and sob loudly. Her father's Arab partner came to her side and put his arm around her shoulder. "Prithi, it is hard for me to say these words. Your father is dead. He was a good man" Sinking into a lounge chair that had been vacated by one of the women, Prithi, too, put her head in her hands and wept.

In a daze, Prithi accompanied her mother to the funeral. Within hours of his death, the company had arranged to fly the body to India to be cremated in his hometown of Poona. Family, relatives and friends crowded into his brother's home on the day of the last rites.

Nearly as swiftly, they were back on a plane headed for Dubai. For reasons mostly unknown, Prithi's mother had decided to stay there. Perhaps there would be less pressure from her family to remarry or even share some her husband's wealth. Initially, she had said it was to finish Prithi's education, but Prithi knew that wasn't true. Often, the Arab partner would come to their home late at night for a meal and stay even later.

In truth, she had hated her mother since the day of the funeral. In a moment when they'd been alone, her mother had cornered her. "You did this," she had screeched in Prithi's ear. "You did this. When you got pregnant, it weakened his heart. You killed your father."

After her exams, Prithi carried out her mother's wishes and went back to India to study at university for a business degree. Living on the campus, she would go to her uncle's for the weekends. From time to time, Franz would still creep into her dreams. On those occasions, her hand would slip between her legs and she would cry out his name as her passion rose then subsided, almost without waking her. Otherwise, she met no other men, nor did she show any interest in any.

After graduating, she returned to her home in Dubai. Rarely speaking to her mother, she stayed mostly in her room. Eventually, through the influence of the Arab partner, she got a job with Dubai Petroleum Company as the secretary to the chief geologist. It was a good salary and included her accommodation.

Moving out of her mother's home, she rarely returned to see her again. Her work with the chief geologist was interesting and at times exciting. Originally from Dallas, Texas, he was a kindly man in his mid-fifties. Although he never said so, Prithi got the impression he had a lot of money. Like many in high positions in the company, his family lived back in the States and he flew over to spend a week or more with them on vacation. From time to time, he invited her to come with him to meet his family. Tempted, she wasn't brave enough. Settling down to live on her own, she kept mainly to herself. Staying home, she watched TV, read or just enjoyed her flat, rarely going out.

Months after she had joined, she befriended an Australian woman who was somewhat older than her and worked as a secretary. At lunchtime, the two of them would work out in the company gym. Encouraged by the Australian, she changed her diet, lost weight, trimmed her hair and started dressing in western dress, usually tight jeans and designer T-shirts. Men still didn't interest her, and she had decided to save money so that she could migrate to Australia, away from India and its culture for good. Every now and then, her company would send her on a training course—first it was word processing and then data management. She was becoming highly skilled.

"Take this to engineering, please Prithi. It's the report from the new rig. Initial rock core survey. The engineers will be interested."

Smiling, Prithi took the report and headed off to the senior engineer's office. Being American, he was friendly and she often chatted and joked with him. Inside his office, she noticed he was busy with someone she'd never seen before.

With a smile, she placed the report on the table. "From geology, sir. They think you'll be interested." When she left, she glanced at the stranger. Tall, he didn't look American. Probably a Brit. She didn't like them much—too racist. But she did like his smile. From the way he sat in the chair, he appeared to be fit and more than likely tough. It didn't matter; she wasn't interested.

# Chapter Twenty-One

# Dubai Dry Docks

Mike stepped out of the plane onto the gangway platform and couldn't believe the heat. It was only March and it was nighttime. Perhaps he was mistaken. Maybe he was in the exhaust of another jet engine somewhere. As he descended the steps, he realized that the heat was still all around him. When he reached the bottom of the stairs and stepped off, he noticed two policemen standing on guard. Both wore khaki uniforms. One was half-asleep while the other held his hand. Submachine guns hung loosely from both their shoulders. With a soldier's eye, he noticed with horror that both the safety catches were off!

Hurriedly, he headed for the terminal that, although only a short walk, in the stifling heat seemed miles away. At the spiraling ramp that led up to main hall, he waded through a sea of dark faces and sweaty bodies heading in the same direction. Near the top, to his surprise, he heard his name being shrieked out in a shrill male voice.

"Meester Hunteer, Meester Hunteer, visa, visa." Looking up, he saw a grinning brown face surrounded by a mass of others leaning over the parapet. With a wave of his arm, he acknowledged the greeting, then watched as a flimsy sheet of paper floated down towards him.

Leaping slightly into the air, he caught it. It was covered in Arabic writing and he didn't have a clue whether the right way was up or down.

Inside the barely air-conditioned main hall, another ocean of bodies swayed and heaved towards the Immigration counter. Out of it appeared a policeman who ushered him towards the only empty reception desk amongst the twenty odd that were crowded with a shouting, unruly mob of brown faces. He dropped his passport and the flimsy sheet of paper in front of an Immigration clerk who was dressed in a traditional Arabic *dishdasha* (long, one-piece tunic).

To his surprise, it was quickly processed. "Costains?" A bit taken aback, Mike gasped, "Yes." The Arab nodded. "*Yallah.*"

Within minutes he was in the baggage collection area. Slightly bemused and very confused, he watched as heaps of bags arrived and were strewn across the floor by waiting porters. The would-be owners were clambering over the heaps while arguing and squabbling for possession. As he stood back, a voice whispered in his ear.

"Meester Hunteer, welcome. I am Suresh. I am your man. Come with me. The bus is waiting." Pushing him off, Mike growled, "My bags?"

There was a flash of white teeth as the Indian smiled then waved his arm towards the heap. "Of course, Meester Hunteer. One moment. Which are yours?"

Miraculously, Mike spotted his two bags and quickly pointed towards them. Yelling and shouting, Suresh waded into the seething mass with two porters at his heels. Almost by magic, within minutes, Mike, his bags and Suresh had charged through the crowd and landed in the waiting minibus.

It took off and headed at breakneck speed down a road that was devoid of even a single streetlight. In the blackness and rocking wildly at each bend, the minibus wound its way through a sleepy village towards a glow on the horizon. Twenty minutes later it braked to a vicious halt, throwing its unsuspecting passengers into the back of the seat in front of them.

Still dazed, Mike climbed out and found himself in the middle of a dirt square surrounded on all sides by blocks of three-storey flats that were unlit. Several more brown faces appeared and he, along with his bags, were swept up to the second floor and let into a flat by Suresh, who grinned broadly.

Snapping out orders in hushed tones and in a language Mike didn't understand, Suresh directed the porters into one of the two bedrooms in the flat. The door to the other bedroom was firmly closed. To Mike's relief, an air-conditioner rattling in the wall had driven away most of the night's heat.

Suresh bowed and grinned. "In the morning, Meester Hunteer, bus will come. I will come with bus and take you to your office. You want anything, sir, I am your man, Suresh."

Mike groped in his pocket for some loose change for a tip but found nothing. Suresh glowered at him. "Meester Hunteer, sir, I am in public relations. I am not a servant. You do not need to give me anything." Blushing, Mike tried to apologize. Suresh grinned, shook his hand and disappeared.

Still bewildered, Mike noticed a fridge by the sink. He opened it. It was almost empty apart from a few vegetables, a loaf of bread, a carton of milk and a six-pack of Heineken.

"Help yourself to a beer. See you in the morning." Startled by the booming voice that emerged from the closed door, Mike jumped back. Then, desperation taking over, he coyly reached in and took a beer. It opened with a slight hiss when he pulled the cord. "Thanks," he muttered back to the still shut door.

The first beer didn't hit the sides. After two more, Mike felt guilty and headed for his bedroom. To his surprise, his bags had been unpacked and his clothes stowed carefully away in the wardrobe. Cleaning his teeth, he realized that three quick beers and the heat had gone to his head. By his bed stood a bottle of water that he swilled in almost one gulp down his throat. Turning the air-conditioner that hummed in his bedroom down to full cool, he slumped naked between the sheets.

His dreams were full of strange policemen holding hands and firing off machine guns. Finally, Val came into his early morning reverie and paraded naked in his mind. Awakening sexually aroused, he masturbated himself to a climax with practiced ease. He slipped back to sleep and, in what seemed moments later, was rudely awakened by a heavy knock on his bedroom door.

"Meester Hunteer, it is Suresh. Bus is waiting, sir. I will take you to the site. Please hurry, Meester Hunteer."

Mike glanced at his watch and realized he'd slept for nearly ten hours. It was midday, local time.

The minibus entered the site in a cloud of white dust. A sleepy guard at the primitive barrier casually waved them through. By the gate stood a large sign that was slightly askew and covered in white dust. Along with advertising that it was the Dubai Dry Dock Project for the Ruler of Dubai and was being built by the Costain–Taylor Woodrow Joint venture with Halcrows as the consultants, it also recorded the latest safety figures.

A mere thirty-odd fatal accidents! Mike gulped. Hopefully, this bus ride would end soon before he was the next number.

Shortly after, having jolted down a construction road surrounded by half-built steel and concrete structures, earth-moving equipment and hundreds of laborers, the bus jerked to a halt outside of two stained and dirty, cream-colored portable cabins. Above the doorway of one, another dust-covered sign welcomed him to RDL Middle East Dock Gate Project. Beyond the cabins, the huge steel forms of fabricated steel lay in the sun as dozens of workers scrambled over their black surfaces.

Mike was nearly overwhelmed by the heat and the noise as he left the bus. Compressors whined and roared as men dressed in heavy blue overalls blasted clean the rusty steel. Clouds of black, evil-looking dust swirled around them. Almost at a run, Mike entered the cabin door. Inside, a tea boy sat half asleep on a stool. When the door was flung open, he leaped to his feet in shock. On both sides of the entrance was an office. In one stood a desk covered in papers and drawings. The other was full of files stacked on drums of paint. A phone rang incessantly on the desk in the first office. Instinctively, Mike picked it up.

"RDL?"

Curious, Mike responded, "Yes." The heavily accented voice continued. "Meester Hunteer?" Mike recognized it. "Yes." Sitting down on the dusty chair, he held the equally dusty earpiece a little distant from his ear.

"Ah, Meester Hunteer, it is Suresh. Mr. Crowley wants you to come to his office. I will send the bus."

Just as he hung up, a tall Indian burst into the office, followed by two sheepish- looking, dark-faced laborers.

"Fucking useless! Fucking useless!" Mike was stunned by the language of this seemingly benign Indian man.

"These men are terminated. Sign these papers, sir!" Bewildered, Mike signed the somewhat dirty and crumpled papers that had been thrust in front of him. Immediately, a squabble broke out in a language he could not make head or tail of. Eventually he understood that these laborers would be on a plane back to India tomorrow, but before he had time to think about them, the bus arrived outside his cabin with a loud, sharp, tooting of its horn.

Again the bus swerved wildly along the dusty white road past huge trucks full of rocks then stopped outside an old disused villa. Later Mike would learn that it was originally the Sheik of Dubai's former beach villa where he'd sat and decided to build this multi-million pound project. He got down from the bus, crossed a broken mosaic tile entrance and pushed through the rough, wooden ply doors.

Immediately he was greeted by Suresh who ushered him through a door bearing a sign that said "Mechanical & Electrical Manager." Seated behind a wide desk with only a solitary piece of paper on it was a thin man with an eagle-like stare who peered down a similar eagle-like nose.

"Mr. Hunter, please be seated. I'm David Crowley, M. & E. manager." Before sitting, Mike held out his hand in a gesture of friendship. It was ignored. Slightly abashed, he sat silently in front of this distinctly unfriendly man.

"Well, Mr. Hunter, where is it?" Mike looked bewildered. "Where's what, Dave?" The man opposite him looked harshly down his nose.

"Mr. Crowley will do fine. Your program, Mr. Hunter. Your plan whereby your company intends to meet its contractual obligations." Somewhat stunned by the reception, all Mike could do was blurt out the first thing that came to his head.

"Er, I've just arrived, Dave, I mean Mr. Crowley. I'm not too sure."

Again, the harsh gaze of the man opposite him increased his discomfort. "Mr. Hunter, your company is now sixty-three days behind schedule. Your project engineer has buggered off. I have had great difficulty in contacting someone responsible from your company office in London. Let me remind you that we hold considerable monies on your account along with a serious bank guarantee. Forty-eight hours, Mr. Hunter. Forty-eight hours… that's all you have before I make arrangements to have your bloody work carried out and bought back on schedule by others at your cost. Do you understand me? Have you any questions? If not, bugger off and get your company's act together!"

Breathing heavily, Mike stood up and without another word left the office. Outside, he jumped back into the minibus.

"Take me to my fucking office." Unfairly, he took his temper out on the driver, who was used to that and merely drove a little faster and wilder. Storming into the porta-cabin he began scrambling through the drawings that were loosely scattered on the drawing board. His hands were shaking in frustration and anger. Roaring at the top of his voice, he startled the tea boy. "Get the fucking foreman, now!"

Scrambling to his feet, the Indian fled for the door. Within seconds, the tall Indian he'd briefly met before was standing in front of him.

"What's your name?" Trembling slightly at Mike's tone, the Indian lowered his eyes as he answered. "Singh, Sahib. Amir Singh." Pointing fiercely at the drawings, Mike went on. "Right, Mr. Singh. What the fuck is going on here?"

Still trembling, the tall man answered humbly, "Not knowing, Sahib. Not knowing. Mr. Jim had all papers in his room. Big problem." Mike growled at the foreman. "Show me the site, then we go to Mr. Jim Turnbull's fucking room. Okay?" They headed for the door. "Big problem, eh? Fucking big problem!" The foreman stayed silent.

An hour later, Mike sat back at the desk in the cabin. The air-conditioner noise added to his stress headache. What sort of shit had James dropped him in? A shambles, a complete fucking shambles! The temptation to get on the next plane home was almost overwhelming.

With a sweep of his arm he cleared the desk, then picked up the drawings and studied them. With a yellow marker pen he outlined the items he had seen on site. With a red marker pen he noted what was obviously missing. The end result was more red than yellow. It was becoming plain why Crowley was so upset.

Still seething, he listed all the part numbers of the missing sections and materials then sent a strongly worded telex back to John James. Calling the Sikh foreman back in, he sat with him till the early hours of the morning, going through alternative construction schedules based on what they had on site. It wasn't a pretty picture.

Without eating, he sank a beer back in his flat and hit the sack. By sunrise he was up again and met his flatmate for the first time. "You look like shit. Williams. Ron Williams, Electrical. You must be Hunter from RDL."

Wearily, Mike nodded. "Yes. Mike Hunter. Thanks for the beers. What a shit hole!"

Williams laughed. "I gather you've already met Crowley. They call him 'eagle beak' for obvious reasons. Tough bastard, but knows his job." A wan grin crossed Mike's face. "Tough! Jesus, I've been in the SAS and I've not met much tougher."

The look on Williams' face changed. "SAS? My brother was in the SAS."

Mike looked up. "*Was?*"

Williams' response was flat and unemotional. "Killed in Northern Ireland."

For a moment Mike was silent. "Sorry."

After a quick breakfast of omelets and toast washed down with black coffee, they briefly sorted out some living arrangements. Shortly after, the minibus arrived to pick up the two men along with others from the bachelor apartments, all British expatriates. One by one, they were dropped off at their offices on the site.

Mike got off the bus and strode at a fast and angry pace around the work area with the foreman. Here and there he stopped to check out the work. His anger rose. Very little of it was being done properly.

Back in his office, he made a list of priorities to be carried out then told the Sikh foreman to fuck off and make sure they were followed exactly. At midday he was on the phone to James in London.

Mike's tone was plain. Stunned and embarrassed at first, the London-based project engineer agreed to all of Mike's harsh demands. That evening, he received a telex with an estimated arrival date of the outstanding material.

Mike and the foreman worked to complete a revised schedule. Before dawn he grabbed a couple of hours sleep then headed back to the site. While he slurped down a cup of coffee, he checked the telexes and his schedule then arranged to see Crowley mid-morning.

Crowley perused the proposed schedule that Mike had thrust in front of him, laid it meticulously on his polished desk and peered at the tired but determined man in front of him.

"Thank you, Hunter. This schedule looks reasonable. I just hope your company can keep to it this time. Don't let me hold you up. You're a busy man. Good day."

Without saying a word, Mike turned and walked out of the office. His step was more firm than it had been on the first encounter. That night he fell fully clothed on the bed at eight o'clock and didn't stir till dawn next day.

## Chapter Twenty-Two

# The Housegirl

They worked six days a week for ten hours a day in the blazing sun. Never having worked with Indians before and not understanding a word of their Hindi language, Mike relied heavily on the foreman. Every day he sent a sharply worded follow-up telex to London, demanding an update on material supplies.

One day, he tried checking the files for any backup information but there was very little recorded. But going through the drawers of the desk that his predecessor had occupied and where he now sat, he found a small photo album in the bottom drawer. Opening it, he flicked through the photos of Turnbull, his wife and children in front of a house then others of Turnbull with the workers, Turnbull on the beach and other mostly boring stuff. When he put it back, he felt a brown envelope tucked in the back of the drawer. Extracting it carefully, he opened it. Inside were more photos, but this time of a more interesting nature.

First there was a naked Asian girl, then two naked Asian girls, followed by a naked Turnbull with the naked girl and another with Turnbull and the two naked girls. Finally, there was one with the first girl and Turnbull doing things that Mike and his wife wouldn't have even talked about. For sure, by the look and smile on Turnbull's face, he wasn't coming back to Dubai and definitely not to his rather fat and plain-looking wife. He put the photos back into the envelope with his flat keys. He would keep them at home for future reference.

To cool himself down, he swallowed a glass of iced water then strode around the fabrication yard. The heat and dust were nearly unbearable. As he inspected the new work, especially the welding, he felt himself getting angrier and angrier.

"Singh, get your fucking arse in my office!" Coming after him at a run, the Sikh gasped in concern, "Yes, Sahib. Yes, yes, Sahib." Inside the office, Mike stared hard into the Indian's face as he stood apprehensively in front of him, and then bawled him.

"Welders! Fucking welders! Where did we get them from, the bloody jungle? I haven't seen one welder I'd accept! Tomorrow morning, six o'clock, they'll be here for one hour's training!"

The tall foreman trembled and there was fear in his voice. "But the bus, Sahib. The bus?" Almost leaping on the man in front of him, Mike snarled, "They can fucking well walk! If they are not here by six in the morning, they'll be back in Bombay tomorrow!"

Again the foreman's voice had a quaver in it. "But they're from Kerala, Sahib." Not pacified, Mike continued in an angry tone. "Well, they can fucking well walk there from Bombay. Have them all here by six!" Then he stormed out of the cabin.

The next morning, Mike lined up the ten welders by a test piece, and one-by-one checked them out. One, only one, could barely pass the test. My God, how could he keep on schedule? He could guarantee that it would be the same with the blasters and painters. Thank you, Turnbull! Hope your Asian whore gives you the clap, you wanker!

Every day, first thing, Mike trained his welders then supervised their work up until seven at night. Back in the flat in the evening, he'd eat something out of a can. Ron Williams occasionally left him a little of what he'd cooked, but he was usually too late and exhausted to reciprocate. It embarrassed him, but he had to get the work done.

After he had eaten, he'd sink into the sofa and watch one of Ron's tapes of English football, usually falling asleep with a can of beer still clutched in his hand.

It took him three months to sort the project out. Although still slightly behind schedule, he could be sure that the work would be approved by the consultant. Despite the pressure of work, he was putting on weight and that depressed him.

Finally, he decided to finish the men at six o'clock. The extra hour meant he could do his exercises and share in the cooking. His workout consisted of a hundred press-ups and sit-ups along with his old SAS exercises. Ron welcomed the company at the evening meal. A week later, he stopped the early-morning training sessions. What they didn't know now they'd never learn. He could sleep in a little longer and not feel so tired during the day.

Now with Ron, he could stay awake watching the football tapes and the occasional blue movie borrowed from God-knows-where by his flatmate. On Fridays, he started to go to the contractors' club on the beach. Known as the Costay club, it had a pool, a bar and a restaurant. With Friday being the day off, there would be a lunchtime barbecue and a movie at night.

The senior engineers were on married status and their young wives, daughters and friends would frolic in the pool or lounge on the sun beds in the briefest of bikinis. After some time, it started to get to him.

One night, after a blue movie session and a few more beers, he broached the subject with his flatmate. "Ron, I'm fed up with the hand jobs. What do you do for a bit of the real thing around here?"

Getting another beer, Ron laughed. "That desperate? You can't wait till you get home to your wife?" Mike sat silently, not knowing how to answer. "Oh, like that with the wife, eh?"

Almost imperceptibly, Mike nodded his head.

"Well, there's always the house girl." He'd never given much thought as to how the flat was cleaned and the bed made. Obviously, there had to be a maid or some sort that came in while they were away.

"No, you're joking! Have you tried it?"

Ron looked at him sidelong. "Do bears shit in the forest? Of course! Cheap, as well. Tip her a couple hundred chips and she'll love you forever. Otherwise, it's off to the Intercontinental Hotel. Got a few thousand to spare?"

Shocked Mike shook his head. "Fuck, no. I'm not that hard up."

Finishing his beer, Ron winked at Mike. "Then try the house girl.

Take the morning off. Nobody will notice. Anyhow, I'll cover for you."

Next morning, Mike missed the minibus on the pretext that he had the shits. Nothing uncommon on the site. Sitting around in the flat, he half-read a book that had been lying on the sofa. Nervously, he made a cup of coffee. Two more cups came and went. At about ten o'clock, a key turned in the door. In came an Indian woman clutching a broom and a bucket.

She was probably in her early thirties. She had a rounded shape, long, black hair and wore an old blouse and floral skirt. Barely noticing him, she shuffled around the flat in her rubber thong sandals. Mike looked her up and down, shook his head, got up, left the flat and walked to the site. Ten minutes later, he was in the porta-cabin sitting behind his desk checking the telexes and wondering whatever made him think he could do that.

A week later, he and Ron had a card night in the flat. About eight of them drank a lot of beer, played cards, won and lost money, ate hot, spicy Indian takeout and finished it off with blue movies accompanied by their not-very-funny, lewd remarks and raucous laughter. Early in the morning, Mike padded out naked to the refrigerator and swilled down nearly a liter of water, followed by two aspirin to ease his headache.

Slipping back to sleep, he woke again about nine o'clock. Ron had cleaned up and left for work on the minibus. He relaxed back in the bed and decided not to go to work. He'd worked three Fridays in a row and deserved a break. In this mood he thought of the girl back in Melbourne. Gently, he became very sexually aroused.

There was a click in the front door as it opened and closed. The house girl had arrived. She shuffled around cleaning outside then entered the bedroom where Mike lay. Surprised, she went to back out. Waving his hand, he beckoned her in. Hesitant, she came close to the bed. Mike reached out and caught her by the wrist then dragged her onto the bed, the sheets falling back, revealing his naked body.

"Ooh, you bad man like Mr. Ron." Going through the motions, she ineffectively tried to push him off as he removed her blouse and bra. Brown nipples hardened as Mike's mouth found them. Groaning slightly, the woman ceased all resistance and Mike removed the rest of her clothes. Hungrily, he slid himself inside her.

Out of control, driven by his overpowering desire, he rapidly climaxed. At the same time, the Indian woman grasped him around the neck and pulled him closer in her passion. It was enough to drive him over the edge and with a loud gasp he climaxed and collapsed onto the brown naked body. Rolling over, he lay breathing heavily as the woman climbed from the bed. "You very bad man. You just like Mr. Ron." She gathered up her clothes and ran to the bathroom.

Pulling on a pair of underpants, he went to the drawer, took out his wallet and lay down two one-hundred dirham notes on the bed.

Immediately after the woman had left the bathroom, he entered, showered, put on fresh clothes and made for the front door. Glancing back, he saw the two notes had disappeared. Before he left, he stuck his head into Ron's room. The house girl was making the bed.

"Thank you. I didn't hurt you, did I?"

Straightening up, she looked at him. "No, sir." She smiled. "Thank you, sir." Shaking his head, Mike headed for the site.

While he was watching another football tape with Ron, Mike leaned forward and grabbed another beer from the table. There was a break in the soundtrack. "Ron, how do these house girls stop getting pregnant?" Turning down the volume on the set, Ron turned and stared at him. "Give her one, then, did you?" Smiling, a little embarrassed, Mike nodded. Ron looked at him harder.

"And you didn't use a condom? You fucking idiot!"

Mike looked sheepish. "What if she gets pregnant?" His response was barely audible. Ron's head went back as he laughed. "Not *that*, you fool. You! You could have caught something. You'd better go to the quack first thing tomorrow."

Sitting in the clinic waiting room, Mike flicked through an old yachting magazine. Hoping against hope, he dreaded the thought that it would be the female doctor. To his dismay, it was the woman. "You men amaze me. Simple, really. Just use protection, or isn't it macho enough? I'll have to do a blood test. In the meantime, I'll give you a shot and I can assure you it will hurt!"

Despite gritting his teeth in anticipation, Mike let out a yelp as she plunged the needle into his exposed naked bottom. Back in front of her and sitting uncomfortably in the chair, he listened shamefacedly as she harangued him again. Told him of a new disease coming out of the States for which there was no cure. "Now, next time use one of *these!*" Instinctively, he caught the packet of condoms that she threw at him.

When he left the clinic he decided that he'd had enough. He would wait till he got back to the U.K. where sex was safer. A week later, he stayed back in the flat and waited for the house girl. This time he used the condom. This time she didn't call him a bad man.

## Chapter Twenty-Three

# Mike Unloads a Cargo Ship

Day after day, Mike worked his men on a ten-hour shift. It was now late summer and temperatures were regularly around forty degrees centigrade. Humidity, dust and the erratic support from head office were draining his resolve. Crowley would stride into his porta-cabin at a quarter past eight every morning.

"Well, Hunter, still behind schedule, I see. All will be reflected in the next monthly certificate. I hope your company's not anxious for their money."

Nothing could be further from the truth. Continually he was under pressure from head office to improve the cash flow and as Crowley left, Mike would curse under his breath. In spite of the heat and his unskilled labor, he had managed to claw back forty days in less then four months. In another three months, God willing, he expected to be back on schedule. Better still, in another month he would be due three weeks leave that he seriously needed, if for no other reason than to get away from Crowley and the house girl who was becoming a habit, a bad one at that.

Stepping out into the blazing heat, he walked down the rows of huge, black, painted steel structures. Provided the correct materials arrived from the U.K, within the next week, he would be ready to start erecting the dock gates on this huge project. Before he went on leave, he hoped.

For an occasional change, some Fridays he'd go with a couple of friends he'd made down to the Intercontinental Hotel on the Creek for a sumptuous breakfast then a stroll through the *Souk* (traditional market). "Stroll" was not quite the word. On Friday mornings, the *Souk* would be heaving with pajama-clad Pakistanis or *lungi*-clad Indians.

He'd stride alongside one of the young engineers, Barrie Charmsen, and his young blonde wife, menacing the leering, lecherous males as they tried to touch the woman. Charmsen was an Australian whose acquaintance he'd made on the site. Wild and outspoken, he was one of Crowley's senior staff on this massive project. Clever and smart, he drank too much, and invariably his wife had to almost carry him from the unrestrained Thursday-night parties.

Mike enjoyed Charmsen's wicked sense of humor and the gossip he brought from Crowley's inner sanctum. It was Charmsen who introduced him to the Dubai Desert Hash House Harriers. In spite of his injured leg, Mike enjoyed the sociable Sunday evening runs through the desert. To keep his sanity, he felt he had to keep fit, even to the extent of playing squash twice a week after work. Usually he played Charmsen. Although he was slower around the court because of his leg, he quickly learned to position himself for the return. Perhaps because of his sharp reflexes, he gained enough skill to play in the local B-grade squash league.

After one of his daily tours of the fabrication yard, he returned, sweating profusely and covered in dust, to the porta-cabin where a message from Crowley greeted him on his desk. With a tissue he lifted the receiver and rang Crowley's office to be told by the secretary that Crowley wanted to see him at midday.

"Please be seated, Mr. Hunter. Coffee?"

Surprised by Crowley's hospitality, Mike accepted the offer. The tea boy scurried away and quickly returned with a cup of fresh coffee. No expense spared in Crowley's office. As Mike relaxed back in the comfort of the clean, air-conditioned office, Crowley looked out of the dust-covered window of the old beach villa and lit up a cigarette, blowing a cloud of smoke into the air.

"Leave due soon, Hunter? Who's replacing you?"

Mike was speechless. He'd not thought of it.

"Well, Hunter? Presumably that idiot James. Better the wanker you know than no wanker at all, eh, Hunter?"

Nodding dumbly, Mike's mind raced. Why hadn't he thought about a replacement? Shit. Immediately after the meeting, he'd telex James.

"Need to know soon, Hunter. By the way, those two sixty-ton crawler cranes in your yard...we'd like to borrow them for a couple of days."

Caught off guard, Mike readily agreed.

"And, of course, you'll supervise them." Now he wasn't too sure of his ground. "Supervise what, Mr. Crowley?"

Crowley stubbed out his cigarette and leaned forward. "David will do fine. Supervise the unloading of the charter vessel. It will dock alongside our temporary quay. Of course, you will. Some of its cargo is your material. It arrives tomorrow. Any problems?"

Totally confused, Mike merely nodded.

"That's it, Hunter. Don't let me hold you up." Rising quickly, Mike was still confused. "Yes, Mr. Crowley, er, David. Yes, tomorrow, okay."

Leaving Crowley's office, he crossed the corridor to see if Charmsen was in. He was.

"So, Mike, what's new?" Grabbing a metal seat, Mike dropped into it in front of Charmsen's desk.

"Crowley wants to use my cranes to unload a charter vessel." Charmsen looked at him carefully. "And naturally you said no." Still not sure of himself, Mike stared at the ground. "Er, no, I said yes." Charmsen almost leaped from his seat. "You fucking idiot! Now the responsibility will be on you. Crowley's been trying to find some dimwit all fucking week to do this. Obviously, he's found one. *You!* You're the sucker!"

Hanging his head, Mike could only mutter curses under his breath. "Come on, Mike. We'd better go down to where the ship's going to dock and see the problems."

Jumping into his Toyota pickup, Mike followed the young engineer, who, despising the company's supplied vehicle, rode his own bright green Yamaha trail bike. Arriving at the recently constructed temporary dock, the two of them walked carefully over the rough preparations.

"Not good, Mike. Not good." Charmsen kicked some of the loose stones into the water.

"Too late. I've agreed and the ship is on its way in."

Two days later, Mike followed his crawling cranes down to where the special charter ship had now arrived—three thousand tons of loose cargo to be unloaded in three days. It was a special concession from the Government of Dubai so that the ship didn't have to be in the queue of the hundred odd ships outside of Port Rashid. Due to the boom in development, cargoes could take up to twenty weeks to be unloaded! The only problem with this was they were forced to use the labor supplied by the Port and not their own trained men.

At quayside, Mike positioned the two cranes. Both of their booms had been extended the day before and he hadn't had enough time to check the skills of the operators with the new arrangement. First they unloaded the four large boilers strapped to the deck. Next, with the additional help of the ship's derrick cranes, they started on the one thousand tons of steel-reinforcing bars that were urgently needed. With two wire slings attached to their hooks, the two cranes would hoist thirty tons at a time off the deck and lower the bars onto the twenty-ton low-loader waiting on the dockside. Totally unsafe and illegal, but who was around to say no?

Unable to control the contract labor, Mike tried to maintain control of his own crane drivers. It was a nightmare. A myriad of Asian voices yelled instructions at each and every operation. Almost in slow motion, Mike saw it coming but was powerless to stop it. The lift of the two cranes was out of synchronization. As they lowered the load, the sling on one end started to slip. In seconds, the heavy bundle of steel bars slid out and hit the low-loader with a loud bang.

Thirty tons of rebar spilled uncontrollably from the tray of the vehicle onto the ground where two laborers ineffectively held up their arms for protection and died in a howl of hideous screams till their deaths silenced them.

At first there was stunned silence. Then a swarm of yelling and shouting laborers leaped forward and tried to drag the bars from the heap by hand. Wading in, Mike managed to gain control and got them to reposition the slings around the bundle. Slowly the cranes lifted the load from the ground, revealing the mangled, bloody corpses of the two laborers. One of their heads was spilt open with a grey mess of brains oozing over the bloodied sand. The other lay twisted, staring lifelessly at the sky, blood and gore dripping from what was once his face.

Before Mike could stop them, a crowd of men leaped forward, unceremoniously hoisted up the bodies and threw them into the back of a nearby pickup. Promptly, about a dozen of them leaped into the back with the broken bodies and the pickup sped off with its tray drooping dangerously to the ground, its lights flashing and its horn blaring. Within seconds it had disappeared in a cloud of dust, headed down the road to the distant hospital.

Shocked, Mike stood helpless. "Shit, if they weren't dead, they're bloody well dead now!"

A little later, much to his dismay, Crowley's white Toyota Cressida arrived.

"Problems, Hunter?" Still shaking slightly, Mike sighed. "You might say so, David." Lighting a cigarette, the manager looked across at the scene of milling workers.

"Yes, you might. I'll get it sorted. Hopefully, that damn fool of an admin manager won't fuck it up even more. Still, not your fault, Hunter. Get on with it. We can't afford any more delay."

Thanks to his military training, Mike pulled himself together and went on unloading the vessel. Two days later, it cast off its moorings and sailed off empty back to the U.K.

## Chapter Twenty-Four

# Miriam

After the vessel left and too exhausted to cook that evening, Mike went with his flatmate to the Costay club. Meeting up with Barrie and his wife, he brooded over a pint of beer while the others fiercely attacked a hot Indian curry. Try as he may, Mike couldn't dismiss the image of the two dead workers from his mind.

"Plenty more where they came from," had been the stock response to the accident. All right for those who weren't there, but for him it wasn't so easy. That their deaths bit so deep surprised him a little. After all, in Vietnam dead enemy was a common sight. Barrie tried to make light of it and told one of his notorious bad jokes.

"Don't laugh. Please don't laugh," pleaded his wife. "He'll just tell another one." Undaunted, he started off again. "I'll tell another one anyhow. That reminds me of the rusty salmon joke." This time looking serious, his wife snapped, "No!"

Soon after, they left. His wife was pregnant and Barrie was nodding off to sleep. Ron and Mike retired to the upstairs bar where amongst the teeming throng of expatriate engineers and supervisors, Mike was the centre of attention and the free beer flowed. Not much later, his tongue was well away and soon he was very drunk. Before he got into trouble, Ron guided him out to the pickup.

Next morning, with a pounding head, he walked around the site. The new delivery of materials was welcome, and if they worked overtime they'd be back on the dreaded schedule that Crowley still checked every morning. Cursing the heat and dust, he hurried back to his air-conditioned office. Swiftly he downed two painkillers then followed them with two quick cups of coffee. "Shit, I have to play squash tonight." Sitting holding his head in his hands, he could hardly look up as the door opened.

"Well, old boy, you were well and truly pissed last night." Tony Clifford's frame filled the door. He was in charge of the construction of the large dock cranes and commanded a section of formidable hooligans who worked hard, played hard and whose drinking habits were legendary.

"Tony, I have to say I'm not a drinker." The big man guffawed. "You can say that again, you miserable fucker. Want to go fishing tomorrow morning?" Mike was shocked. "Bloody hell, is it Friday already!"

Clifford shrugged. "All fucking day."

In his conscience, he felt perhaps he should work in the morning but he really needed a break after this week's drama. "Okay, what time?" Tony smiled evilly. "Five." Mike's eyes opened wide. "You must be joking." Still smiling, Tony was ready to leave. "Think the fish will wait for you, arsehole?"

Mike was still pleading as the big man left. "Six?" Waving as he stepped out the door, Tony's voice boomed back, "Six, and no later."

His head still ached as he put together the telex telling James that Crowley wanted him out to replace him while he was on leave and then drove down to head office to pick up the mail. After handing the telex to the dispatch clerk, he waited to make sure it was sent.

Leaning on the counter, he looked idly out the window. While he watched, one of the young wives pulled up in her car. As she climbed out of the four-wheel drive, she displayed a pair of long, slim, tanned legs that went on forever. When she bent over to get her young child out of the safety seat, she exposed her brief, thin lace panties. Throwing her child over one shoulder, she flicked her long black hair out of her face and headed off next door to the site bank. Mike felt the blood rush from his head down to between his legs. No matter how hard he tried, his trousers still bulged. "Shit, I've got to get out of this place!"

Gently the bright yellow hull of Clifford's cabin cruiser slipped through the sparkling blue water of the Gulf. Out behind the stern of the boat, the small auxiliary outboard motor caused barely a ripple. They'd stormed out to his favorite fishing spot in less than an hour with the use of the two 250-horsepower Johnson outboards, but now they lazily trailed two lines behind the boat.

Munching on a fresh bread roll filled with bacon, lettuce, tomato and a fried egg, Mike nursed a cold Heineken in the other hand. Even though it was nearly eight in the morning, the sun was still not too vicious and they lolled around wearing only shorts.

Suddenly Tony shouted and dropped his roll and beer as he grabbed a rod. With much shouting and cheering, the others watched as he reeled in a good-sized fighting barracuda. After landing it, he picked up his roll and opened another beer. Ron, along with Peter, one of Tony's crew on the site, chopped off the head of the fish and dropped it into the water. Gulls and a single tern wheeled and dived on the entrails. Across the sea, carried by the gentle offshore breeze, came the faint whiff of early morning barbecues and cooking. A warm relaxing feeling swept through Mike.

Then, without warning it was his turn. The reel next to him started to screech as the line spun out. Amidst more cheering and shouting, Mike played the lunging, leaping fish to alongside the boat. This time it was a kingfish and it fought like hell. Peter finally gaffed it and hauled it on board.

"That's enough fish for lunch," Tony said, laughing. They pulled up the auxiliary as the main engines burst into life at the skipper's touch, then headed back. Over the calm sea they streaked, leaving behind a frothy white wake. On the approach to Dubai, the silhouettes of the mosques stood out. As they slowed down, a school of dolphins joined them, frolicking and diving in front of the cruiser's yellow salt-flecked hull. After pulling the boat out of the water onto the trailer, they headed back to Tony's villa.

When they entered the house, Tony barked out orders and two houseboys scurried to their tasks. Within minutes, the merry little group was sitting around a small pool and fountain drinking champagne and orange juice while munching on freshly chopped pineapple and mango.

"We'll have the fish for lunch," Tony declared. "The boys will marinate and barbecue them. Let's have a beer then go to the Costay club for a swim."

Perched on a small sand dune, the Costay Club was the social heart for the hundreds of expatriate senior white-faced staff working on the Dry Docks. After the long working day and on the one day off a week, they crowded into the small two-storey building with its bars and restaurant. Overlooking the bright blue, sparkling Arabian Gulf waters, it was the life and soul of the expatriate entertainment. Its heartbeat stopped only when the last drunken occupant swayed out of the gate. Helped by the ever-subservient Indian staff, the drunk would fall into the company car and sleep until it was time to drive back to the site to work again. Hunter often wondered how the fuck they ever got the project built.

Peter, Ron and Tony were big men carrying plenty of weight, although most of it was fat. On the contrary, Mike was still slim and muscular, conscientiously keeping fit. The large quantities of alcohol didn't seem to affect the big men. Heading to the club, Mike felt quite pissed. Normally, he didn't go swimming in public; he was very self-conscious about his scarred leg.

He slipped into the pool and tried to swim a length but gave up. All around him, the young children of the married men splashed and shouted. Alongside him, a teenage girl and boy teased and ducked each other. Every now and then, the girl would emerge with her bikini top askew; a hard little breast with a bright pink nipple would be briefly exposed before she pulled the material over it. In his mind, Mike struggled not to reach out and touch her. Enough was enough. He desperately needed his home leave.

Back at Tony's villa, the houseboys ladled out spoonfuls of savory rice onto a plate full of succulent curried barbecued fish. The food literally melted in Mike's mouth, and as he ate he swilled down yet another beer. Several beers later, he was well gone and pouring his heart out to the other three who were barely listening.

"I say, old boy," Tony said, reaching for another beer, "I'd say you're a bit of a mess. You need sorting out. Going on leave soon, I believe? Stop over in Beirut is what's needed. Do it. Call me before you go. I've an old chum there. Edouard, good fellow, knows the lay of the land, if you know what I mean"

In the morning, as he staggered around the fabrication yard, Mike swore that never again would he go fishing with Clifford. This was the granddaddy of all hangovers. Not only did his head pound, but the hot, spicy fish was playing hell with his arsehole. Never! Never again!

On top of it all, he had received a telex advising him that John James was arriving early next morning. He'd have to be out at the airport with Suresh to meet the bugger. Immediately after he got back to the flat he hit the sack, leaving Ron strict instructions to wake him up before he went to bed. Fortunately, he did. The minibus arrived with Suresh five minutes after he'd finished showering and dressing.

As usual, the airport was heaving. A sea of brown faces surged in and out of the building. Suresh yelled and shouted his way through the terminal, dragging Mike behind him. Thirty minutes later, they had a sweating, red-faced man in a suit in tow. Leading him like a bullock on a nose rope through the entry procedures, they quickly bundled him into the minibus and twenty minutes later he was in the cool interior of the Intercontinental Hotel.

"Like to join me for a beer, Mike?" Mike looked at his watch. "No, thanks, John. Got to be on site by seven." This time, James glanced at his watch. "My God, is that the right time? You've only got about four hours."

James sat in Crowley's office. It was nearly midday when he finally arrived on the site. Sitting next to him, Mike watched with mounting irritation the British class system rear its ugly head. Crowley and James had gone to the same public school and lived within twenty miles of each other. By one o'clock, James was off to lunch with Crowley as Mike headed back to the site cabin. He kicked the door open and entered the dusty room that was now almost like home. With an angry sweep of his arm, he cleared the drawings off the desk and slumped into the old metal chair. Recovering his aplomb slightly, he growled to nobody in particular, "Who gives a shit? So long as I can go on leave."

# HUNTER'S GOLD

True to his word, Tony had arranged for Mike to meet up with his contact in Beirut when he stopped over on his way home to the U.K. He was everything Mike expected a Lebanese like him to be: fat, dressed in a white suit, and with gold bracelets that were overshadowed by the hugely expensive gold Rolex watch hanging from his limp wrist.

Cruising to the hotel in a dark-windowed Mercedes Benz, Mike listened as Edouard extolled the virtues of Tony Clifford. It was obvious that both of them had worked outside of the law on more than one occasion. Late that night, his Lebanese escort guided him through the casino, where he was more than well known. Later, Mike would find out that he was part owner.

Several hours later, having enjoyed a fine meal and wine, Edouard shook his hand and took his leave. No longer interested in the glittering gambling house, Mike made his way back to the hotel in the chauffeur-driven car that had been left for him. Edouard's parting remark about a small gift awaiting him back in his room left him a little apprehensive.

When he reached his room, his concern deepened at the sight of the largely built but smoothly groomed, oily creep that met him. To Mike's surprise, he offered his hand in friendship and Mike shook it cautiously. With that, the man produced a house key, opened Mike's door, showed him in then left, closing the door softly behind him.

Inside, he moved cautiously then almost jumped out of his skin when he saw a figure sitting on the edge of his bed. When he saw it was a girl, his heartbeat slowed but not for long. In one fluid movement, she stood up. She was beautiful, long-legged and dressed in tight designer jeans and a T-shirt.

Dream-like, she was in front of him. "Bonsoir, Monsieur Mike. I am Miriam." Mike took the outstretched hand that was offered him. Gracefully, she led him to the bed.

Lowering himself onto it, he tamely let her undress him. From a near side chest of drawers, she produced two vials of scented oil. Then she stood and let her clothes fall to the floor. Mike let out a gasp of admiration. Never before had he seen such a taut, lovely, honey-colored body.

115

Naked, she went to the mini bar and poured a long gin and tonic. Offering it to him, she gestured that he should lie face-down on the bed. The massage was out of this world. By the time he'd finished his gin and tonic, he was floating on air.

He rolled over, pulled her to him and without any resistance entered her body. Twisting and turning, she did unbelievable things to him. When he fell back sprawled across the bed and she was preparing to go, he couldn't remember how many times he'd climaxed, but it was more than just twice.

Before he drifted off to sleep, he couldn't believe what had happened to him. Any more of that treatment and he would have given all the money he had and more to spend just another hour with Miriam.

Twenty-four hours later, he stepped from the plane onto the exit ramp at Heathrow. Through the glass panes he could see it was cold, wet and raining. The UK hadn't changed. Suddenly he needed the sun in Dubai.

"Hell, fuck it. I want to go back!"

## Chapter Twenty-Five

# Mike's Holiday

B eside Carol was a slim young girl with long, blonde hair. Almost beyond recognition, she stood in tight denim jeans with a duffle coat top. Mike gasped when he realized it was his daughter. Only a little over six months had passed since he'd seen her, but what a difference. Carol looked the same, perhaps slightly heavier, but his daughter had changed beyond belief.

Upon seeing him, Elizabeth left her mother's side and ran to her father. Throwing her arms around his neck, she smothered his cheek in kisses. "Daddy, daddy, I missed you!" With one arm clutching his carry bag, Mike responded by wrapping the other around her slim form and hugging her to him. Carol stood half-smiling, waiting for them to come to her.

"Hi, Carol. Miss me?" Dropping his daughter, he hugged his wife to him. Almost casually, she returned his embrace. "Yes, Mike. Welcome back."

As his wife drove him home in the new Cortina, Mike became aware for the first time how bleak the countryside was in early November. Most of the leaves had fallen, leaving the trees and shrubs bare and stark in the half-light. Although it was midday, the dark sky with its drizzling rain made it seem like night. Cars drove by with their headlights shining on the dull, black, slippery road.

Driving through the high streets, Mike listened to Elizabeth's endless chatter as Carol concentrated on the traffic. Pedestrians leaned into the cold rain, coats and jackets wrapped around them. Only the lights of the shop windows brightened the bleak day. The bright sunshine and sparkling blue waters of Dubai seemed a lifetime away.

When the car drove in, Mike barely recognized the house. They'd bought it just before he left. When he got the contract to go to Dubai, he agreed with Carol to sell the old house and move to a new one. It had been a good deal and Carol had driven a hard bargain. With the money they'd made on the old one, they'd nearly paid this one off. The mortgage was small and his pay packet was large.

Large enough to also send Elizabeth to a nearby public school. Their new status was reflected in Carol's choice of furniture and Elizabeth's new public school, cultured accent.

Despite the warm welcome, he felt like a bit of a stranger. He placed his case on the bed, opened it and took out two small, red velvet bags with their drawstrings pulled tightly around their necks. Undoing the strings, he emptied the contents onto the bed. Two bright gold necklaces snaked out onto the coverlet.

Both women gasped with glee and picked out one each. The young girl chose the heavier, chunkier one—she could get away with it—and the finer chain suited Carol. Mike smiled as they paraded around in front of the mirror. Without drawing attention to himself, he reached into his case, plucked out two little red boxes and placed them open on the bed. Two pairs of exquisite pearl earrings glistened as they lay on their white silk cushions.

Suddenly his daughter saw them. "Mummy, mummy, look what else! Oh, Daddy, thank you!" Running to him, she kissed him on the cheek several times. Once they'd put on all their jewellery, Mike reached into his case again and retrieved a brand new Canon camera.

Faces wreathed with joy, Carol and Elizabeth posed as he took endless photos with the flash. Finally he handed the camera to his wife. "This is yours as well."

Carol, excited, turned it carefully over in her hands, "Oh, Mike, can I work it?" Mike smiled. "Of course. It's automatic." Then with a broader smile, he produced another package from behind his back. His daughter shrieked with happiness when she saw her latest toy, a Sony Walkman radio cassette player.

That night during the evening meal, Mike told them both about his job. After their daughter had skipped off to her room to study, they began to talk in all seriousness. It was about the money and the future. Another two years and they'd have paid off the house, but Elizabeth had at least five years to go at school and it was expensive. Then there would be three more years at university, and if she didn't get a grant, that would be expensive as well.

Carol wasn't happy that he wanted to stay out there longer, but despite this, granted it was a good idea. Later in bed, struggling, they made dutiful love. It was an effort for both of them and finally they ceased with an air of futility. "I'm sorry, Carol. I'm tired. Must be the plane trip."

Mike lay awake in the dark, listening to his wife's regular breathing. Thoughts of the Lebanese girl kept flitting through his mind, and as he dozed off, the house girl crept seductively into his dreams. In Dubai he needed to get back home, and now he wanted to get back to Dubai!

Two weeks seemed to drag. To please Carol, he redecorated the spare room, cleared out the garage to make room for storage cupboards, supervised the installation of a new gas boiler for the central heating and put paving stones down in the backyard. During the evening meals they chattered away like a family, but when Elizabeth disappeared, Mike and Carol sat silently together watching TV.

Just before he left, he went to Elizabeth's school for parents' evening and listened to several teachers extol his daughter's virtues. The day before he was due to leave, he watched her ride in the local gymkhana. It was a far cry from his childhood. Still, he wouldn't have wished that on his worst enemy.

On the final night, the three of them went to an expensive restaurant where he ordered champagne. Mike drank little and Elizabeth was restricted to one glass. Carol finished the rest. By the time they got home, Carol was quite tipsy.

Shooing their daughter to bed, they sat on the lounge watching a late movie. It was a love story and his wife became more and more amorous as the film went on. Before it ended, they made love on the lounge room floor. This time Mike's performance was better and his wife went up to bed naked, wiggling her bare bottom with a smile on her face.

## Chapter Twenty-Six

# Mike Meets the Queen

As the plane flew high, Mike looked out the window while he enjoyed his meal. Below, a carpet of white fluffy clouds appeared solid enough to walk on. Incredible to believe that it was only in this century we could look down on the clouds. In the end, he'd been glad to leave, but the tears and supplications of his daughter had gotten to him.

Carol seemed almost pleased for him. In spite of her initial unhappiness at his intention to continue working abroad, after two weeks it was obvious he got under her feet. The weather had depressed him and he looked forward to the warm sun of Dubai.

Back on site, he found the entire project was bustling. With only four months to go until the formal completion date, the pressure was on. To his disgust, he found James and Crowley nearly close friends. Fortunate, though, while he was away, James had basically done nothing, leaving it all up to the Indian supervisor to press on with the work.

Through the window of his porta-cabin, he watched Crowley and James stroll around the yard as one of the last dock gate modules was being loaded onto the transporter. It was apparent that a lot of mutual verbal backslapping was going on. Mike felt almost sick. Both of them were tall men, physically unfit, smokers and walked with their feet turned out, their backs slightly stooped.

During this time of the year the weather had began to cool, but still both of them returned sweating profusely. Entering his cabin,

Crowley snapped at the tea boy to bring the coffee and water, then, along with James, slumped ungraciously into one of the worn-out metal chairs in front of Mike's desk.

"Good thing James was here, Hunter. Sorted it all. Back on schedule. Don't let it slip."

Mike had to forcibly restrain himself from leaping over the desk and strangling the bastard with his bare hands. James sat there lapping it all up with a supercilious grin on his pale but red, flushed face. Fucking old school tie. The sooner they poisoned all these arseholes, the better off they'd all be in the U.K. Bet they all voted Tory.

With the cooler weather, the mornings on the site were refreshing but hectic; the pressure was really on now. A week after he arrived back, the large one hundred-ton crawler cranes lowered the last of the massive, black painted modules onto the low loader. Creeping past the almost completed buildings and steel structures, it made its way down to end of the pier. Little remained to complete the three huge dry docks.

Protecting the works from the sea was a large earth dam on which a giant grab was beginning to remove the top rock cover. Mike watched with satisfaction as the module was finally positioned, ready to be bolted into place. Two weeks later, the three essential dock gates stood ready to take the full force of the sea when the earth dam was finally removed. Arguably as strong as the concrete walls of the docks, they would eventually be lowered into the water to let the first of the large super tankers in for dry-docking.

Down the piers, the giant yellow cranes that had been recently completed by Clifford and his gang maneuvered back and forth under trial. Preparations were being made to complete and pave the remaining roads. By the end of December, the whole project took on a finished appearance, although much work remained to be done.

The notice was posted on every board and arrived in every in-tray. It had been confirmed that Queen Elizabeth II would open the project at the end of February 1979. Shortly after, Mike received his gilt-edged invitation to attend the reception after the opening. Drinking his coffee at his desk, he was browsing through the last crop of telexes from London when Crowley strode in.

"Morning, Mike." Looking up, Mike face remained expressionless. He didn't have a lot of love for Crowley and even less for James, but at least the latter had pissed off back to London and he didn't have him hanging around the fabrication yard all day.

"Morning, Dave. Coffee?" Pulling up a chair, Crowley plunked down. "Yes, why not?" Lighting his pipe, the manager stared blankly out the dusty window. "Time to demobilize, eh, Mike?" Still reading the telexes, Mike barely paid attention. "Yes, Dave, it's in hand."

Sucking on his pipe, Crowley blew a cloud of smoke into the air. "Good, good. How long are you intending to stay?" Finishing his reading, Mike laid the documents on the table. "Until March, end of contract. James wants me to finish, sell the plant and finalize the payments."

Taking another draw on his pipe, Crowley blew yet a larger cloud of smoke into the air. "Payments? What payments? You owe *us* money for the pleasure of working out here!"

Laughing, Mike picked up the coffee that had just been placed in front of him by his ever-attendant tea boy. "Pleasure? I would have had more fun if a shark had chewed my foot off!"

Crowley looked at him sidelong. "Come on, Hunter, don't be like that. You've enjoyed every minute." Spluttering his coffee back into his cup, Mike began to laugh again. Crowley was a different man now the project was nearing completion; he was beginning to show a human streak.

"Anyhow, Hunter, haven't time to sit entertaining sub-contractors. Must leave." Draining his cup, Crowley took one more puff of his pipe, stood up and went to leave. Reaching the door, he turned around to face Mike. "By the way, Hunter, I've put you on my list to meet the Queen. Hope you bought a suit and a decent tie." With that, he disappeared out the door.

Most of the plant was sold and the fabrication and paint sheds removed a week before the opening. The earth dam in front of the docks had been removed and the gates had been a success, holding back the water with barely a leak. Not long after, the huge basins of the three docks were flooded for the first time. Most of the workforce stopped and watched in awe as the water sped across the concrete floors and rapidly filled the vast, empty space. At last, the whole project had an air of completion.

A gentle wind blew from the sea on the day of the opening ceremony. Wheeling above the glittering sea, the white seabirds contrasted against the bright blue sea and the slightly lighter blue sky. Along the roadside, Union Jacks and UAE flags flew from myriad flagpoles. Every road had been cleaned and swept, buildings freshly painted. Gangs of laborers had been cleaning and polishing for days. Plants and trees in pots sprung up overnight, and new grass lay in bright green strips of turf. Tiers of temporary seating had been erected at the head of the main dock. In the centre of them facing down the dock was a dais on which stood a control panel containing one large push button. This dock had been emptied but the other two were full, and in them floated several freighters that had been towed in overnight from neighboring Port Rashid.

Families and friends all decked out in suits and fine dresses crowded onto the seats shortly before the appointed hour. Friendly, khaki-clad policemen guided cars and onlookers to their designated places. Barely were they seated when two white Rolls- Royce cars accompanied by an entourage of police cars and motorbikes with flashing lights rolled into the area in front of the dais.

A sprightly Arab with an erect bearing leaped from the first vehicle. With a dark beard, glinting eyes and wearing a light black cloak over his traditional white dress, he was an impressive figure who dominated the whole proceedings. It was the first time that Mike and many in the audience had ever seen the legendary and revered Sheik Rashid. Spontaneously, loud applause broke out. Following him were several notable Arabs including the fabled Midi Al Tajir. The door of the second Rolls-Royce opened and an equerry in ceremonial uniform also leaped from the still-moving car. When it stopped, he stood at attention and held the door as the Queen, dressed in a light yellow dress and white hat, emerged into the bright sunlight.

Again, applause broke out and Prince Phillip stepped out behind his wife with a broad smile and a friendly wave. Following them were the contracts manager and the project manager. Quickly the speeches were over and the Queen, along with Sheik Rashid, stepped up to the control panel and pushed the button. At the far end of the empty dock, a rush of water foamed into the dock. Instantaneously, the crowd broke into cheers and applause. The Dubai Dry Docks were formally opened.

Mike stood stiffly at attention in the line of managers and engineers being inspected by the Royal party. Occasionally the party stopped and the Queen or the Duke chatted with an individual. To Mike's amazement, the Duke stopped in front of him. "You're ex-Army, aren't you, young man?"

Stunned into silence, Mike could only nod. "Can always tell. Bearing. Military bearing. Never leaves you." Finally finding his voice, Mike responded nervously, "Yes, sir!" The Duke continued. "What part of the project were you involved in?" A little surer of himself, Mike replied confidently, "The dock gates, sir." Nodding, the Duke went to move and then stopped. "Well done, well done. Be in trouble if they leaked, eh?[1]" Laughing mildly at his own joke, the Duke then caught up with the rest of the party.

---

1    Author's note: some twenty years later, one of the gates failed with a catastrophic loss of life.

## Chapter Twenty-Seven

# The Split

The day after the opening ceremony, Mike sat with John James, who'd come out with several of the directors from RDL for the festivity. A number of options were open to him. He could return to the U.K. and work on one of their new projects for the oil industry up in Scotland; he could go to Nigeria where they were building a number of bridges for the government road project; or the one RDL weren't offering, he could leave and find another job in Dubai. The last one was the most appealing and he'd put out feelers amongst his contacts.

An offer from Dubai Petroleum Company could not be refused: almost double the money, training in the States and much better leave conditions. Although he would be technically working for Conoco from the U.S.A., he wouldn't be getting as good conditions as his American peers. But still, what he was going to get suited him. It was a position as an operator on the rigs in the Rashid field fifty miles offshore in the middle of the Arabian Gulf. For every month he worked, he would have ten days home leave. *Not bad*, he thought.

Although his wife seemed consoled that he would stay in Dubai when they last discussed it on his leave, her last letter expressed her concern and disappointment. It was then that he had the bright idea to bring her and his daughter out for a holiday at the end of his contract. Even though it was the end of March and fairly hot, he could take them up into the Hajar Mountains and show them the

Hatta pools. Then there would be fishing in the early morning and maybe a trip to Oman. At night when it was cooler, they could shop in the local markets for gold and trinkets.

As expected, they both jumped at the chance and two weeks later Mike picked up his family at the usual teeming and humming arrivals terminal.

Yet again, Mike almost didn't recognize his daughter who'd grown even taller and ran to him from the barrier to fling her arms around his neck. Dressed in tight jeans and a T-shirt, she was followed by myriad pairs of admiring eyes and some not-so- savory ones.

"Daddy, daddy, I'm so happy!" Holding her at arm's length, her father looked her up and down. "My God, you've grown so tall." Behind her, Carol stood smiling. She'd aged a little and put on more weight. Mike disentangled himself from his daughter then hugged his wife. "Hi, Carol. Glad to see you." Kissing him, Carol hugged him back then stepped aside to let her daughter grab her father around the waist.

Wiping the sweat that had already formed on her brow, his wife took his free arm. "Ooh, it's so hot and crowded, Mike. Will we be long?" Right on cue, Suresh appeared with two porters complete with trolleys. Grabbing Carol's hand, he shook it vigorously. He had a grin that stretched from ear to ear.

"Missus Hunteer, so pleased to meet you. I am Suresh. Misteer Mike is a good man. It is my pleasure to meet you." Turning, he greeted Elizabeth in a similar manner and when he had finished, barked out orders to the porters. Forcibly, they thrust their way through the noisy, smelly crowd of Asian workers till they retrieved the two bags that Mike pointed out to them. In no time, they were in the air-conditioned minibus that rocked and swayed at its usual high speed through the night. Occasionally, it swerved erratically around the traffic to the accompaniment of shrieks from Elizabeth. Finally they arrived at Mike's flat.

The next morning Carol and Elizabeth had a traditional English breakfast cooked by Mike. They were all in good spirits after a long sleep-in and quickly warmed to Mike's suggestion that they tour Dubai before it became too hot in the day.

Together they wandered the *souqs* with Carol and his daughter marveling over spices and perfume oils from many exotic places. From there they entered the gold *souq*. Shop after small shop of gold jewellery of every kind greeted his stunned visitors. Nonchalantly, Mike led them from one quaint door to the next while they were astonished by the fragile construction of such treasure troves. Finally tiring of the continual displaying and bartering of the merchants, Mike bought them both an expensive twenty-four-carat gold piece.

From there they made their way through the narrow lanes and passageways out into an open-air vegetable, fish and meat market. Lines of fresh fruit ended with stalls filled with baskets of fresh and unusual vegetables. The air was laden with a curious mixture of the scents of lime, parsley, mint and the nearby sea.

Further along, a flock of hapless-looking goats and sheep waited, mournfully bleating their miserable future. Nearby, a group of Arabs bartered over a goat. Then, to Elizabeth's horror, the deal was struck and with one swift movement, a knife was produced and without ceremony the animal's throat was cut where it stood. Blood poured onto the cracked and stained concrete floor and flowed into the gutter as the stricken goat kicked its last.

Carol was almost sick on the spot. Elizabeth shrieked again and again, attracting a crowd of concerned and curious dark faces. Quickly Mike led them away, hailed a taxi and sped off to the nearby magnificent Hyatt Regency that towered over the sea. Looming over the corniche, it offered a cool, safe seclusion to the still-mortified party.

Carol and Elizabeth were stunned by the contrast to what they had just seen. Small children in winter clothes skated around a huge, colorful ice rink under a multi-patterned atrium that swooped high up to the top floor of this multi-storey building. Inside this luxurious air-conditioned hotel complex, they were ushered into yet a more exotic coffee shop and shown to seats of plush red cushions on erotically-carved teak chairs.

Above them, another atrium swept up to the roof. From each balcony floor hung bright green creepers, and in the centre a fountain whispered and tinkled as it dropped into a crystal clear reflection pond. Swimming languorously in its cool water were lazy, fat, red-and-gold Chinese carp.

With a sigh, they finally relaxed and sipped on spiced coffee while eating ripe dates stuffed with almonds. Elizabeth had quieted down and wiped the tearstains from her cheeks. She was glad to be away from the real Dubai, and her face glowed as she opened the blue velvet bag containing her necklace. Carol reached over and clipped the long golden rope around her throat. Mike looked in amazement at how suddenly his daughter had turned into a young pretty woman.

At night they ate in the open at the Costay club. Stars twinkled in the dark sky as the sound of the surf rolling onto the white moonlight sands relaxed them almost as much as the ice-cold white wine in their glasses. Dining on fresh barbecued Gulf prawns and crisp green salads, the horrors of the day were long forgotten. Returning home, they swiftly went to bed, exhausted by the day's activities. To Mike's great relief, Carol quickly dropped off to sleep. It was no good; he didn't have any desire left in him for her body. Hopefully, for the rest of their holiday they would not have to confront it.

One trip followed another. One day they were off to Oman and diving in the deep waters of the Arabian Sea. Next, they bumped over the long sweeping dunes in the desert.

On another, Mike took them into the *wadi* (dry riverbed) in the Hajar Mountains. Winding down the torturous rocky bed of the dried-up stream, they marveled at its tall sides where trickles of water still stained the rock face. Green oleander shrubs sprouted from the cracks. A small stream flowed intermittently through the pebble floor bed. Rounding a bend, Mike stopped the four-wheel drive and they paddled in a small, cool shallow lake as little silver fish darted between their toes.

With the sun starting to set early in the mountains, Mike drove cautiously down another track over a rocky hill until they halted in a small deserted valley. Surrounded by rocks, myriad small pools flowed into each other to finally become a stream that became a waterfall that dropped down into a dark chasm. By now it was night and the moon crept over the purple mountaintops. Spreading a blanket out over a smooth rock, they ate a meal of salad, cold chicken and fresh bread.

Their daughter, exhausted by the drive, curled up in the backseat of the wagon and slept. Mike and Carol finished the bottle of white wine then walked beside the pools that glinted and sparkled in the moonlight. Without a word, when they reached a slightly deeper pool, they slipped off their clothes and waded into cool water. Instinctively, they reached for each other and on the soft muddy bank under the moonlight made feverish love. Carol's passion surprised Mike as she arched her back and called out in her final moments.

Later, Mike carefully drove the vehicle back toward the main road. His daughter still slept and his wife sat with her head lolling on her shoulder as he negotiated the rocky terrain. Eventually they hit the hard road and in a little over an hour were back in the flat.

It was after midnight when his wife went to bed and Mike sat out on the balcony drinking an ice-cold beer, watching the lights of the Dry Docks. The physical relief of their sex had left him relaxed, but deep down inside he knew there had been no real feelings between him and his wife. He was fairly sure that she felt the same.

Almost before it seemed to have begun, the holiday was over. Mike had received his letter of appointment and was due to fly to the States for training the following week. Elizabeth's new term at school was to start the following Monday.

The evening before Carol and Elizabeth were to leave; they dined at the French restaurant in the Intercontinental Hotel overlooking the lights of the Creek. It was said to be the finest French restaurant outside of Paris. They had Champagne, caviar, lobster and anything else that took their fancy.

After dining, they walked along the Creek in the warm night and boarded an Abra to cruise slowly up and down the calm waters to admire the scenery along both banks. Elizabeth was asleep in the taxi when they arrived back at Mike's flat.

After seeing her to bed, Mike opened a beer and sat out on the balcony. To his surprise, his wife joined him. Together they sat in silence. Finally, Carol spoke in a choked whisper. "It's over, Mike."

Taking a sip on the can, Mike looked out to the sea as he replied. "The holiday. Was it good?"

There was a gap in the conversation. "No, Mike. The marriage. The holiday was too good for words. I loved every minute. But you and I were not together."

There was another gap. "Not even in the mountains?" Carol gently shook her head. "Not even in the mountains. Mike, we were very young when we got married. We've grown apart. I'm still young and so are you. I want to meet somebody who I can love."

Mike realized Carol was crying. He was nearly moved to tears himself. Struggling to control her emotions, Carol continued. "Mike, I don't hate you. It's just that I don't love you. I want a divorce. I want to be free to meet somebody."

Mike sat motionless, still staring out to sea. "And Elizabeth?" Sobbing, Carol reached over and took his hand. "She'll always be ours, Mike. Don't fight this. Let's part as friends."

Silently they sat watching the night sky. Mike now grasped that his wife meant what she said. It was probably what he would have said if he'd had the courage.

"Okay." Mike's whispered answer masked the emotion he felt. Not bitterness, but sad relief.

## Chapter Twenty-Eight

# The Rig

Gently the big 747 Pan Am jet touched down on the runway, then with a roar of its reverse thrust engines, shuddered almost to a halt further down the concrete strip. Steadily it bumped over the expansion cracks to finally stop near the new extensions to Dubai Airport.

Mike stepped out into the familiar heat and headed quickly down the gangway steps to the low-level bus waiting to take the passengers to the comfort of the terminal. Inside it was crowded, but not as badly as before. A little more organized than when he had arrived over a year ago, he was quickly through and in a taxi off to his new flat. Relaxing back in the seat of the cab as it sounded its horn continuously and swerved its way through the traffic, he thought about the last two weeks.

His training course in Houston with Conoco had gone rapidly. It was mostly about safety procedures on the rig, and his previous Army discipline had come in handy, understanding the necessity of rigid order during a crisis. At night he'd drunk and sometimes partied with the others on the course. The American girls had proved to be very friendly and very accommodating, slightly amused and occasionally bowled over by his English accent. Several had shown themselves to be more than friendly, and he felt a trip to the medical clinic was a matter of priority.

Upon entering his flat, he was pleased to see that Suresh had moved all his furniture and left the new place neat and tidy. There were even half a dozen cold beers in the fridge. It had been worth paying the keen little Indian a few extra hundred dirhams to make sure that the job had been done properly.

On the table was his mail that had accumulated in the post box while he was away. There was a thick brown envelope with his address in his wife's handwriting on the front. Opening it, he grabbed a beer and sat down on the sofa under the gentle breeze of the air-conditioner.

Its contents were brisk and to the point. Carol had enclosed the legal papers for a separation. In her letter she went on to say that she felt no bitterness and that they'd grown apart. She would keep the house for Elizabeth's sake and only expect a reasonable extra amount for her and their daughter's upkeep.

At first angry, Mike opened another beer and read the letter again, then the legal papers. "Oh, what the hell! What's over is over."

Muttering and cursing a little more under his breath, he found a pen and signed the separation documents. Then, tired after his trip, he stripped to his underpants, slumped on the bed and slept till late that evening.

Hungry, he wandered down the Satwa high street to Ravi's where he sat and ate a hot spicy chicken *tikka*. While sitting there, a crowd he knew from the rugby club arrived.

One of them joined him for a chat. There was to be a Desert Hash House Harriers run next Sunday night; why didn't he come? Started at five, wear shorts and a T-shirt and be prepared to drink a lot of beer.

Several nights later, he found himself with a group of about twenty runners— some of them girls—all ready to run madly around the desert dunes following a trail of straws laid earlier in the afternoon.

Running enthusiastically despite his bad leg, he cried "On, on!" with the rest of the pack as they dashed from one straw to another. Finally, some forty minutes later, he arrived back at the cars, hot, sandy, covered in sweat and very thirsty! Quickly, a plastic rubbish bin filled to the brim with ice and cans of beer was produced. Equally as quickly, Mike scoffed two of them, the first not even touching his sides.

A shout went up, and the young engineer whom he knew from the Dry Dock began to amuse the merry crowd with a crude and foulmouthed description of the run and the runners. In keeping with the tradition, new runners were obliged to down several more beers at one go. One of these included Mike.

Afterward, slightly drunk, he began talking to a young woman who was equally covered in sand and sweat. Her name was Clare and he thought her quite pretty. She was a brunette with a little-on-the-fuller type of figure.

The group split up, made for the cars and headed homeward out of the dunes. As he left, Mike noticed one of the four-wheelers stuck in the sand. It was Clare's. After an hour of struggling, he managed to free it. In gratitude, Clare asked him back to her flat for a beer and a chili.

To his surprise, he realized that his flat was just around the corner. Inside her flat, she directed him to the bathroom, threw him a silk kimono and told him to shower while she put the frozen chili in the microwave.

Showered, he emerged wearing only a blue Kimono and nothing underneath, He was embarrassed. Clare looked at him, gave a wolf whistle and handed him a cold beer. Gathering up his running clothes, she tossed them in the washing machine before she disappeared into the bathroom to shower.

"Your running gear will be dry and ready by the time you leave." Bursting into a laugh, she looked him up and down. "Don't worry, I wasn't going to send you out into the street dressed like that!" Pulling the gown more tightly around him, Mike grimaced. "Thank God! I'd never have made it past the first Arab coffee shop!"

Not long after, Clare emerged from the bathroom, showered and perfumed. She wore a light cotton cheesecloth long dress and it was obvious that also there was nothing underneath.

Mike's eyes followed her as she went into the kitchen, the neat folds of her buttocks clearly visible through the fine material. They sat at a small table eating the chili. Clare had produced a bottle of red wine and it slipped pleasantly down both their throats.

After Mike had told her of his broken marriage, she revealed that she'd been married before. Six months it had lasted. Her husband had been an Arab national and, in keeping with tradition, could not stay away from other women. Clare had found him in bed with a Lebanese woman when she had returned home early from nightshift at the hospital where she worked as a nurse. She'd packed her bags and left on the spot.

The night drew on and Clare bought out a bowl of peaches. Slicing them, she leaned over and popped a piece into Mike's mouth, then slowly and deliberately ate one herself.

Again she repeated this and as she leaned further forward, the opening at the neck of her dress revealed two firm, round breasts with pink, erect nipples. As she put the last piece in his mouth, he held her wrist, pulled her around the table and kissed her firmly on the mouth. His kiss was returned with passion, and as he held her closer his kimono fell open, exposing how excited he was.

Clare's hands closed over his rigid penis. Within seconds, her dress was over her head and he was kissing the hard nipples of her breasts. In one movement, he lifted her in his arms, swept into the bedroom and in an instant they were making frantic love.

They collapsed, gasping, into each other's arms, then lay still and silent in the dark. A little later, they made love again, this time more slowly and deliberately.

Dawn was gently breaking as Mike slipped out of the bed, found his still slightly damp shorts and T-shirt, pulled them on and crept out the front door. Driving home in the cool of the morning, he felt relaxed and happy. Next evening he would take Clare out to diner then back to her flat before he left for the rig in the morning.

Mike stood at the door of the helicopter ready to step in as the blades whirled over his head. The dinner with Clare had not been a late affair but she had stayed all night in his flat. They had decided that whenever he was off the rig they'd stay together. Climbing into his seat, Mike buckled ready for another stint on the rig. Abruptly the chopper rose from the ground reminding him of Vietnam, something he'd like to forget.

# HUNTER'S GOLD

As the chopper flew over Dubai City, they could see the Creek, the Dry Dock and then they were out over the glimmering, bright blue sea. Half an hour later, the helicopter hovered gently over the landing pad before touching down. Ducking to avoid the still rotating blades, Mike and the other men ran to the steps. Five minutes later, he had stowed his bags in his cabin and stood in front of the control panel in the operating room, ready for his first shift on the rig.

# Chapter Twenty-Nine

# The Storm

Out on the high platform of the rig, Mike watched two large manta rays swimming languidly in the clear water between the legs of the structure. They were frequent visitors to this area and Mike pondered whether or not they were territorial or something. Probably they found food there and returned when they were hungry.

In the distance, the dirty yellow flame with a plume of black smoke that marked the location of the flare stack rose vertically to smudge the clear blue sky. It was early morning and a gentle, warm breeze blew off the land that was out of sight to the east.

Not far off could be seen the low dim outline of Sir Abu Nair island. Several of the operators on the rig had motored out to it on their days off. Only fifty-five miles from Dubai, it was popular with fishermen and divers. During the Second World War it had been a firing target range and some unexploded shells were believed to still remain.

The cool of the morning was to his liking. It gave him a chance to get out of the air-conditioning. But when the heat of the summer's day was upon him, standing outside was uncomfortable and in no time his shirt and trousers would be dripping in sweat. Life on the rig was routine and tedious, almost boring. Nearly three months had passed since he first arrived and he'd now adjusted to the shifts.

Life onshore was much more pleasant, as he and Clare had all but moved in to each other's flats, although Mike mostly stayed at

Clare's. Living there permanently, she'd made it much more of a home in contrast to his stark furnishings with little else to adorn the empty space. Another three months from today and he'd be due leave, and they'd planned to go to Jordan together.

Looking out across the sea, he watched idly as a service vessel appeared on the horizon headed for the rig. It was the normal delivery boat full of supplies and spare parts. A gantry crane perched high on the platform would lower its hook and with the usual practiced efficiency the boat would be unloaded.

In a few hours, the boat would then head off back to Dubai that day. Before it arrived, Mike went back into the control room.

"Shit, it's hot out there today. Dry, though. Very dry. Not like the last few days." Not really speaking to anyone in particular, he didn't expect a reply. Back at the control panel, he watched the array of gauges and meters as their indicating needles stayed resolutely at the correct position on the dials. Every minute, more oil was pumped out from underneath the sea into the large underwater storage tanks that were emptied from time to time into huge ocean-going supertankers.

Later that afternoon, he went back out onto the platform again. Having lain off to avoid the sweltering midday heat, the service vessel had now maneuvered alongside. It was completely calm with no breeze at all and an almost perfectly flat sea. Men moved around on the open deck securing the cargo onto the gantry crane hook that had been lowered. Speedily as possible, each load was discharged.

Mike watched them, barely noticing the rapid drop in temperature. Out in the distance, the flare, that had been vertical now burned strangely at an acute angle. Suddenly there was a faint roar as if a plane was passing overhead. Then, without warning, the rig was hit with a strong gust of cooler air. Rapidly, its strength built up, whipping up the flat sea into streaks of tiny foam-covered waves.

Lying in the lee of the platform, the vessel continued to unload, although by now the skipper was using the engines to keep the boat positioned. Mike peered down. A sharp, short swell was beginning to swirl around the rig's legs. Surprisingly, the gantry crane's safety switch had not cut off in the strong winds. Perhaps, Mike thought, the operator had overridden it against regulations, or maybe the little anemometer whirling around the top of the jib had jammed.

Clouds formed in the sky—long, streaky white ones that scudded across at low level. The service vessel had started to pitch and roll in the swell, and the men on the deck struggled to keep their feet as they worked quickly to finish unloading the last of the cargo. Every now and then, a wave would break under the rig, its crest surfing through the legs and covering the vessel with wind-driven spray.

Night was falling, and along with the cloud cover it had become dark. Spotlights on the rig and the vessel lit the deck. Only two men in soaked overalls and bright orange life jackets were left battling to hold their feet as they wrestled with the last of the cargo. Shoving slings around the box of spare parts, they signaled with a wave of their hands and the load lifted off the deck. The two workmen clutched the safety rails as they began to make their way back to their cabins.

Abruptly, the stern of the vessel dropped into a trough. A large wave broke through the legs, sending a wall of water rushing over the open deck. To Mike's horror, when it had flowed clear, the men had disappeared. Frantically, he ran to the alarm button and slammed it with his fist. Loud horns instantly hooted the alarm and operators raced from the control room, grabbing safety rescue equipment as they left.

"Man overboard!" Mike shrieked into the screeching wind. An emergency crew rushed to the railings to hurl orange life rings over the side into the foaming water below. Several of them charged down the steps to the lower deck that was now awash with the rising waves.

Aboard the vessel, the crew had been alerted, and searchlights swept the white surf astern of the vessel. A shout went up as a yellow safety helmet suddenly appeared in the swirling waters behind the vessel. But just as rapidly, it disappeared.

After about an hour and with no further signs of life, the search was abandoned. The vessel drifted back from the rig and sat with its bow into the waves on its engines, a lone spotlight continuing to forlornly sweep the turbulent sea.

During the night, the storm abated. In spite of his experiences in Vietnam, Mike found it difficult to get over the sudden deaths of the two seamen.

Early next morning, all was calm except for a lazy swell that rolled under the rig. The previously clear water was now opaque with churned-up sand. A warm breeze blew off the land as usual. From the workboat, a small craft was launched and several crewmen spent a fruitless morning searching for the bodies.

Two police officers arrived on the morning helicopter and carried out a brief investigation. Mike signed a statement as one of the witnesses. By midday, it was all over. Sedately, almost mournfully, the service vessel moved off, heeled slightly over as she bore away from the rig and headed back to Dubai Port.

Arriving back in Dubai after the end of his shift, Mike had a telegram waiting for him. His mother had died. He got on the next plane and flew home to her small and quiet funeral.

# Chapter Thirty

# Another Storm

Clare and Mike's relationship had deepened. They could barely wait to be together when Mike was offshore. Within minutes of his return, if Clare was at home, they would be in bed making passionate love. Together they went to the gym where they worked out or played squash, Mike's leg making them almost equal partners. Otherwise, they would swim at the club, go to the beach or simply sit at home and talk to each other.

The physical activity did wonders for Clare. She lost weight, gained muscle tone and grew her hair long. Mike would marvel at her lithe, sinuous body as she came out of the shower into the bedroom where he was usually waiting. On one occasion, they were on the Hash and after turning in different directions ended up meeting each other in a small valley amongst the dunes.

With the light fading and the runners moving off into the distance, they were alone. In a moment of madness, they frantically removed their clothes and made furious love in the warm, soft sand, their passion heightened by the fear of being caught any moment. At the gathering after the run, the hash leader had guessed their escapade. To their great embarrassment, his ribald comments caused much hilarity and they blushed red. Later that night in bed, they laughed so much about the incident that they almost couldn't make love again…almost!

Not long after, Mike's six-month leave was due and they packed their bags for a journey to Jordan. They'd bought a new four-wheel drive and decided to travel by road through Saudi Arabia. Despite having all the correct visas and vehicle passes, their confrontations with the officious and arrogant Saudis were almost too much to bear. Mike's patience was stretched to the limit. Finally, hot and dusty after three days on the road, most of it spent at border posts, they drove wearily into Amman.

To their delight, the small hotel they booked into was comfortable and pleasant, although only three-star. The owner, who had been educated in the U.K., spoke excellent English and was warm and friendly. Within minutes they were in the shower and not long after, enjoying a cold beer on the tiny balcony while munching dates stuffed with pistachios. Down below them, a noisy passing parade of local Arabs bustled back and forth. Though it was early afternoon, it was not hot by Dubai standards and the wind felt cool on their faces.

As the sky reddened then darkened, Clare gazed at Mike's face. When night fell they were still sitting there. Clare felt she'd been in love before but not like this. Maybe it was time to settle down, marry and have kids. But would Mike want another family? Probably not. Well, she could forego the kids, Mike would be enough.

"What are you thinking?"

Clare jumped a little as Mike spoke.

"Nothing." She took his hand. *Yes, this is the man for me.*

"You were thinking you love me and I'm the best man you've ever had." Mike laughed to himself as Clare squeezed his hand.

"Maybe."

Clare fell asleep straight away. Though the window, Mike watched the twinkling stars against their carpet of purple. He didn't know much about Clare, but he did know he wanted her and the rest didn't matter. What he did know he liked, no...*loved.* Life with her was so different from his life with Carol. No baggage, no knee-jerk emotional reactions, no scratching old scars that would lead to yet another disagreement.

Probably she'd want a family. No big deal. He'd cross that bridge when they came to it. He rolled over, gently kissed her then slipped off to sleep.

Early the next morning, they headed off to the ancient city of Petra. Hiring two horses, they rode through the majestic valley with its huge sandstone carvings in the rock face. It was breathtaking!

Their guide bought a small charcoal stove and they lunched on Arab bread and grilled kebab then fruit followed by bitter strong Turkish coffee. In the shade of the rocks, they watched the carvings darken as the sun lowered itself in the sky.

That night back at the hotel, they lay naked on the bed with the windows wide open. Drinking the champagne that the owner had managed to find for them, they gazed out at the starry night. They were unbelievably happy. Languorously they made love, then slipped off to sleep in each other's arms. Next day they headed back on the long journey to Dubai.

Back in Dubai, Clare had to return to work so Mike, who had another week of his leave to go, climbed on a plane and went back to the U.K. It was mainly to see his daughter but, as well, to make peace with his wife. His daughter's reception was as warm as ever and, surprisingly, his wife was cordial, although a little standoffish. Mike looked at her. She'd aged, but then again, so had he.

During the week they kept up appearances, but when Elizabeth had gone to bed the conversation became stilted and difficult. Mike slept in the spare room. On the day before he departed, he took his daughter to the movies and then to dinner.

"You and Mummy are going to part, aren't you, Daddy?" Mike almost choked on his steak in surprise.

"Your mother never told you?"

The response was immediate. "No, but I can see. You don't like each other anymore."

Mike put down his knife and fork. "Well, that's a bit harsh. We don't get on and we've decided to separate."

Anger tinged his daughter's voice. "She's got another man. I don't like him. I want to come with you." Tears started to roll down her cheek. Mike called for the bill then took her, sat beside her on a bench in a nearby park and put his arm around her. Sobbing, she buried her head in his shoulder.

"Don't go, Daddy. Don't go. Stay. I don't want Mummy to marry anybody else." Mike remained silent then finally he whispered, "I'll always be your father. Your mother wants that. She won't hurt you or let you down. I have to go back and make enough money for you to go to university. I'll have a word with your mother."

Later that evening when Elizabeth had gone to her room, Mike spoke to his wife. It wasn't a happy scene. For some reason she wanted to blame him for everything. Struggling to contain his temper, he listened. The woman opposite him was a complete stranger.

"Carol, do what you like with whomever you like, but while I'm paying for you to support yourself and Elizabeth, at least try to be considerate to her and a little more subtle. I don't care what you think about me anymore. That's not important, but our daughter is!"

With that he left the room and went to his own. The next morning as he departed for the airport, Elizabeth was once again in tears. Carol took her by the hand and kissed Mike goodbye on the cheek. "I'll look after Elizabeth, don't worry. I'm sorry. I hope I didn't spoil your holiday." Mike sadly shook his head. "No, it's alright. Bye, Elizabeth. I love you. I'll be back to see you soon."

Lying back in bed with Clare, Mike told her the whole story. "You should bring her out here more often, Mike. Don't lose touch with your daughter. Besides, I'd like to meet her. How old is she?" Mike's hands started to roam. "Nearly fifteen." Playfully, Clare pushed them away. "Not much younger than me!"

Leaning on his elbows, Mike looked her in the eye. "Get off. Come here." Burying his head in her breasts, his hands started to wander again, this time with more success, especially when he touched the spots she particularly liked. "Mmm, doesn't feel like you're fifteen." Clare began to respond to his touch. "Oh, don't stop. You're a beast." Moments later they were making love. Mike never ceased to wonder at Clare's sexual appetite. It equaled his, and from time to time their lovemaking was so noisy he thought the neighbors must hear. Serves them right for listening!

With the months slipping by, they drifted into a routine. Occasionally, they discussed getting married. It was still more than a year to go before Mike's divorce was final. At Christmas when he went back to the U.K. for Elizabeth's sake, Clare at the same time made a brief trip to be with her parents. Both were back in time to enjoy a flamboyant and wild New Year's Eve celebration at the local yacht club.

Several weeks later, Mike caught Clare in a pensive mood. Asking what the problem was only resulted in being in bed again with Clare even more passionate than ever.

"Mike, I love you. You know that, don't you? You'll never forget that, will you?" Sensing a change of mood, Mike was quiet for a moment. "What the hell are you talking about? Of course I know you love me. What's up?" Clare didn't answer.

Sitting up he stared down at her small, naked body outlined in the dim light. "What's the problem?" Pulling him to her, she held him tight. "Nothing, Mike. Nothing."

When Mike opened the door to her flat, he sensed there was something wrong. Before he left, Clare had been strangely possessive, almost as if she didn't want him to go out to the rig. Dropping his bag, he strode briskly into the living room. The pictures had gone. Running into the bedroom, he flung open the wardrobe doors. All of Clare's clothes had gone. He looked at their bed. In the middle of his pillow was an envelope with his name scrawled on the front. Tearing it open, he sat heavily on the bed and started to read. A chill ran through his heart.

"My dearest, darling Mike, I'm so sorry I could not face you before I left. My ex- husband has been harassing me for the last two months. He has been coming around while you have been away. Last time he tried to rape me and said he was going to make trouble for us. He said he would report us to the police for adultery. Darling, I am so scared. If I told you I know you would have probably killed him. I know you could. I have gone to Australia and when I have settled I will let you know. I am sorry, Mike, so sorry. I love you so much. Please forgive me. Loving you forever, Clare."

Again and again he read the letter as a storm brewed in his brain. Screwing up the letter, he hurled it at the wall with all his might. The chill around Mike's heart turned to a raging anger. Clare was right. He'd kill the Arab bastard and tear his fucking heart out if he could've laid his hands on him. In wild anger, he kicked and lashed out at the furniture, breaking a chair with a vicious chop. Tears of sorrow and anger mingled with sweat as they flowed down his twisted face.

He tore open the refrigerator and snatched up a beer, drained the contents and hurled the empty can at the wall. Repeatedly he did the same until he'd consumed the five that had been there. In a half-drunken state he stormed from the apartment, threw his bag into the pickup and drove wildly back to his flat.

Yanking his door open, he raged into the bedroom and collapsed in a heap on his bed. Minutes later, still sobbing, he rose and staggered to the kitchen where he drank more beer. Then, exhausted by emotion and drunk, fell asleep fully clothed.

The next morning he dragged himself into the shower, his head aching with a fearful hangover. Showered and changed, he went back to Clare's empty flat and searched for clues of where she may have gone in Australia. While he was at it, he tried to find out who the Arab was to whom she'd been married. If he could find him, he'd sort the bastard out. Sadly, there was nothing. He rang her mother, but she knew nothing about Clare's departure and was equally as shocked.

For the next two days he moped around his flat. Inside he felt a hollow, lonely emptiness. For hours he sat and stared at the few photos he had of Clare. Time and time again he read her note, vaguely hoping it was a nightmare from which he'd awaken. Thankfully, his shift day came around. At least out on the rig he'd not be around all the familiar things that reminded him of Clare. It was worse than her being dead. She was somewhere on this earth and he couldn't reach her.

# Chapter Thirty-One

# The Rifle

When his shift was over, he returned to his flat. It was a prison. As night fell he had to get out. He walked around the streets trying to rid the thoughts of Clare that tumbled and turned endlessly around in his mind. Each day it got worse instead of getting better. He stopped playing squash and going on the Hash because they had too many memories of Clare. He was very much at a loose and dangerous end.

Eventually, one of his fellow operators, Don Johnson, a big American from Louisiana, talked him into going to the Dirt Donks, a club of trail bike riders. They needed marshals on their courses on the Friday scramble races. He went. It was a new crowd and new faces. At least he wouldn't be reminded of Clare at every turn.

On the rig, he put his heart and soul into the job to avoid thinking of her. He started a correspondence course on welding and structural engineering, as it still interested him. During the time that he was ashore, he spent all his time pulling down and reassembling trail bikes with Don or helping organize the races. Don talked him into buying a 250 c.c. bike for himself. With practice, he could overcome the problem with his stiff, injured leg. With trepidation, he entered his first race, coming last but proud of the achievement.

Amongst his mail, he instantly recognized the writing on one of the envelopes. It was Clare's. Frantically he tore it open. With a sinking heart he read the contents.

"Darling Mike,

# Hunter's Gold

I don't know how to tell you this. I have a job in Australia and I have decided to stay. I don't want to hurt you and the memory of our good times together still pains me. You know I can't come back to Dubai with that bloody ex of mine. I have met someone really nice here, an Australian, and he wants to marry me. Forgive me, Mike. I still do love you, but it is impossible.

All my love forever,

Clare."

When she had left, he'd feared the worst and now it had happened. Anger and hurt welled up inside of him. Cursing and swearing with rage, he went to the fridge and downed a beer. Life wasn't worth living without Clare. All that had kept him going was gone. Wild with emotion, he went out to his trail bike. Kicking it over, he rode fiercely into the night wearing only a T-shirt and jeans, no helmet and no boots.

For about half an hour, he sped aimlessly out of town. Large sand dunes loomed on either side in the desert. Moonlight shone eerily down, creating patterns of somber brown and dark shadows.

Without thinking, he wheeled his bike off the road into the sand and tore up and over one small dune after another. At the top of a huge dune, he accelerated as hard as he could. The bike flew into the air, gliding like a small plane then dived down into the trough below.

Although he'd wanted to die, he instinctively clung to the handlebars of the bike. Hitting the ground on its front wheel, it buckled, and at the same time the muscles in Mike's left shoulder gave way. Instantly, his chest hit the top of the front forks, breaking two ribs. As he collapsed to one side, the bike fell on top of him, its exhaust pipe searing the flesh on his leg. With a scream of agony, he wriggled from beneath it. Rolling around in distress, he finally sat up, put his head between his knees and sobbed his heart out. The pain there was much worse than his injuries.

About an hour later, he had recovered sufficiently enough to stagger back to the road where one of the ubiquitous taxis invariably trolling for passengers picked him up and took him home. Reaching his flat, he stumbled in, found some money to pay the cab driver then made his way to the kitchen.

He shuffled through the drawers until he found the illegal packet of codeine that Clare had stolen from the hospital. The recommended dosage was two tablets. He took three and washed them down with another beer. In agony, he limped to the freezer, grabbed a packet of frozen peas then staggered to the bedroom.

Tentatively, he lowered his bruised body onto the bed and pressed the packet of peas to his burnt flesh. He gasped in pain, then wrapped the sheet around it. Exhausted, he fell into a codeine-and-alcohol-induced sleep, dreaming violently of sand dunes, bikes and Clare's face.

In the morning, the dawn light seared through the open curtains. Waking, the pain wracked his body. He'd not realized he'd grazed his face. Now the oozing blood had stuck to the pillow. Hardly able to move from the agony of his torn shoulder and broken ribs, he managed to call Don from the phone by his bed.

When Don entered the room, he stood, shocked. "Shit, man, what happened? Did you get the number of the truck?"

Dressed in jeans and a Harley Davidson T-shirt with his belly hanging over a wide leather belt, he towered over the bed.

"Fucking hell, man, you're a mess! I'll get you to a doctor. What the fuck happened?"

In a whisper, Mike tried not to start sobbing again as he told the story. Pain throbbed through his heart. The big man listened in silence. When Mike had finished, he sat on the edge of the bed.

"Don't worry about the bike, Mike. I'll get Bobby to pick it up with the trailer." With that, the American picked up the phone and rang his son. "All done. Now to get you to the quack."

With great difficulty, Don eased Mike from the bed, loaded him into his massive American four-wheel-drive pickup and drove him carefully to the Dubai Petroleum Company doctor.

"Two broken ribs, a torn shoulder, badly grazed face and second-degree burns to the leg, but you'll live. Not bad for a night. Tell me, were you drinking? No, don't answer that. I don't want to know."

Mike had blurted out to the doctor a story of going for a joyride. The real story hurt too much to tell again.

"Well, you don't talk much. Anyhow, it'll be sometime before you're back at work."

Suddenly Don spoke up. "He was in the Army, special services."

Eyeing him, the doctor smile grimly. "Tough man, eh. Well. those ribs will keep you quiet. They'll be strapped up like that for at least three weeks."

Instead of flying out to the rig the following day, Mike reported in to the office. Expecting the worst, he was surprised by the reception from the maintenance supervisor.

"Fortunate, damn fortunate. Been looking at your personal file, Mike. See you've got construction experience and a welding supervisor's ticket. By the way, how'd you hurt yourself?"

Looking a bit sheepish, Mike didn't respond. His boss was another American, this time from Dallas. Slim, well-educated and in his mid-fifties, he'd been a petroleum engineer for thirty years.

"Don't tell me. Got pissed at a stag show or something? Been there myself. Got the T-shirt. Nothing serious." The tea boy interrupted them. Drinking his coffee was painful, but it gave Mike a chance to recover.

"Yeah," the Dallas engineer drawled. "As I was saying, damned fortunate. This rig that's being built by McDermott's is nearly finished. So's our damned supervising engineer. Got himself tanked up. Trashed the flat and his wife. We've had to get him out fast. Marital problems. But you'll do. You're not an engineer, but it's all welding and scheduling. I'm sure you can handle it. Start next Monday, if that's alright with the Doc."

Mike didn't check with the doctor but went straight to work. Lying on its side, the big tubular frame was in the fabrication yard at the top end of the creek. With only two weeks to go to the completion date, workmen swarmed over it night and day.

Mike picked up the x-rays of the welds and glanced through them. His eyes widened as he flicked through them, one after another, on the screen. Not one of them met the specification.

Calling in the McDermott's engineer, he went through them again. The silence was deafening. A brief but tense meeting was held with the consultant and the project engineer. Dye and ultrasound tests were rapidly carried out on all the welds. Seventy-five percent failure!

"What do you intend to do?" Mike's boss's tone was harsh and steely tough as he addressed the McDermott's project manager. There was an icy silence across the meeting table. "Well, I'll tell you what you're going to do. You're going to fly welders in from the States and they're going to work all damned night and day. It'll be at your cost and there will be penalties as well."

Flustered, the project manager started to explain. "But your engineer approved…." His voice trailed off as Mike's boss stared him down. "I don't care what our man may or may not have approved! It's not fucking approved now! So move. Meeting closed."

Leaving the meeting, his boss pulled him to one side. "Good work, Mike. Good work. Keep on top of it. There'll be a bonus."

Two days later, a team of ten welders arrived from the States. Most of them were black and tough. They took no orders but they knew their jobs.

"Find one bad weld and you can weld my balls to the rig!" Their foreman was the biggest of them all. The thought of finding a bad weld amused Mike. Welding this man's balls to anything would require the help of the U.S. Army!

Within a week, over fifty percent of the remedial work had been completed. The men worked straight eight-hour shifts through the day and night and they did know their job. Not one failure! Each welder did the work of at least three of the Asian welders in one day. Only two weeks behind schedule and the work was finished. The clients were so pleased that they didn't impose any penalty for that portion of the work. However, the most crucial part of the contract was yet to come.

Six massive crawler cranes waddled into position around the finished structure. Later, they lifted the huge complex of pipes onto a rolling frame. The next day it was winched onto a barge moored alongside the yard in the creek. Finally, it was ready to be towed out to the offshore field at the first window of opportunity in the weather. Along with a very handy bonus, Mike was to accompany the rig to its destination out in the Gulf. The work was great therapy; it took his mind off Clare.

It was a Friday when the opportunity presented itself and the barge left the mooring. Ahead, one of the largest oceangoing tugs available pulled it forward while two smaller tugs attached to the stern of the barge controlled its movement down the narrow waterway.

On the bridge of the lead tug, Mike watched as the Creek traffic came to a standstill while the massive barge and its load dominated their water. Normally, it was bustling with water taxis and coastal trading dhows going to and fro, but this morning, under the bright sun, all was stopped. Along the banks, crowds of laborers on their day off stood and watched this spectacular procession. Passing the *souq* and the Ruler's Palace, many of the occupants waved. Mike waved back.

About an hour after leaving the moorings, the barge entered the flat, glittering waters of the Gulf. The smaller tugs threw their towing lines and the larger tug gradually accelerated and headed off at a steady pace of around four knots. It would take roughly fifteen hours to get to the oil fields.

From the bridge, Mike could see their tow with its tall structure streaming out behind them. While the engines thumped rhythmically below them, Mike carried on a conversation with the skipper.

Another American, only this time from Louisiana and he spoke fluent Creole. One of the other skippers from a nearby service vessel was from the same region and Mike listened, bemused, as they spoke to each other over the radio in a curious mixture of French and English with a deep drawl.

On occasion Clare had slipped into his mind, but for the most part the activity of the project kept his melancholy away. Not like before, when he could think of nothing else. At one stage he'd rung her parents to try and find out where she was in Australia, but they couldn't or wouldn't tell him. Lying in bed at night all alone, he'd worked out in his mind the different ways he would have killed her ex-husband if he only knew who he was.

Tirelessly, the vessel churned through the calm blue sea. Above them, the occasional seabird wheeled and dived into the wake. Come midday, he and the skipper sat down to eat in the captain's private mess. To Mike's surprise and delight, a bottle of red wine appeared on the table.

"My father was of French origin; his grandfather was from Marseille. My real name is Jacques, but call me Jack."

Mike grinned. "Right, Jack. I like the idea of a glass of red wine for lunch!"

Jack's smile showed a couple of missing teeth as he poured him a glass that was nearly overflowing. Over lunch, Mike learned that Jack had been in Vietnam about the same time as him, only with the U.S. Navy on river patrol.

"Never forget it, Mike. Never. Every morning, bodies floating down the river. Some without heads; others twisted and mutilated. A few with their hands tied behind their backs. I don't believe it was all Cong. Think some of our boys were behind it. Have to admit, the girls were good. Caught a dose a couple of times, but worth it. How about you?"

Mike tried to make light of his experiences. "Never caught a dose, but caught a bullet." Jack roared with laughter. "Give me a dose anytime!" Mike nodded wryly. "Same here." Watching the American enjoy himself, he felt the warm atmosphere wash over and he began to laugh as well. It was the first real laugh he'd had since Clare had left.

By early next morning, under the stars, the tug and its fully laden barge arrived at its destination. Not long after, another two service vessels arrived. All lay at anchor in a blaze of lights till the sun rose.

By seven in the morning, the divers were in the water to check out the seabed where the rig legs were to sit. More anchors were needed for stability, and the two service vessels motored to exact positions then lowered them to the bottom. Attaching them to the barge, the tension was taken up on the cables and the barge was located to where the rig was to be dropped.

Workmen scurried around the barge, removing the holding down lashings and shackles while others cut the temporary welds that fixed it to the rig. Rollers were positioned and thoroughly greased. Several highly experienced technicians were left on board, the others leaving by small runabouts back to the service vessels.

On board, the valves in the barge's hull were gradually opened and water flowed into one end. Almost imperceptibly, the large vessel began to sink at the stern. Calmly and predictably, it tilted more and more. Then suddenly, almost taking the observers unaware, the great structure slid with a huge splash off the barge and down to the sea bottom.

Freed of its load, the barge bobbed back up, wallowed a little in the foam then sat motionless again. Behind it, all that could be seen were the tips of the legs that protruded slightly above the surface.

Aboard the tug, the crew cheered and cans of Coke were passed around in celebration. Tidying up, the service vessels lifted anchor and were soon off. Back on the barge, pumps spewed water out over the side as it slowly regained an even keel. A couple of hours later, the tug took the tow again and headed back to Dubai.

Doggedly the tug cruised eastwards. Dinnertime came around and another bottle of wine appeared on the table between Mike and Jack. "Very civilized." Jack smiled and nodded, easing his big frame into the small chair.

Finishing the meal, Jack leaned back in his chair and lit a cigar. "Got something that might interest you." With a puff of smoke he rose, lumbered to his cabin, stuck his arm into the wardrobe and reappeared carrying a rifle.

"Don't shoot! I surrender," quipped Mike as he held up his hands. "Take it." Catching the rifle as it was gently tossed to him, Mike turned it over and cast a professional gaze over its mechanism.

"Never seen one before, but I guess it's an AK47." Then, quickly opening the breech, "And it's loaded!" Jack nodded. "Right both times." Closing the breech, Mike laid it on the table. "Where'd you get it?"

Jack's tale of his adventurous and dangerous trip to the Gulf of Aquaba even had Mike whistling in admiration. "Damned Royal Colombo. Shot up by an Exocet missile. Iranian. We took supplies up to a Dutch rescue tug that had it in tow. Bloody dangerous. Those Dutchie bastards were fucking mad towing that scrap metal. Money, that's what they were after."

Mike gave him a sideways glance. "And you?" Slowly the American drew on his cigar then blew out a cloud of smoke. "Well, of course, but I wasn't a sitting duck. At least I didn't have a tow and could maneuver. Anyhow, they were armed to the teeth— rifles, machine guns and even grenade throwers. They gave me a couple of these little beauties and a few boxes of rounds. Had them ever since. Like a tryout?" Picking up the weapon, Mike eyed the barrel. "Sure!"

Turning in his chair, the skipper ordered the head boatman to have an empty oil drum on deck. Drinking the last of the bottle of wine, they strode out onto the wide afterdeck. The heavy cable, to which the empty barge was attached, was still streaming out behind. Waving his arm, the skipper had the vessel gradually slow to a stop. Before it completely slowed, the crew threw a drum overboard, where it drifted into the water between the tug and the barge.

"Have a shot." Shaking his head, Mike handed the rifle back. "You first." Jack fired off half a dozen rounds that splashed viciously around the bobbing drum. "Ah, never was any fucking good at it. You have a go."

Squeezing the trigger gently, Mike aimed and let off two rounds, the report of the rifle echoing off the hull of the trailing barge. "Shit, you missed, too!" Lowering the rifle so it hung loosely by his thigh, Mike muttered, "Watch."

Leaning on the rail, they stared at the drum. It began to list, and then it quickly stood upright before it slid out of sight below the water.

Drawing in a heavy breath, the American growled, "Jesus, you're fucking good. What'd you do?" Grinning, Mike shouldered the rifle. "One in the waterline, one in the top to let the air out."

Straightening up from the rail where he was leaning, the big man pulled out another cigar. "A damned professional. What were you in?" Mike didn't look at him. "SAS." Lighting the cigar, Jack blew another cloud in the air. "Pity the fucking gooks."

Back on the bridge, the skipper ordered "slow" ahead and the vessel vibrated forward under their feet. In the cabin, Mike put the safety catch back on the rifle and handed it to Jack. Raising his big paw, the skipper shook his head. "No, no, you keep it. You know what to do with it! It's yours."

Surprised, Mike cradled the weapon in his arm. "How'll I get it off?"

Jack's eyes narrowed. "What? Through the dock gate. Fucking easy. Those dumb bastards…I could drive a tank up to them and they'd wave it through." Sure enough, Mike dismantled the rifle and placed it in a canvas bag in a toolbox. He emptied about a hundred rounds into another bag and stuck them in a different toolbox. Throwing them into the back of his pickup, he covered it with other equipment and then a canvas tarpaulin.

At the gate he stopped as the guard lazily strolled over to his vehicle. Seeing Mike, he grinned and held out his hand. Taking it, Mike shook it firmly. The guard started towards the back of the pickup, muttering to himself in Arabic. Before he was about to lift the corner of the canvas cover, there was a sharp toot. It was Jack.

Looking back, the guard waved his hand, directing Mike to move on. From his rear view mirror he saw Jack shake the guard's hand then hand him a brown leather bag. Two bottles of whisky, no doubt.

Back at the flat, he carefully unloaded the two tool kits, and then, after reassembling the rifle, stashed it, well hidden, on the top shelf of his wardrobe. The canvas bag full of rounds he hid in the back of a drawer in his chest of drawers. That night, after a couple of beers, he dropped off to sleep wishing he could locate Clare's Arab ex-husband, bastard that he was. Now he really had the right tools to fix the arsehole!

The next day, he headed straight to the project engineer's room. Without knocking he entered, smiling as the older man looked up. Leaping to his feet, the engineer offered his hand in warm welcome.

"Mike, sit. Sit down." Coming from around his desk, he patted Mike on the shoulder, sat him down and ordered coffee for two over the phone.

"Well done, Mike. Well done. Barely a week behind schedule. It will reflect in your bonus next month. Upstairs they're really impressed. McDermott's owe you one as well. No penalties. They were damned lucky. We've got another project for you."

Mike shook his head slightly. "Er, I'd rather not." Surprised, the engineer stared at Mike. "What's that, Mike?" Clenching his hands together between his knees, the younger man looked down. "No, thanks. If you don't mind, I'd like to be back on the rig. My ribs are okay now and I'd like my old job back." Sighing, the engineer leaned back in his chair. "No problem, Mike. No problem."

When he went for his coffee, Mike heard someone enter the room behind him. Turning, he caught sight of a pretty Indian girl. She was tall, had long legs, long, dark hair, almond eyes and wore jeans, a designer T-shirt and high-heeled sandals. All told, she was enough to get his heart started.

"Good morning, sir. Here's the report." Mike's boss raised his eyes at the voice. "Oh, good morning. Thank you." With that, the girl dropped a file on the desk, turned and walked out.

Mike's gaze followed, and then he swiveled back to the other man and raised his eyebrows. "Not bad, not bad. Who's that?" Continuing to read the file he'd just opened; the engineer's voice was barely audible. "Oh, Prithi. She's the chief geologist's secretary. Nice girl, but aloof. Typical, typical."

Mike leaned forward. "Typical?" Putting down the file, the engineer looked at Mike. "Oh, yes. You know these Indian girls… guarded by their family. Can't go near them. Saving them for the right marriage. Some rich merchant probably. You've no chance."

Laughing, Mike stood up to leave. "Too bad. I could do with some spice in my life." The older man started to laugh as well. "Stick to the white girls. They're spicy enough." Reaching the door, Mike looked back. "Yeah, you're right. Spicy enough. See you soon." As he headed off to his pickup, Mike found himself humming for the first time in a long while.

# Chapter Thirty-Two

# The Nightclub

There was a change of work roster that changed Mike's lifestyle. Instead of thirty days on, then ten days off, the company decided on a system of seven days on and seven off. This meant he had only a week on shore to fill in his time.

Those from the States and some from the U.K. still continued to fly home to be with their families. But apart from his daughter, Mike didn't have any family. Except for when the divorce papers came through, he hadn't heard from his estranged wife Carol. He'd signed the papers automatically, without even reading them.

Later, speaking on the phone to her when she'd rung to thank him, there was no rancor; just politeness with a tinge of sadness. When his daughter had made a short visit to see him, he learned that she'd met yet another man and was thinking of marrying him. Mike didn't feel angry or any emotion at all. Any that had been in him was driven deep into his subconscious by his affair with Clare.

Since her last message, he'd hoped against reason that he'd hear from Clare at least one more time. He never did. It was a serious wound and would take a long time to heal, or so he thought. Other women didn't interest him. Once, on an urge and encouraged by one of the young men who worked with him and who wanted company, he went to Bangkok. From the moment they arrived, they were beset with young, attractive Asian girls with only one motive.

Finding it almost too much to bear, he accepted a proposition for one night. In his hotel room, he had barely time to unpack before the young, lithe girl with a boyish figure had undressed and was beckoning him into the shower. More bemused than sexually aroused, he followed her through her every move.

In the morning, she told him she loved him and wanted to stay. It was a good act, but Mike realized it was only for the night. "Stay? For how much?" Unabashed and as quick as a flash, she was back on him. "Five hundred dollars and you can do everything to me."

Smiling, she kissed him and touched him in places where she thought it would arouse his interest. But it didn't. "Here's another one hundred for you to go now." For a second she frowned, then quickly smiled again and handed him a card. "You good man. If you change your mind, you ring me. Other girls no good. Only do for money. I love you!" Laughing, Mike pushed her out the door.

During the rest of the week, he was fairly bored. The city was dirty, noisy and he got sick of touring temples. A short trip into the countryside was his only relief. Huge teak trees covered the road with their foliage as vines twined around their trunks. High above, monkeys screamed and cursed. Patches of cleared areas revealed paddy fields full of water and dotted with peasants who, knee deep, worked at planting rice. Continually bent, they wore woven bamboo coned hats and from distance looked like some strange animals grazing.

At the end of the holiday as the plane lifted off, he swore to himself he would never come back.

Back in Dubai, Mike was still involved with the Dirt Donks, but there was time on his hands. He bought a fishing boat to help pass the time. Over twenty-five feet long, it came with a trailer and had two powerful outboards and a cabin that slept two. With the change in work pattern, Don could also spare the time to go on a fishing trip with him, particularly as his wife and boy had moved back to the States for the summer.

Mostly it was just the two of them that fished, although on occasions they took other rig workers with them. On each trip they would catch far more than a fair share of fish and invariably ended up giving them away to the nearby servants and watchmen. Their reward for such generosity was often a mouthwatering, spicy fish curry in return.

Apart from watching TV or reading, his only other activity was drinking with Don and several cronies at the Dubai Petroleum Company club. Once or twice they would all end up slightly drunk in a nightclub. As the men would consistently outnumber the women by a factor of three to one, it was not very satisfying. Mike had sworn he wouldn't do it again when Don asked him to try it one more time. This time they would go early and by themselves. Since Don's wife was due back for a holiday the following week, Mike agreed to go.

"Come on, Mike, let's party. I want a bit of action before Sandy's back in town." Dressed in a cleaned and pressed black shirt, fashion leather jacket, tailored jeans with a leather belt and silver buckle, along with his Cuban-heeled cowboy boots, Don really looked the part. Mike dressed down. In a simple white shirt, sports trousers and a jacket, he paled in Don's shadow.

Upon entering the nightclub, they could see it was already starting to fill with young people. "I'm ready to party, Mike." Looking him up and down, Mike grinned wryly. "I'm too old and you're too ugly." Heading for the bar, the big man dragged him along. "Get fucked. I'm going to have me a ball."

Standing in the crowd, Mike felt out of place, although Don was thoroughly enjoying himself. Lavishly buying drinks for all and sundry, he'd attracted the attention of a couple of airhostesses. Standing no chance with them didn't stop him from trying. Out of the corner of his eye, Mike thought he saw somebody he knew.

"Hey, Don, who's that over there near the end of the bar?" Glancing over, Don chortled, "Hey, it's that Aussie chick from the office. Her husband's out of town. She must have the same idea as me." Still staring, Mike pulled Don's elbow. "Who's that with her?" Don peered through the smoke haze. "Ah, yes, she's managed to tow that Indian chick along, too. What's her name? Pretty or something." Mike tried to catch their eye, but it was too late; they were surrounded by what looked like a couple of expensively dressed, wealthy young local Arabs.

Towards midnight, Mike decided to leave, as he was bored and tired. The music was too loud and by now Don was slightly drunk, the airhostesses having left some time earlier. As he tried to convince Don to leave, his attention was caught by the angry tone of a woman arguing. Moving towards the sound, he saw the Australian woman pushing away one of the Arabs, whom was trying to drag the struggling Indian girl with him. Suddenly it turned ugly. Another Arab shoved the Australian woman to the floor and started to viciously kick her. Without hesitation, Mike strode over, Don's slightly weaving bulk following him.

"That's enough!" Grabbing the woman's assailant by the shoulder, Mike pulled him off and sent him flying across the floor. Turning on the other, he wrenched the Arab's hand from the Indian girl's wrist and pushed him back into the crowd. "The girl doesn't want you." By this time, Don had helped the older woman to her feet. With a bleeding nose, she looked a mess. She needed to go to a hospital. Meanwhile, the Arab who had grabbed the Indian girl was back in Mike's face.

"Hey, whitey, fuck off." Holding his ground, Mike coolly snarled, "You fuck off." With that, Mike shoved him again. Falling back into the now larger and agitated crowd that had now gathered, the Arab cursed loudly. Suddenly in the half-light, a knife flashed. Several of the women in the crowd screamed as they backed off, leaving Mike and the Arab in the clear.

Watching him carefully, Mike let the Arab come at him. Slashing with the knife, the wild-eyed younger man lunged. Neatly, Mike stepped to one side and let the knife and arm fly past his ribs. At the same time, in one fluid movement, he swiveled, grabbed his arm, twisted it and then dropped to one knee, sending his attacker soaring over his shoulder. Hanging onto the arm, he twisted it again, and with that, the knife fell to the floor.

Pulling himself to his feet and dragging the Arab along with him, he drove the flat of his other hand forcefully into the man's face. Connecting hard, the hardened palm broke his nose and drove bone and cartilage deep into his skull. All his military training returned as he stamped viciously down on the instep of his opponent. With a scream, the man doubled over as Mike brought his knee up into his groin. Another cruel twist and he broke the arm he still had in a vice-like grip. As the Arab fell towards him, he was about to drive his fist into his foe's heart. It would have been a killing blow. Reason stopped him and instead he delivered another crippling jab to the man's head, causing it to jerk painfully back. By this time, the Arab was unconscious and his body slumped to the floor.

With his hands held ready at his side, Mike looked around, breathing heavily. "Who's next?" The other Arab looked meaningfully at the knife lying near him on the floor. Before he could move, Don's big cowboy boot caught him fair in the groin. He, too, dropped and landed by his companion with a screech, writhing in agony as the crowd moved further back. "Nice work, Don!"

;By now the music had stopped and the lights had come on. A large security guard closed in, followed by another. Taking one look, the first of them faced Mike. "Quickly, come with me. Bring your friends." Rapidly, they departed out the back door. Reaching the parked car, they stopped briefly.

"Don, you take the woman to the hospital. Use your friendly Yankee accent to convince the cops it was an accident. I'll take the girl home in a taxi." Bundling the shaking Indian girl into a nearby cab, he asked where she lived. In a frightened voice, she started to apologize. "I'm sorry. It was my first night out. I'm sorry for any trouble I caused." In the faint light of the cab, Mike could see the tears streaming down her cheeks. "Don't worry. It wasn't your fault. Now, where do you live?"

To his surprise, the girl clasped his hand. "Please, if you don't mind, I'm too scared to go back to my flat. What if they follow? Can I stay with you and your wife?" Mike took a deep breath. "I live alone." For a moment there was silence, she let go his hand. "But don't worry, I'm safe. Yes, you can come back for the night, sleep in the spare room." This time, holding out his hand, he grinned in the dark. "I'm Mike. Pleased to meet you." Softly, she took his hand and shook it. "I'm Prithi." Again, there was a little silence. "I know." The whispered reply nearly went unnoticed.

Finding the light in his flat, Mike showed the girl in. "Don't mind the mess. Would you like a drink?" Wide-eyed, Prithi glanced around the large room. "Just water, thanks." Bringing her a glass,

Mike showed her where the spare room was. After the door closed on the spare room, he showered, took out a beer and stood on the balcony looking out at the dark. Faintly in the background, he could hear the girl crying. Tempted though he was to go in, he shrugged his shoulders, downed the beer and went off to his own room.

## Chapter Thirty-Three

# Prithi Moves In

Early the next morning, as he waited for his coffee to brew, he was on the phone to Don.

"What happened at the hospital?"

Don's voice sounded confident down the line. "Not a lot. She'll be alright. Broken nose, cracked ribs, a few bruises, but she'll live."

Still concerned, Mike wanted more information. "Police? What about the cops?" His concern was met with a nervous laugh. "Oh, that, eh? Not really. One came in while the doc was bandaging up Janine. Couldn't speak English, so the quack translated. Bit embarrassing at first. I didn't know her name. Thank God she quickly twigged. We told him some bullshit about her being my cousin and falling out of the wagon. He bought most of it, filled out some forms in Arabic, and then Janine, the doc and I signed them. No hassle really."

Mike breathed a sigh of relief. "Shit, that was fucking lucky. What about Janine?" Don answered quickly. "Oh, she's still in hospital overnight for observation. I'll pick her up at lunchtime."

There was silence on the line for a moment. "Suppose that means the fishing's off."

Down the phone came a loud laugh. "Fuck off, Mike. You're a hard bastard."

While he was speaking, the spare bedroom door quietly opened. Stepping out cautiously, Prithi looked around. Seeing Mike, her gaze went to the ground. She brushed the hair she had washed but not dried properly away from her face, revealing big brown eyes that had done a lot of crying. Wearing the clothes she'd worn the night before, she felt wretched and ugly.

"Talk to you later, Don. My guest just came out from under a rock."

Surprise was in Don's voice. "The Indian girl?"

Mike's head was nodding as he spoke on the line. "Prithi. Yeah, Prithi." There was a low whistle on the other end.

"You got the best deal!"

Mike was immediately on the defensive. "Nothing in it, Don, you dirty old bastard. She slept in the spare room."

For a moment there was silence. "Watch your step, old buddy." Smiling to himself, Mike had the last word. "Piss off, Don." With that, he hung up, stood up and walked over to the young girl, who watched him carefully with a lost bewildered look then lowered her eyes as he got closer.

"Hi. Good morning." Last night's red dress caught his eye. In the full morning light, the red was a lot brighter. Slightly low cut, the hem stopped about a hand's width above her knee. He glanced admiringly at her long legs then her shapely figure. With her head hung down, she didn't notice. Standing in front of her, he lifted her face with his finger under her chin. "Okay? Not hurt or anything."

Almost on the verge of tears again, she shook her head. "Sorry. I'm so sorry I caused all that trouble. I don't want to cause you any more trouble, sir."

Mike was slightly shocked. "Sir? Sir? That's a bit bloody formal. The name's Mike, Prithi. I guess you could do with a hair dryer." Subconsciously, she put her hand to her head as Mike lifted several dripping strands with his other fingers.

Returning with a drier, he handed it to her. "There's a plug in the bathroom. When you finish, there's coffee on the table."

As she turned and left for the bathroom, Mike resumed admiring her young shape.

She finished drying her hair then came and sat at the table. Mike poured her coffee then passed it to her.

"Want some breakfast?" Shaking her head, Prithi put the cup to her lips. Several sips later she looked at up. "Please don't look at me. I'm a mess. I left my bag and everything in the nightclub."

Mike couldn't stop himself from smiling. "You look pretty good to me. Sure you won't have some breakfast?" Prithi looked embarrassed then concerned. A comment like that from an Indian man could mean trouble. But this man seemed different, and last night he'd saved her.

For the first time there was a brief hint of a smile. "Just a little toast, if that's okay." Mike struggled to drag his eyes away from her face with its honey brown skin, almond eyes and soft pink lips as he strode to the kitchen worktop and flicked a couple of slices of bread into the toaster.

Prithi's hunger got the better of her and after nibbling at the first slice, she gave up the pretence and quickly ate another three covered in butter and jam. Feeling better, she began to talk about the previous evening.

That was the first time she had been to a nightclub, but it was Janine's birthday and she'd been talked into it. All they had wanted to do was have a few drinks then leave. Before they could, the Arabs had accosted them. Not wishing to cause offence, they talked to them. Mike knew the rest. Preferring to watch her as she talked, Mike listened patiently. Gradually, Prithi came down from her high emotional state.

This encouraged her to talk more, and he listened as she told him about her job, the difficulties of living alone as a single Indian girl and then drifted into the problems she had with her mother.

While she spoke, Mike couldn't take his eyes off her. Prettier than he had first thought, he was amazed by her clear skin and glinting eyes. Finally, she drew to a halt then asked him about himself. Watching him talk, she was reminded of Franz. An older version, but he had the light-colored hair, animated and good looking face, and seemed interested in her. There was a toughness about him, and she knew from last evening that he could more than handle himself. When he spoke about his job, she realized with a shock that he was the same person she'd seen in the engineer's office.

About an hour later when they'd exhausted the coffee, Mike suggested that he take her home. Suddenly, her eyes widened with fear. "Please, I don't want to go." Puzzled, Mike stared at her. "But why?"

There was a tremor in her voice. "I'm scared. They might find out where I live." Mike's look was scornful. "No way. One of them is in hospital and the other's too bloody sore. Don't worry, Prithi." Still the fear remained in her face. "Alright, you can stay here for a few days. I'm off to the rig tomorrow, but you can use the spare room. Come on, we'll go back to your place for some clothes." The look of relief in her face warmed Mike's heart, and they headed out the door into his pickup and off to her flat.

Hastily, she entered her flat and very rapidly reappeared with an overnight bag stuffed with clothes. She looked around in fear as she left the flat. Almost leaping into the pickup, she slammed the door. "Go quickly, please. His friends might be watching." Shaking his head in disbelief, Mike put the vehicle in gear and drove off.

Back at his flat, she changed then came out to join him in the living room. "Prithi, don't worry, you're safe here. Would you like to do something? Get out of here? Try and forget last night?" There was no reply. Prithi sat motionless. "Come on, we'll go down the Creek in my boat. It's still in the water at the marina. Don and I were going to go fishing, so I put it in the water yesterday. It'll be quite safe. We'll stay in the Creek."

Reluctantly, Prithi agreed. She wanted to get the memory of last night out of her mind. Still seated, she watched as Mike, with practiced ease, threw half a dozen cold beers and a bottle of white wine into a cool box.

"May as well eat these also," he said, as he pulled some sandwiches wrapped in silver foil from the freezer.

Bumping over the sand track, the pickup reached the old Grey Mackenzie marina. In truth, it was merely several wooden planks on a raft of empty oil drums floating off the ancient quayside. Her irritation from the sand getting into her high-heeled shoes as she walked from the pickup turned to apprehension as she tried to negotiate the wobbling planks leading to the boat. "Take your shoes off. Hang on, I'll help you." After heaving the cool box onto his shoulder, Mike nimbly bounced down the planks, dropped it onboard then came back for Prithi. Waiting for her to remove her shoes, he then took her hand and guided her onto the boat.

Once on board, she felt safer. The boat was roomy and there were cushioned seats to sit on. Over their head was a blue sun canopy and she could see down into the small neat cabin with two bunk beds. With a slight growl, the engines started then settled down to a soft purr. Casually, with an air born of experience, Mike cast off the mooring lines and they gently slipped out into the Creek.

Firstly, they motored up towards the end of the lagoon where the pink flamingos waded in the tidal marsh. After Prithi had admired them, Mike turned the boat and headed back downstream. Barely idling, they glided through the water past the ship repair yard where old wooden dhows jostled for room as they waited their turn to be lifted out of the water. Leaving the crowded bank, Mike took off his T-shirt and jeans and stood at the wheel of the boat in his brief swimming trunks.

At first Prithi was embarrassed, but he'd done it so unselfconsciously she realized it was part of his normal lifestyle. Overcoming her initial qualms, she cast her eye over his body. It was lean and muscular, hard looking with a slight tan. Bending over to take out a beer, the material of his swim apparel pulled tight, revealing the outline of his buttocks and his private parts. She turned away quickly in case he saw her looking.

Mike offered her a beer and was slightly amused when she refused. "It's all we've got unless you like white wine." Again she shook her head. Scratching around in the ice, Mike came up with a can of soda. "This is pretty plain. Sure you don't want to try it with a drop of wine to give it some taste?" Unsure at first, Prithi finally nodded then watched as Mike deftly pulled the cork from the bottle and poured a mixture of wine and soda into a plastic glass.

They passed under Al Garhoud Bridge and motored into a wider body of water. On the banks were more wooden dhows being repaired by dark-skinned tradesmen stripped to the waist. They used the same tools as had been used hundreds of years before. Next they drifted with the current under Al Makhtoum Bridge into the busy commercial waterway. The Intercontinental Hotel stood on one bank with a row of elegant white-hulled boats moored outside. Next to it was McDermott's yard. Dirty and dusty, it was full of massive steel structures and tall lumbering cranes. On the opposite bank, a motley collection of barges with disheveled accommodation blocks fixed to their decks lay haphazardly moored to each other.

Rounding the bend in the Creek, the old Sheik's palace came into view and they were surrounded by mad, bustling water taxis full of passengers in an array of multi- colored national dress. The taxis plied back and forth at a furious pace as the water foamed around them.

When they passed the landing steps, they could see the milling crowds in the markets as they hurried to and fro on their Friday morning shopping sprees. On both sides, several mosques, their minarets towering over the chaotic mixture of coral limestone and cement block buildings surrounded by dilapidated galvanized iron warehouses, called loudly to the faithful.

Without noticing, Prithi sipped down several glasses of wine and soda. By the time they reached the Creek mouth, she was feeling sleepy and comfortable. Observing the sea state, Mike spoke almost to himself. "Looks like it's calm outside today. Let's go along the Corniche. If it's too much, say so and I'll turn back."

Enjoying the slightly rocking motion, Prithi simply smiled. Cruising past, she gazed up at the huge monolith of the Hyatt Regency Hotel, then Mike turned the wheel and they headed further out to sea. He brought the boat to a stop and they sat enjoying the slight mild breeze. "Let's have lunch and we'll go back."

Half asleep, Prithi rested with her elbows on the edge of the hull and her back against the cushion while she ate the sandwiches. Not exactly to her taste, but she liked them. Another glass of wine and soda helped them go down. The boat was surrounded by the shimmering blue sea. In the distance they could see the shoreline.

"Wonder what the poor people are doing." Prithi laughed softly at Mike's quip. With the sun overhead, she was starting to feel quite hot in her black T-shirt and jeans. Mike read her thoughts. "Too hot? Want to go?" Prithi shook her head. She liked it out here with Mike; she felt safe. "Take your top and jeans off. It's no problem. You can't be seen out here." She shook her head vigorously. Then, as the sun beat down, she had second thoughts. "Are you sure? You don't mind?" Feigning disinterest, Mike's tone was casual. "Not at all."

From the corner of his eye, Mike watched as Prithi removed her T-shirt and jeans Folding them carefully, she made a pillow of them and then lay back on the seat in just her bra and a pair of black panties. Through the sheer material of the bra Mike could clearly see her hard swollen nipples. Despite himself, he began to get aroused. Fearful it would show through his swimming trunks, he turned his attention to the sea.

Magnetically his gaze was drawn back to her long brown legs that ended in the brief black lace panties. Finally, he could take no more. Opening another can of beer, he started the motors. "Have to get back. Work tomorrow." Prithi only nodded. She was nearly asleep, the events of last evening having caught up with her. Back in the Creek, Mike reached over and shook her awake. "Better get dressed. You might start a riot on the banks."

It was late when they finished packing up the boat. On the way home, they stopped at Ravi's restaurant in Satwa to pick up a chicken *tikka*. After devouring it in front of the TV, Mike opened another bottle of white wine. Prithi drank a glass before she started to feel sleepy again. "I'm going to shower and go to bed." Mike smiled kindly as she got up and went off to the spare bathroom. He, too, headed for the shower.

Back into the lounge room, he was pleasantly surprised to see Prithi wrapped in a large white towel sipping another glass of wine while watching TV. He sat beside her and poured a glass for himself. Almost asleep, Prithi leaned back on the sofa and her towel began to slip.

This time it was too much for Mike. Reaching over, he took her head in his hands and kissed her, softly at first, but more firmly as the kiss was returned. Both their towels slid to the floor. Wordlessly, they made their way to his bedroom and slipped in between the sheets. Initially their lovemaking was quite gentle, but then years of starvation overcame them and it ended in a breathless, panting passion.

Almost immediately, Prithi drifted off to sleep. For a while, Mike sat propped on one elbow watching the firm outline of her breasts with their dark nipples rise and fall in the soft moonlight. Not long afterwards, he too, floated off to sleep.

In the morning he quietly rose, showered, changed, packed his bag and left by the front door while she was still sleeping. Spread-eagled, naked as she lay on the bed, it was all Mike could do to force himself to leave.

Upon his return a week later, he was more than surprised to find his flat neat and tidy. When he was out on the rig he'd spoken to Prithi on the phone several times and reassured her it was all right to stay. The last time he spoke, she wasn't sure. By the look of his flat, the answer had been to stay.

Around five-thirty, the door clicked open and Prithi walked in, having been dropped off by the office bus. For a moment they just looked at each other then Mike took her in his arms. "You stayed." Prithi's whispered reply was almost inaudible. "Yes." At that moment the phone rang.

"Mike?"

He recognized the voice.

"Don, your timing's shit."

On the other end the remark was ignored. "About time you were back."

Mike shrugged his shoulders. "What's new?" Don sounded casual. "Not a lot. While you were having a holiday on the rig, a couple of cops visited the office." Mike's concern was aroused. "For you or me?" For a moment Don was silent. "Both. We need to go to the police station tomorrow. No problem, according to Mr. Fixit. Just a brief interview." Mike wasn't convinced. "Trouble?"

Again a slight pause. "No, I don't think so. We have to speak to a Major Ali Essa Al Ghofran. Nice guy, according to all reports. No problem."

Mike tried to make light of it. "Great. I'll sleep on it." Don tried the same. "And something else!" For a second, Mike was slightly puzzled. "What?" There was mirth in Don's voice. "I mean sleep on something else, or should I say some*one* else, you lucky bastard." A slight smile crossed Mike's face. "Goodnight, Don. See you in the morning." With that, he hung up.

Prithi looked concerned. "Are you in trouble because of me, Mike?" Leaning forward, Mike kissed her on the forehead. "Don't be silly, Prithi, Come on and get ready. Let's eat."

The more senior Ali Essa became the more complicated and political his was his life. Today was no exception. Lying on his desk was a file he had to deal with. Furrowing his brow, he read it with annoyance.

The supposed victim was familiar and known to him. Not for the first time had this wild, uncontrollable young Arab man of a prominent family from a nearby Emirate been in trouble. Fights, illegal gambling, alleged rape and drugs—it was all on the form sheet in the file. Now, despite this, the family were putting pressure on to prosecute the *farangis*

However, at this time, the report read that he was in hospital with a broken nose, three cracked ribs, a broken arm, fractured wrist and contusions about the neck. He was lucky he hadn't ended up in a wheelchair or even worse. His equally unattractive companion was in a bed alongside him with a badly bruised groin and crushed testicles.

Ali Essa had no sympathy for the two, but there the pressure on him to make a case of it could not be ignored. Typically, it was in a nightclub and more typically it involved alcohol and women. Cursing under his breath, he called for the duty officer.

"Lieutenant Shebib, go and pick up the two men in this report. Two expatriates. Work for Dubai Petroleum, according to the information. Bring them here and I don't want any trouble, understand?"

Saluting as he left, the officer stopped at the door. "Anything else, *seedi*?" Ali Essa thought for a moment. "*La*, just no trouble, *tammam*."

After the officer had gone, Ali Essa turned his attention back to the file. Flicking through the report, he cursed again. It could have been an even greater problem if one of them had been killed. Trying to keep the peace between expatriates and locals was no easy task,

171

particularly when there was a woman involved. Very tricky. A real balancing act.

Outnumbered in the population by nearly five to one, the local Arab boys had a deep-seated complex about expatriates. Understandable, but all it needed was a woman, alcohol and the night to create a powder keg ready to explode.

# Chapter Thirty-Four

# The Trial

Mike and Don walked into the police station, escorted by the policeman sent to pick them up and accompanied by the company's public relations man, a Palestinian with a Lebanese passport. Inside Major Ali Essa's office, they were surprised to be greeted by a well-dressed, uniformed young officer. Offering them a seat, he paused before he sat down.

"Who are you?" He directed the question in Arabic to the Palestinian.

*"Moh'd Saeed."*

Ali Essa looked annoyed. "You are a lawyer?" About to sit, the other Arab paused for a moment. "No, I'm the company's public relations manager." Now very annoyed, Ali Essa pointed to the door. "Then get out. We don't need you. And Sergeant, leave us and make sure we are not disturbed."

The conversation was all in Arabic. Mike and Don looked at each other, very concerned.

"Good morning, gentlemen. Excuse my manners but I don't want any interference, especially from people who don't know how sensitive this matter is."

Somewhat surprised at the almost impeccable English, Mike and Don simply nodded. Opening the file in front of him, Ali Essa looked straight at Mike. "Mr. Mike?" Mike looked him straight back in the eye. "Mike Hunter, yes."

With a wry grin, Ali Essa sat back in his seat. "Ah, yes, of course. I forgot. You British…it is either Mike or Mr. Hunter. Which will it be?" Slightly more relaxed, Mike, too, sat back. "Mike will do."

Leaning forward again, the young officer began to get serious. "Well, Mike, I have a report in front of me. It is a report of an assault in a nightclub against two Arab nationals, both of whom were hospitalized. The description of the assailant fits you. Can you help me out?"

Hesitating, Mike looked at Don, who merely shrugged his shoulders.

"Of course, you are not under arrest and you are entitled to a lawyer when you are. This is a civilized country. For now, as you say in England, you are helping the police with their enquiries. The more help we get, the more helpful we can be."

Mike relaxed. Ali Essa continued in the same tone. "It is the injuries that are my problem and probably yours. I can imagine him receiving bruises in a sensitive part like his friend in the bed next to him." Pausing, he glanced at Don, who looked uncomfortable and stared at the ground. "But a broken nose, three cracked ribs, a broken arm, fractured wrist and contusions about the neck and severe bruising. Quite a list, Mike, and apparently not a scratch on you or his intended victim."

Stiffening, Mike's eyes went steely. "He had a knife."

Not fazed, Ali Essa returned the look. "And you had your military training. You nearly killed him." Both men sat silently, not lowering their gaze. "Mike, I have no choice but to charge you with assault. Now I do suggest that you contact a lawyer." Calling in the lieutenant, who was waiting outside, Ali Essa spoke to him rapidly in Arabic. "Please go with the duty officer, Mike."

Wordlessly Mike stood up. The duty officer pulled a set of handcuffs from his belt and went to put them on Mike's wrists.

"That's not necessary." Now Don was getting excited. "Don, leave it. Go explain it to Prithi and get a bloody lawyer, fast!"

In the cell, Mike waited impatiently for Don to return. It was some hours later when Don, the company public relations man and a well-dressed, elderly Arab man arrived. The older man was the lawyer, a Lebanese who spoke fluent English and Arabic. Speaking briefly to Mike, the lawyer left them, returning about an hour later in the company of the duty officer.

"Unfortunately Mr. Hunter, it is too late to arrange bail. I have tried my best, but you will have to stay overnight. Don't worry, the officers here are my friends and many would sympathize with you. But I can not change the law."

This was too much for Mike. He leaped to his feet. "Fuck the law! When, tomorrow?" The lawyer's voice was soft as he tried to placate his client. "Oh, early tomorrow. About ten. There is no problem." Far from comforted, Mike was still angry. "There *is* a fucking problem. I have to stay here tonight!" Shaking his head, the lawyer stepped forward. "Mr. Hunter…may I call you Mike?" A snarled grunt was all that was heard. "Mike, calm down. Do not use such language. Please do not make more trouble for yourself."

Without waiting for an answer, the lawyer and the Palestinian spoke to each other in Arabic and then to the duty officer. Don moved closer to the cell. "Cool it, Mike. It's only for the night. Janine and I will look after Prithi and I'll be back in the morning. Play it cool, man. Play it cool." Still angry, Mike shrugged off the hand Don had put through the bars and rested on his shoulder. Then, realizing there was no alternative, he reached out and shook Don's hand. "Thanks, Don. Take care."

As the small group left, the lawyer returned. "They will bring you good food. I have spoken to the officer in charge. This is only the lockup, not the jail. I can arrange these things."

Leaning back against the rough wall, Mike let out a heavy sigh. "All part of life's rich, colorful pattern," he muttered to himself as he stared at the bars of the cell. Alongside him were a couple of Asians wearing grubby old clothes and chattering like monkeys. Tempted to scream at them to shut up, he finally slumped on the bench, his head in his hands covering his eyes while he wept tears of anger and frustration.

Finally calmed, he took his hands from his face. The lockup was silent. His two next door neighbors were staring speechless at him through the grilles that separated them. "What are you looking at?" The threat in his voice caused them to back off, although they probably didn't understand a word. A little later they started chattering again. "Aw, shit! Shut up!" This time, ignoring his threats, the two continued their banter.

Mike paced his cell then eventually sat back on the bench. As the afternoon drew to a close, the warmth of the cell and the exhaustion of frustration wore him down and he drifted off into a fitful sleep. About an hour later he awoke. Darkness had fallen and the lockup was lit by dim fluorescent lights, several of which flickered annoyingly. Surprisingly, he felt refreshed, the anger having left him in his sleep. Unbelievably, he smelt the delicious scent of curry. To his amazement, a guard appeared at his door, opened it and carefully laid out on the floor, a tray of rice, curry, fruit and Indian bread, along with a bottle of water.

Hungrily, Mike hopped into it. With a smile, the guard retreated. Next door, his neighbors were eyeing him balefully in silence as they watched him eat. Unashamedly, he scoffed the lot in front of them and then enjoyed the contents of the bottle of water. "No chance of a beer?" Smiling to himself, he continued to talk out loud to no one in particular. "Won't hurt to have a clear head in the morning."

That night he slept better than he thought he would. After clearing his tray, the guard bought him a clean blanket. Too hot to need it, he folded it into a soft pillow. During the night he dreamed of Vietnam, Prithi, knives, Arabs and an assortment of characters most of whom he didn't remember. Prithi's soft, warm body seemed so real yet so far away.

The noise of the guard woke him. He desperately needed to relieve himself and he rattled his door. Seeing his need, the guard opened it, cuffed him to his wrist and headed him off to the toilet. Smelling so foul, it almost put him off his needs.

Struggling with one hand, he dropped his trousers to try and squat over the hole in the ground. Shaking his head, the guard released the cuffs then stood until he had finished.

Back in his cell again, he was astonished by the arrival of an omelet sandwich and a cup of coffee. Obviously, his lawyer was a man of connections! Around ten o'clock, the guard arrived and released him. Bail had been arranged.

Outside, Don, Janine and a tearful Prithi greeted him. "It's my fault, Mike," Prithi sobbed, holding him tight. "No, no, don't be like that. Come on, don't cry." He hugged her tightly to him. "Hey, Don, too early for a beer?" Heading towards the parked pickup, Don called back, "No way. There's a cold one in the fridge."

Back at the office at the start of the week, Mike stormed into the public relation man's office. "Bloody great help, you were." Smiling unctuously, the Palestinian stood and held out his hand. "Ah, Mr. Mike, you are out. See, I told you not to worry." Ignoring the outstretched hand, Mike went on. "Worry! I spent the whole night in a cell. What sort of a Mr. Fixit man do you call yourself?" Nervously, the public relations man sat down. "Mr. Mike, please, not so angry. The case is serious. The boy you hurt, he is the nephew of a Sheik. Very powerful. It is difficult for all of us. Please understand." Still standing over the desk, Mike was not put off. "All I understand is that I saved someone from having their head kicked in and I ended up in a bloody cell!" Waving his hand, the Palestinian tried in vain to calm him. "Mr. Mike, please, I will speak to the police. Do not worry."

A month later, the same man rang him. "Mr. Mike, Mr. Mike, do not be angry. Your court case is being heard tomorrow. I will come and pick you up and take you to the court. Please wear a suit."

Next morning, with a face like thunder, Mike met the trembling Arab. "I thought you said you would arrange things. You're fucking useless!" Trying not to anger him any further, the Palestinian looked at the ground. "Please, please, Mr. Mike, do not keep using that language. I have tried, really, but we must go to the court."

Greeting them at the courthouse steps, the lawyer shook Mike's hand. It was all Mike could do to remain civil. "Sorry about this, Mr. Hunter. I tried to get the case dismissed, but somebody seems to be causing a problem." Still annoyed, Mike managed a smile. "Not to worry. I'm ready for them."

Striding up the somewhat imposing structure with its sandstone columns and marble entrance, Mike led them through the doors. With mock courtesy, he ushered in the lawyer then the Palestinian in front of him. Inside the main entrance, a crowd milled and pushed as if in a cattle market. Scanning a hand-written board, the public relations man read the Arabic notice board and directed them to the courtroom.

Outside the court, Mike waited impatiently in silence for his case to come up. While he waited, a procession of police and prisoners seemed to come and go incessantly. Despite the air-conditioning, the atmosphere was already oppressive and the smell of body odor overpowering. An hour and a half later, his case was called.

Entering the courtroom, Mike was taken to a table in front of a podium, where an elderly, sweating Arab in a black frock suit, white shirt and stylized black bowtie, presided. His lawyer had changed into similar garb and at a table opposite sat another lawyer dressed in the same manner. With a clout of his gavel, the elderly Arab, who was obviously the judge, began the proceedings.

Conducted in Arabic and in a judicial procedure that left Mike confused, the hearing was over in a very short time. Mike's lawyer hung his head then shook it slightly. To Mike's shock, two policemen were headed towards him. "What's going on? What the fuck's going on!" His lawyer still looked shocked. "They found you guilty. Three months in jail and a twenty-thousand-dirham fine." Mike now looked even more shocked than his lawyer. "*Guilty! Guilty! What bloody guilty? I've not even spoken!*" Mike's shouting bought the court to a standstill. "*I'm not going to jail without being heard. This is not a court; it's a circus!*" Closing in on him, the policemen tried to quiet him. With a push, Mike sent them tumbling backwards. The lawyer stepped between them. On the podium, the judge hammered hard with his gavel. Instantly, the court froze. In a loud voice, the judge called both lawyers to the bar. A heated discussion took place and then the two lawyers returned to their tables. Mike's lawyer had the faintest trace of a smile on his face. "They'll hear your evidence."

Sweating profusely in the heat and shaking in anger, Mike sat in the witness box. In measured tones at the prompting of his lawyer; he outlined the events that had happened in the nightclub. After that, he answered the cross-examination by the prosecution lawyer and then the judge. It was a lengthy procedure as each sentence was meticulously translated into the two languages.

"Where's the Arab I beat up?" he roughly whispered to his lawyer when he was back at the table.

"In jail in Egypt. Drugs."

Mike sat puzzled. "Then why me?"

His lawyer reached over and laid his hand on his thigh. "Shush! The judge is summing up."

After what seemed an age, the judge finally stood up to leave. Surprisingly and to Mike's relief, the policemen did not move towards him. His lawyer turned, smiled and shook his hand. "Congratulations. Fined twenty thousand dirhams and six months' probation."

Barely appeased, Mike extracted his hand from the lawyer's. "Well, that's better than jail, but not much bloody better."

The lawyer shook his head. "Come now, Mr. Hunter, it's much better. You wouldn't like jail. It's not like the lockup."

Recovering his humor, Mike grinned. "Guess you're right. Goodbye. I'm out of here!" Turning his back on the lawyer, Mike strode from the court, pushing the fumbling public relations man to one side as he did.

Seated in the restaurant of the Hyatt Regency that overlooked the sea, Mike, Prithi, Don and Janine sat enjoying their Italian meal. Through the picture window they could sense the dark Gulf waters, although they were unable to see it. Reflected in the window were the images of themselves at the table. Elegant and relaxed, they appeared as if they were in a lifestyle magazine: Mike in a dark shirt; Don in his normal denim shirt, jeans and cowboy boots; Janine in a white, low-cut dress with a gold chain around her tanned neck; and Prithi in a simple, tight red dress. In the middle of the table a bottle of red wine sat beside a flickering candle. Plates of pasta covered in rich seafood sauce lay in front of them. "Better than prison food," quipped Don.

"Wouldn't know, never been there," retorted Mike with a grin on his face. "Second bloody Arab I've had trouble with, though." They all looked quizzically at him. "Really?" Janine looked bemused.

"Yeah, I seem to attract them." This time Prithi looked at him anxiously, her wide, almond eyes sparkling in the candlelight. "Tell us about the first." Filling his glass again, he related the story of

Clare. Careful not to hurt Prithi's feelings, he made it out to be just a light-hearted romance. But as he told the tale, he realized he still missed her.

"Well, I'll be doggone; you have had a string of bad 'uns." Janine winced at Don's outlandish cowboy accent. "Don, just because you are American, you don't have to talk like one." At that they all laughed, and quickly another bottle of red wine appeared. After the meal, Janine and Don left in a taxi.

Stepping out into the night, Mike and Prithi felt it starting to rain. This was rare for Dubai, and they enjoyed the sensation of raindrops on their heads. Before long it turned into a torrent and they ducked into a nearby shop entrance for cover. It was one of the many gold shops that lined the way to the spice *souq*.

Sheltered from the rain, they admired the shimmering gold jewellery in the window. Since it was late at night, the shop was closed but the lights had been left on to display the tempting trinkets. Stepping out when the rain ceased, they splashed through the puddles back to the car park. In the cool of the evening with the light twinkling in the reflections of the pools of water, Mike took Prithi in his arms and kissed her passionately. Returning the kiss, she whispered that she wanted to get home to bed.

With a grin on his face he opened the pickup door, let her in then headed home. On the way, the thought struck him. "You'd look gorgeous in some gold. We will come again tomorrow night and choose something for you." Prithi took his hand off the gear stick and placed it on her breast. Mike couldn't wait to get home!

# Chapter Thirty-Five

# The Plan

They almost had to elbow their way through the Friday night crowd. With barely enough room to move in the hectic crush, they were amazed when a white Mercedes Benz with black windows forced its way down the narrow lane. Stopping outside of one of the many shops in the alleyway, it sounded its horn several times. Instantly, an Indian scurried out and a darkened window was lowered. After a brief discussion, the Indian disappeared. Almost as quickly he reappeared, clutching a tray of ornate gold necklaces that immediately disappeared into the car.

Watching, Mike and Prithi were astounded when the practically empty tray was thrust out of the window to the waiting Indian. Simultaneously, the window soundlessly closed and the Mercedes slowly and deliberately forced its way through the crowd.

Up and down the potholed tarmac road, Pakistanis, Indians, some European expatriates and Arabs dawdled and gawked in front of the glittering windows. Grabbing Prithi's hand, Mike made his way into the shop outside of which the strange transaction had just taken place. "We'll try this one. They obviously have a very select clientele. Even if we don't drive a Mercedes, maybe they'll serve us."

In front of them was an array of cheap glass counters under which lay an amazing, glinting array of jewellery—necklaces, earrings, finger rings, bracelets, ankle bracelets and brooches. Behind the counters all around the walls were more display cabinets of similar construction full of the same. Brightly lit by rows of bare fluorescent lights evenly spread over the ceiling, the effect was almost surreal.

There were only a few customers in the store, mostly Indian couples. Immediately when Mike and Prithi showed interest in the gold trinkets under the counter, a little Indian salesman in a prayer cap appeared in front of them. Prithi ignored him as he spoke Hindi to her and asked in English for a necklace. Pulling a thick chain from underneath the counter, the salesman displayed it across his hand. Shaking her head, Prithi pointed to another.

So it went on until the salesman found a fine, intricately woven light chain. Placing it around her slim neck, Prithi faced Mike. The effect was electric. Lying loosely over Prithi's brown curves, the fine necklace seemed like a stream of golden honey flowing down to her magic treasures. Mike was almost breathless with admiration. "What do you think?" Recovering slightly, Mike whispered softly, "Think? I couldn't tell you what I think in front of everybody. Buy it. You look heavenly." Prithi's eyes sparkled. "No, really, do you like it?" Struggling not to kiss her in public, Mike smiled. "Like it? I love it!"

After some discussion, they negotiated a rate per gram that struck them as reasonable. The Indian weighed the chain on a pair of old-fashioned scales. It was surprising how much such a small chain weighed, but Mike wasn't arguing. He couldn't wait to get home and see Prithi parade around the bedroom wearing the necklace and nothing else.

When they got home, that is exactly what she did. Barely pausing to open a bottle of wine, pour two glasses and slip on a record, the two made for the bedroom. Lying on the bed in just his jeans and T-shirt, Mike watched as Prithi peeled off her clothes.

In the soft, pale light she walked erotically around the bedroom holding her glass of wine. With her dark nipples hardening, her breasts stood high, and in between them lay the sensuous line of gold flowing down to nearly touch her firm, round stomach. Below this was the familiar triangle of dark black hair and her long smooth legs going down to the floor. Almost choking on his wine, Mike had never seen anything so exotic. Within minutes, he, too, was naked and pulling Prithi giggling and laughing to the bed. Winding the chain around both their necks, they made slow, passionate love then lay breathless in each other's arms.

Relaxed, Mike reached for the wine bottle and poured another glass for both of them. Lying back against the pillows with Prithi in his arms, Mike started to muse about the gold *souq*. "How many gold shops do you think there were in the market, Prithi?" Twisting the chain around her fingers, the naked girl leaned over and kissed him. "I don't know. Does it matter? About twenty, maybe."

Mike was silent for a while. "That's what I thought. So many little shops and no security. Each of them must have a small fortune stashed inside their walls. Who buys it all?" Leaning over him, Prithi let her breasts stroke Mike's chest. His attention started to drift.

"Like that?"

Pulling her to him, he began kissing her and then sat up.

"No, who does buy it?"

Slightly disappointed, Prithi too sat up. "Mostly Indians. Why?"

Mike was lost in thought. "I don't know…just thinking. Why Indians?"

Prithi started to play with the chain. "To take back to India, of course."

Mike was puzzled. "Of course?"

Prithi looked at him with her big, wide almond eyes. He was starting to lose concentration again. "For dowries. They smuggle it in. They have been doing it for ages. It's worth almost six times its value on the black market in India."

Suddenly, Mike's attention was restored. "Six times! God, there must be several million dollars or more lying around in those tin pot shacks in the *souq*. It's a wonder nobody's stolen it by now!"

With that, Prithi climbed over his body, hers already warm and willing. Laughing, Mike held her to him. "Obviously, you're not interested. Mmm, that's nice. Don't stop." Thrusting her body down on his, she started nibbling his ear. "Who cares about the gold…?" Her whisper was coarse and full of promise.

Rolling her over and entering her already excited body, Mike gasped, "*I* do. I must buy you more if it has this effect." With her body movements, Prithi silenced any more conversation, and this time, after they'd made love, both of them fell asleep in each other's arms

Back on the rig, Mike couldn't get the thought of all that gold out of his mind. Although he'd been to the gold *souq* on more than one occasion since coming to Dubai, it wasn't until that night with Prithi that he'd realized how much unprotected treasure lay there. Sitting at the control panel, he poured over one of the engineering books from the technical library. Finding out the specific density of gold, he did a quick calculation based on the price he'd paid in the *souq*. Then, multiplying it by six, he sat back and whistled. "Shit! Barely a couple hundred kilos and I'd be a multi-millionaire in India."

The more he thought about it, the more the idea of being a millionaire in India with Prithi started to appeal to him. Back on land, he broached the subject again with Prithi, who laughed and told him not to be so silly. Despite her comments, he sat down and began to formulate a plan. It probably wouldn't come to anything, but the mechanics of planning it amused him.

Firstly, he'd obviously have to get the gold out of the shops. This gave him a few nights of serious thinking. Eventually, he decided that to simply break in and grab handfuls of the stock was the best approach. Secondly, how to get it out of the *souq*. Catch a taxi? Ridiculous. What about a bike. Of course. A bike with saddlebags. A decent trail bike could carry an extra couple of hundred kilos at a push. Bit wobbly and uncontrollable, but it could do it. But what then? He could hardly drive a trail bike to India with a couple saddlebags full of gold. This was his third problem.

More nights of thought and then it dawned on him. Melt it down into something. Something what? Melted down, it would have to be cast into something that didn't look like bars of gold! This problem had him foxed for several weeks until one day when he walked out to the four-wheel drive and banged his knee on the steel bumper bar. The idea literally struck him! Why not cast it into the form of bumper bars of a four-wheel drive vehicle? They had strong enough suspension on them so that it wouldn't be obvious. Exporting secondhand vehicles to India was quite common.

The more he thought about it, the more feasible it became. Now, what had started as a joke had began to have a life of its own. Prithi was starting to get a little scared and more often bored with Mike's preoccupation with his idea. Her only compensation was the now regular trips to the gold *souq* from where she would return wearing yet another piece of jewellery bought by Mike as he checked out one shop after another.

Several months later, Mike had mapped out the entire *souq* and virtually measured, step by step, the distance between each door, as well as the security arrangements. None of the doors had much more than a simple lock and a weak steel grating. Having plotted out the *souq*, Mike put his mind on to how he could burgle each small shop and maximize his catch as if he were a fisherman after sardines. One weekend he bought a new trail bike—the most powerful available—and started practicing to ride again. Just to try his luck, he rode it through the *souq* a little after the start of the afternoon break. It was all but deserted as he accelerated through the empty laneways. Continuing on, he crossed the main road and ended up on the creek bank. Pleased with himself, he headed back to the flat to plan more of the adventure.

By this time, the plan was becoming an obsession. Prithi noticed a change in him, a slight hardening of his attitude. Moments of almost deep silence followed by bursts of hilarity. Although he still sought out her body in bed each night, she didn't feel as if it was the same person. It was as if he had another love, and in reality he did: his plan to rob the gold *souq*. Mike had fallen in love with gold.

Each night after they had made love, he talked to her about how much money they would have and how they would live in India: a flat in Bombay, a villa in Goa, something in the mountains near the Himalayas and maybe even a place somewhere else, perhaps London. To some extent, these plans fired her imagination, and although Mike already had a daughter, she started to think of having a child of her own. When they had the money, she would have children. Mentioning this to Mike, she was a little disappointed when he quickly and casually brushed over the subject.

When Mike was sound asleep, Prithi would sit in the chair near the bed and watch him. Although he was nearly old enough to be her father, that didn't matter. Many Indian women married men like that. Besides, he didn't look it and certainly didn't act it. He didn't neglect her and she felt he'd always protect her. Mike was safe; he made her feel secure. Form what she knew, most Indian men wouldn't or didn't want to make their wives feel like that. Whatever Mike wanted of her she would do.

Mike's next step was to equip his bike with saddlebags that would carry the gold. Down in the old secondhand market, he purchased a heap of used car batteries and stripped them of their lead. In the garage, he set up a couple of gas bottles then melted the lead down and poured it into small, neat moulds. Eventually, he had enough ingots to represent the load he was going to carry. Fixing the saddlebags to where he'd removed the pillion seat, he loaded them with the ingots. Again, he practiced riding the bike. This time it wasn't so easy and it sluggishly twisted under him like an old horse that didn't like the saddle. Eventually he mastered its uncomfortable, unpredictable behavior and was satisfied with its performance. However, it couldn't be ridden any distance.

At this stage, Mike was well and truly committed to his plan. All that was missing was how to get the bike and the gold from the *souq* to where he could work on it and melt it down. The solution became obvious one Friday when he was out fishing with Don in the boat. Use the boat! Bring the boat into the creek, load the gold onto it and take it up the coast to, say, Ajman or Umm Al Quwain, where he could rent a cheap workshop or something. He was so pleased with the idea, he gave a shout.

"What? Got a bite?" responded Don backing off the throttle and slowing the boat. "No, no, Don, not a bite, but the whole bloody fish!"

His friend looked at him strangely. "What the hell are you talking about?" Laughing to himself, Mike cooled off a little. "Nothing, Don, nothing. Let's

Have another beer."

Handing him another ice-cold beer, Don stared at him quizzically. "You'd better get out of the sun. It's cooking your brain!"

During the next shift off the rig, he took Prithi and they toured Ajman and found a small villa with a garage and workshop in the backyard. The rent was more than reasonable and Mike paid a year in advance. When he told Don he was shifting the boat to Ajman, his friend just shrugged his shoulders.

Don had his own problems. His wife was suing him for divorce; she'd found out about Janine.

At the time, Mike was a bit surprised when Don told him. He'd been so preoccupied with his own life that he'd not realized Janine had moved in with the American. "It's going to be more of a problem when Janine's husband finds out."

His friend winced visibly at Mike's comment. "Shit, Mike, don't remind me. I've had that on my mind all week He has!" Patting him on the shoulder, Mike went on. "Just get divorced and forget it. I've had one. It wasn't so difficult." Don looked surprised. "With a grown kid! See how easy it is? Not a scar to be seen."

Spending their lives between the flat and the house in Ajman was very wearing on Prithi. Although she liked the idea of having a lot of money in India, all this plotting, planning and scheming was starting to get on her nerves. In the back of her mind, she knew it would be dangerous, but not until Mike took her out on the boat one day did it dawn on her how dangerous.

When they were finally out of sight of the land, Mike disappeared below and emerged with a rifle. Prithi cowered in the seat at the stern. Laughing, Mike pointed the gun away. "I'm not going to shoot you, not with this at least." Slightly mollified, Prithi sat up. "What do you need it for?" Mike gave her a sidelong glance. "What do you think? If I'm stopped in the *souq*, do you think the guards or the watchmen will shake hands with me?" Prithi paled. "You mean, you'll...?" This time Mike looked straight at her. "Kill them. Yes, what else can I do?" Tossing a plastic barrel over the side, Mike backed the boat off and fired several rounds into the floating target. "Not bad. Still got my eye in."

On the cruise back to shore, Prithi stayed silent. Even Mike's gentle teasing couldn't get her out of her somber mood. Part of her wanted to quit now, leave Mike and get out, but the other part, a lot deeper, wanted the money. Finally, she perked up at the suggestion that they go to the Hyatt for dinner and book a room for the night.

Up in their room in the top floor overlooking the Gulf, Mike opened the bottle of champagne he'd ordered. Sitting naked on the double bed, they looked out over the dark sea and the even darker sky dotted with its bright stars. "To us, Prithi. To us. We deserve to be rich." Turning to her, he kissed her lips then moved down to her nipples. Giggling, she tossed back the glass of champagne before they made love.

"Prithi, I love you," Mike's voice whispered in her ear.

Prithi closed her eyes to stop the tears from falling. It was the first time Mike had said he loved her. Apart from Franz a long time ago, no man had ever said that to her.

# Chapter Thirty-Six

# Rajan

Seated at her desk, Prithi continued to work as two technicians entered her office. Trailing lines of white cable, they poked and prodded around the walls. The company was installing the latest in office business systems along with new intercommunication equipment. Already she had the latest IBM word processor and it was rumored that all machines would be interlinked. While they worked, Prithi glanced at them from time to time. One was an older man who seemed to be the foreman; the other was young, tall and slim. Both were dressed in white overalls and worked methodically.

Finally they approached her desk. The younger one addressed her politely in Hindi, asking her to move. Choosing to ignore his Hindi, she replied harshly in English, "What do you want?" Somewhat crushed, the younger one tried again in halting English. "Excuse, Madam, we work on desk. Please shifting, please."

Begrudgingly, she rose and moved. When she passed by him, the younger one smiled. Scowling outwardly, she thought he was quite good looking. His face was as lean as his body and he had bright white teeth and sparkling, white almond-shaped eyes. On top of his head, his hair was dark, thick and slightly wavy. There was a slight resemblance to one of the current Indian stars of the Hindi musical films that she hated.

Leaving them to it, she went and had a cup of coffee. Upon her return, she noticed the older man had gone and the younger one was tidying up her desk. Feeling slightly sorry for her cold reaction to their presence, she thanked him in Hindi.

"Sorry, I was a bit rude. Thank you." His smile flashed "No, Madam, I am sorry we disturbed you. Unfortunately, I must come back one or two times to check the equipment." Prithi shrugged. "I don't mind." A little bolder, he held out his hand. "My name is Rajan." Coolly ignoring the hand, she sat down. "Thank you, Rajan. Now I must get on with my work."

The next day, she went to the canteen for lunch. This time she sat alone. Her friend Janine was in Australia trying to sort out her affairs with her husband. Eating without much thought, she was staring into space when a voice jolted her back into reality.

"Hello, Madam, may I sit here?" Looking around, Prithi saw that most of the tables had been filled and in front of her was the young technician with a full tray. The pleading look in his eyes softened her attitude and she nodded her acceptance.

For most of the meal, they sat in silence. Finally, the young man spoke. "I am sorry I upset you." Somewhat haughtily, she peered at him. "No, you don't upset me. It is just that I'm busy and not interested." Taking a chance, the young man went on. "Not interested in me, or not interested in my work?" Giving him a second look, Prithi realized that perhaps she was a little interested in him. "No, just your work." This bought a smile to his face. "I'll try not to interfere with your work. Do you remember my name?" This was a bit cheeky, Prithi thought, but she wasn't too annoyed. "Rajan." Again, a flash of a smile. "That's right. What was your name? I can't remember?" Prithi pushed her seat back. "I didn't tell you."

With that, she rose to leave, then with a slight smile, turned back to him. "Prithi. Goodbye."

That night as she lay beside Mike, she listened to him talk about his plan. But just before she slipped off to sleep, Rajan's smile drifted into her mind.

When he wasn't working out on the platform, Mike spent most of his time refining his plans for the raid on the gold *souq*. In the workshop stood an old Land rover he'd bought. Removing the front and rear bumper bars, he fabricated moulds from them and using scrap lead, he melted it down then poured it into the moulds. It took him several tries before he got it nearly right. Although the lead wasn't quite as dense as the gold would be, it was close enough to give him an idea of what would be needed.

With Mike becoming more and more engrossed in his project, Prithi was becoming more and more confused. Almost every lunchtime Rajan sought her out. From time to time, she refused to let him sit with her, excusing herself when he arrived.

But slowly she became friendlier and actually enjoyed having his company. All the same, she was glad when Janine returned and gave her a reason to refuse to sit with him.

About a week later, seeming to work on the intercom equipment, he shyly whispered to her, "Prithi, will you come out with me?"

For a moment she was shocked. "No!"

Crestfallen, he tried one more time. "Just for a cup of coffee?'" It was almost the end of the day. "Alright coffee on the way out."

Mike was away on the rig and she felt that this was an opportunity to get rid of Rajan. Seated at a table in a small Indian tea shop, she disdainfully held her cup of coffee as Rajan tried to make conversation. "Rajan, I came with you to tell you I already have a man. An Englishman. I live with him. I'm not interested in you."

Surprisingly, he wasn't all that upset with her statement. As he drank his coffee, he smiled and looked at her carefully. "But if you really like him, you wouldn't be drinking coffee with me." With that, Prithi was stunned. There was more to this young man than she had thought. Shaking her head, she finally gave a laugh. "Maybe you're right, but what makes you think I could be interested in you?" This time he simply fixed her eyes with his. "I just know." Struggling, she finally broke their eye contact. She'd had enough; he was really starting to get to her.

That night she lay in bed really confused. If Mike were successful, they would be rich and living in India. If he wasn't and he was caught or even worse, what would she do? Maybe she'd be caught with him. Then there was their age difference. Not that Mike was really old, but she knew he already had a family and if she wanted one, he wouldn't. But Rajan? He was only a tradesman, but he was good looking, and young! When he'd stared into her eyes, she'd felt weak and unsure. Twisting and turning in bed, she came to no conclusion and eventually fell into an exhausted sleep.

Practically every week Mike had off was spent in the villa at Ajman. Closer and closer, his plan became finished in all of its details. He had decided that he would carry out the raid on the first day of Ramadan. This was the same time Israel had commenced their successful war against the Arabs in the sixties. Being the major religious festival of the year, in the early hours of the morning everyone would be asleep and quite unprepared for anything but fasting for the next twenty-eight days or so. On top of that, the gold shops would be fully stocked, ready for the buying spree that took place at the end of that time. It was ideal and still about a month away, sufficient time to finish all the preparations.

One Friday, he took Prithi out on the boat and cruised gently down the Creek. Timing everything, he carried out a trial mooring near the rocks on the bank while trying not to attract attention by pretending he had engine trouble. Prithi was beginning to get fed up with his obsessive planning and, for the first time in their affair, became short- tempered and whined to be taken home. That night, she barely spoke to Mike, and when she awoke he had already left for the platform.

About midday, Rajan rang. This time he asked her out that night for a meal. Still annoyed with Mike, she decided to accept. When he asked her where she lived, she gave him her old flat address, although she rarely stayed there now.

Nearing eight that evening, a taxi arrived and the bell rang. Both of them were equally surprised when the door was opened. Wearing a simple black dress with a gold necklace, Prithi looked stunning. Equally, Rajan had dressed in a white shirt with dark trousers and looked quite handsome. They dined at the Dubai Durbar; a sumptuous Indian restaurant that Prithi was sure was beyond Rajan's means.

After the meal, the two of them returned to Prithi's flat. Standing at the door, she was of two minds then finally opened it. "Come in, Rajan. Come in for a drink before you go." He followed quickly. Upon entering, he was somewhat overawed by its lavishness, although it was plain by Prithi's standards. Going to her small bar, all she could find was a bottle of whisky. Pouring a small quantity into two glasses, she went to the fridge, found a little ice and plunked two lumps of it into each glass.

Sitting opposite to Rajan, she sipped her whisky as she listened to him talk about himself. Born in Bombay of wealthy parents, he had gone to the best college in the city. When he was seventeen, his father went bankrupt, his partner having run off with all the money. After selling his mother's jewellery, they had enough money to keep him at school until he passed his final exams. With what was left, they paid an agent and he got a job in Saudi Arabia as a clerk. He stayed five years and sent all his money back to his parents so that his brother could finish college. Eighteen months ago, he'd managed to obtain a position as a trainee technician in a Dubai company. Although it was less money, it was better than Saudi. At school his English had been good, but in Saudi he never used it, only Hindi and some Arabic. Now he wanted to save money and go back to university.

By this time the glasses were empty, so Prithi poured another two. The sound of his voice and the whisky was having an intoxicating effect on her. Nearing the end of the second glass, she felt quite relaxed. Not really listening, she vaguely heard him say how pretty she was. Next thing, he'd stood, walked over and pulled her to her feet by one hand.

Meekly she followed as he led her into the bedroom. Like a rabbit caught in the headlights of a car, she stood wide-eyed, almost paralyzed, quivering with fear and sexual apprehension. Deftly, Rajan reached around her and undid the zipper of her dress, and when it fell to the floor she was naked except for her panties. Equally as deftly, he swept them to floor and she unconsciously stepped out of them. With their eyes locked together, he swiftly removed his clothes.

Prithi gasped softly as she looked down at the evidence of his excitement. Gently, he pushed her onto the bed. Then, without a word, he fell on her. Almost brutally they made frantic love that was over nearly as quick as it had started. Rajan rolled away from her body and lay silently on his back. Alongside him, Prithi breathed heavily.

When he regained his strength, Rajan rose, went to the bathroom, washed then returned and dressed. With a brief kiss on her lips, he left her naked spread over the bed. Exhausted by the heightened excitement and a little drunk from the whisky, she dropped off to sleep. Later during the night she awoke with a headache and a maddening thirst. Gulping water from the fridge and aspirin from a bottle, she returned, showered, then slipped under the sheets and slept till morning.

Awakening, she remembered what had happened. Was it rape she asked herself? Not really, but if it hadn't been for the whisky and her excitement it may have been. Hating herself for having betrayed Mike, she swore she would never see Rajan again.

During the day, Rajan tried to speak to her but she ignored him, and again the next day. Alone at night in her flat where she had decided to stay for a while, she began to rationalize that what she had done wasn't wrong. After all, Mike had been married and must have had other women. Wasn't she entitled to try another man? Wouldn't he do the same if the opportunity presented itself? On the following day, Rajan tentatively tried to speak to her again. This time she replied with a smile. In return, his smile brightened her day. She asked him around again that night.

Meeting him at the door in T-shirt and shorts, she saw him raise his eyebrows. After a simple meal, they had one whisky and she let him take her to the bedroom. This time, the lovemaking was gentler and Rajan stayed until well after midnight. Leaving, he begged to see her again. "Maybe," was her response. "Not next week, though." She needed time to think. Mike would be back. Crestfallen, he turned to her angrily.

'You'll stay with *him* now?" Without hesitating, she replied, "Yes." With a snarl, he whispered, "Whore!" under his breath and stormed off. Shaking her head, she watched him go. Next week would be the start of Ramadan. Mike most definitely would be back

# Chapter Thirty-Seven

# The Raid

After she had showered, Prithi looked at her body carefully in the mirror. There were no marks. Curiously she wondered if Mike would know whether she'd been with another man or not. As usual, he'd want to make love as soon as he was home. Finishing work, she returned to his villa. Kissing her passionately, he took her to the bedroom and without hesitation, she stripped and they fell into bed. When they had finished, she waited with baited breath, but Mike didn't make any comment. On the contrary, he remarked how good she'd been and inwardly she smiled to herself.

Two days before the start of Ramadan, they moved to the house in Ajman. Ramadan would begin when a chosen committee sighted the new moon. Nobody could really be sure on what day it would commence. Each day, Prithi had to drive to and from Ajman to Dubai along the crowded highway to get to the office. It wasn't an enjoyable experience.

Even less enjoyable was the anxious waiting while Mike prepared, over and over again, the equipment needed for the operation. He overhauled the bike, the motors on the boat, his AK 47 and every other item. It would be late in the evening before the committee declared Ramadan. They would have to move fast.

There was not much in the plan for Prithi's role except that as a driver. First, she would drive to Dubai to pick up Mike after he had ridden the bike and parked it opposite the gold *souq*. It would be covered with a tarpaulin, which he hoped wouldn't be too obvious.

Then, after a high-speed drive back to Ajman, they would jump into the boat and power down to the creek. They would be into it then!

On the first night, they waited impatiently for the traditional sound of a cannon firing and the wail of the mosque. There was nothing. The next day was business as usual. Ramadan must surely be the next night. Without waiting for the sign, Mike took off on the bike, followed by Prithi in the four-wheel drive. Parking the bike where he had planned, he waited for Prithi. Just before she arrived, he heard the dull thud of a cannon and the cries from the mosques. Ramadan had started!

Driving back to Ajman, Mike went over the plan again and again in his mind. Occasionally, he'd stop thinking and tell Prithi yet again what she must do. As soon as they reached the slipway where the boat was moored at anchor in shallow water, he waded out with Prithi in his arms and helped her aboard. Firing up the engines, they raced out of the Ajman Creek and headed for Dubai Creek. Reaching the open water, Mike backed off the throttle and handed the helm to Prithi.

Down below, he changed into swimming trunks then pulled a black T-shirt and tracksuit bottoms over top. Over his head he tugged a black balaclava. Around his waist he clipped a combat belt with a knife and two additional clips of ammunition for the AK 47. On his feet he wore black trainers. Taking out a tin of dark boot polish, he blackened his face and arms. Emerging from the cabin, he was greeted by a squeal of shock from Prithi. Laughing, Mike took her hand. "You've never seen me in combat gear before. Don't worry, I'll never be recognized." Calming down, Prithi handed the helm back to him. "Not even by your own mother." Mike gave a short laugh at Prithi's wit.

At the entrance of the Creek, he turned off the navigation lights and slowed the boat to a crawl. A bit early yet; it was only two-thirty in the morning. With the new moon having disappeared, the only light was the loom of the city. Three o'clock would probably be the best time. It would take no more than sixty minutes if everything went to plan.

He cut the engines and the boat glided to a stop alongside the rocks. Leaning over with a boat hook, Mike caught one of the rocks.

He passed the hook to Prithi and she held the boat in the slight current while Mike silently secured it fore and aft with mooring lines. Lifting the outboard motors out of the water to minimize the drag on the lines, he then pulled out a plank that he had tied to the back of the stern. With some effort, he pushed it onto the rocks. It would be his gangplank for loading the stolen cargo. Resting for a moment, he listened for any unusual noise. All he could hear was the trickle of the tidal water around the rocks. Going below, he readied himself for the sortie.

Checking his kit bag, he made sure he had the crowbar, sharpened bolt cutters, specially padded steel hammer, WD 40 spray and a pair of light leather gloves. Picking up the rifle, he came out into the stern area. He paused and pulled Prithi to him, kissed her hard on the lips then disappeared at a run up the gangplank.

In the cover of the shadows from the trucks parked along the creek he made his way cautiously to the car park where he'd left the bike. He removed the tarpaulin and put the key in the ignition and turned. Instantly, the bike started. Effortlessly, he climbed atop the saddle, flicked it into gear and rode quietly into the gold *souq*. It was just as he had anticipated; not a soul was around. The shops were dimly lit by one or two lights left on inside. A few lights glowed faintly in the main laneway so that it, too, was dim and in the shadow. Stopping the engine, he slipped silently to the ground. He was ready to go into action.

With caution he approached the first shop. Slinging the AK 47 over his shoulder, he reached into the kit bag, pulled out the lubricant spray and squirted both sides of the track holding the old folding grating. Then, with the aid of the bolt cutters, he sliced through the locks that secured the gratings to the ground. The hardened Wiltshire blades went through them like a hot knife through butter. Leaning on the crowbar he'd thrust in between the jamb and the door, he gave it an extra shove and the door popped open. He'd made it into the shop with barely a sound.

He took out the cloth-covered steel hammer from the bag and rapped it sharply on the glass countertop on the first cabinet. With a dull thud and a tinkling of glass, it broke. All was silent again.

Putting on the pair of gloves, he rapidly gathered up the loot of necklaces and dropped them into a canvas sack.

Repeating the actions, he went from display cabinet to display cabinet. Soon the bag was filled with gold jewellery. He checked his watch. It had taken four minutes—a bit slow; he'd allowed himself only three minutes per shop.

Silently he scurried from the shop and emptied the contents of the canvas bag into the saddlebags fixed to the bike. Although it was early morning and quite cool, he was now sweating profusely. Moving on quietly, he hit one shop after another in the same fashion. Working in a crossways fashion, he ransacked the shops from one side of the road to the other. The bike was hidden in a shadow on one edge. He didn't dare start the motor until he had finished.

By the time he got to shop nine, the physical exertion and fear were taking their toll. Despite his fitness, his legs felt like jelly. The only bonus was that the saddlebags were filling faster than anticipated. He estimated that he already had over a hundred kilos.

Just as he left the tenth shop, he caught a slight movement in his peripheral vision. With professional skill, he dropped to one knee and brought the AK 47 to his shoulder. Through the sights, he could see an old caretaker in a dark *dishdasha* carrying a camel stick and shuffling towards him.

Lining him up carefully, Mike saw the figure raise the stick and open his mouth ready to shout. As he did, Mike pulled off two quick shots. The figure slumped and lay motionless on the road, a dark pool of blood starting to form around the body. Mike waited for a few moments looking around for any more unwelcome visitors. There was no other movement. Quickly he regained his feet and continued his task.

But by the time he got to shop number fourteen, he heard a voice calling in Arabic. It was the caretaker's companion searching for him. Again, Mike took a crouching position and as the new arrival came into the lane, he waited until he was clearly in his sights. When he reached the roadway, the newcomer saw the body and ran towards it. Bending over it, he was about to let out a cry when two bullets from Mike's rifle silenced him forever. He, too, slumped to the ground dead, alongside his companion.

With his heart thumping like a steam engine, Mike called on his adrenaline reserves to keep him going. Four shops later, he'd nearly filled all the saddlebags. Then, down the road, there was a faint flash of blue light reflected in a shop window. Police! Backing into a shadow, Mike realized that someone had alerted the police.

Slowly, a green and white Mercedes Benz emblazoned with "Police" in both English and Arabic down both sides and with its blue light flashing, crept into view. With his last few grains of energy, he steadied the rifle on his shoulder and took careful aim. Two more shots cracked out. The first took out the driver. Without control, the car veered and smashed heavily into a shop window. His second shot caught the other policeman in the passenger seat as he raised the radio to his mouth, ready to call for help. Ripping through his wrist, the bullet smashed the man's jaw, knocking him unconscious.

"Shit, I hope he didn't get the call out!" Gasping for breath, Mike headed for the bike. Enough was enough. Breathing heavily, he hoisted himself onto the machine and turned the ignition key. To his massive relief, it started instantly. "Thank God!" His rasped cry of joy faded into the night as he slipped the bike into gear and headed out of the lane.

It was more of a struggle than he'd expected. The extra weight caused it to waddle more than he'd planned, and it was almost too difficult to ride. Wrestling with the bike, he left the *souq* and headed for the dark creek bank. To avoid attention, he kept the engine speed as low as possible as he made his way past the parked trucks to where the boat was moored.

He immediately cut the engine when he arrived. It took the last of his strength to get it up on the kickstand. Unhooking the first saddlebag, he staggered under its weight towards the gangplank.

"Mike, Mike, is that you?" Prithi's scared whisper was full of tension. "Shush, Prithi! Yes, it's me. Quiet. Hold the boat steady!" Almost tripping, he only just made the stern with his load. Dropping it on the floor of the cockpit, he ran back to the bike. Three more times he made the trip. As he did, he became weaker and weaker. On the last one he thought he wouldn't make it. Inside his chest, his heart pounded like it never had before in his life. With lungs on fire, he staggered like a drunk up the wooden plank to the back of the boat and then fell with the saddlebag to the floor. Gasping and heaving, he thought he would have a heart attack.

Resting for as long as he dared, he stripped down to his swimming trunks then ran back across the gangplank. He yanked it out from the boat and dragged it to a slightly elevated rock. Placing one end firmly on the top, he checked it for stability. Not happy when it wobbled slightly, he jammed another two rocks beside it. Sweat was pouring down his face and into his eyes, stinging them fiercely, almost blinding him. Satisfied with the arrangement, he went to the bike. Then, taking the AK 47 in one hand and placing his kit bag on the tank, he started the machine. With difficulty he tried to operate the clutch. Frustrated by the rifle, he finally pushed it back onto his shoulder and in this manner squeezed in the clutch handle and slipped the bike into gear. At the same moment, he wrenched on the throttle with the other hand and aimed the speeding bike at the plank. With the engine screaming at top speed, he managed to change up to second gear and give the throttle a final wrap. Reaching the far end of the plank, the bike flew into the night air over the black creek waters. In mid-flight, Mike hurled himself from the saddle and flung the rifle from his shoulder. All three fell into the swirling waters together.

As he sank down into its cool water, Mike started to feel refreshed and then suddenly he realized he was being swept away from the boat. Panic set in. Furiously, he swam towards the bank and after what seemed an age reached the side of the boat. With one gigantic effort, he hauled himself, slippery and wet, into the stern cockpit. Without a word to the shocked Prithi, he lowered the engines, started them, ran to the bow, released the line then ran back to the stern and did the same.

Quickly and silently the boat drifted out into the tidal stream. Cautiously Mike slipped the motor into forward and the boat rapidly moved ahead towards the entrance of the Creek. Gritting his teeth and despite the temptation to run, Mike kept the boat at slow speed until the flashing red lights of the container tractors working in the port alongside were amid ships. Only then did he lean forward and push the throttles to fully open.

Responding by almost leaping out of the water, the boat hurled through the still, dark night and even darker waters until they were well out to sea. With the land now a mere string of lights behind them, Mike cut the engines. Silently, the bows sank gently down and the boat cruised to a halt.

"A beer, Prithi, a fucking beer!" Frantically Prithi scrabbled around in one of the cool boxes, found an ice-cold can and handed it to Mike. Shaking violently, he pulled open the ring top then spilt more than he drank. "Another fucker. Quick, before I die!" In a similar fashion, he sank another two before slightly calming down

Reaching for a fourth, he grabbed Prithi and hugged her close. "We're rich, Prithi! We're fucking rich!" Like Mike, she was shaking like a leaf. In his arms, she finally quieted down then joined him in a beer. Adrenaline still flowing in his blood, Mike kissed Prithi hard on the lips and at the same time removed her bikini top. Lips cold and wet from beer closed round her nipples as he guided her into the cabin.

Without any more preliminaries, he stripped off his trunks then her bikini bottoms. Mike was unstoppable and although she wasn't prepared, the heat of his passion was infectious and she, too, raised her body in desire as they made frantic love.

When he'd finished, Mike went out into the cockpit. Standing naked at the helm, he started the engines and let the boat cruise gently into the cool, early-morning air. "Here, Prithi. Come here. Bring another beer." Naked as well, she stood by him in the soothing breeze as he sipped the beer she handed him. She reached up and took the can from him and finished it herself. Laughing, he put his arm around her. "Champagne next." Snuggling close to him, they remained like that as the sun rose in the east and the boat cruised sedately northwards towards Ajman Creek.

Before they arrived, Mike emptied the contents of the saddlebags into the cool boxes. Covering the gold with fish and ice they'd previously bought from the fish market, he then hurled the saddlebags over the side, followed by his tracksuit. With the light of day upon them, he and Prithi dressed in jeans and T-shirt.

They were early at the slipway and nobody was around. The pickup was where he'd parked it. Mike hitched up the trailer, hauled out the boat dripping with water, and headed off home. After parking the trailer in the backyard, he and Prithi went into the house.

In bed, Mike finally relaxed. Prithi sat down on the bed beside him. "No hurry, Prithi. We'll play it cool. You go to work as usual and I'll stash the cool boxes somewhere safe." Worried, the girl looked at him intensely. "Nobody saw you?" Mike shook his head. "I thought I heard shots." Looking her straight in the eye, Mike didn't hesitate. "You did." Prithi looked even more worried." What happened?" Mike lowered his gaze. "You don't want to know. But there are no witnesses." A shocked tone crept into Prithi's voice. "You didn't...?" There was silence for a moment as Prithi's voice trailed off. Mike's look was direct and hard again. "Kill someone? Yes, several." Shocked, Prithi recoiled. She'd not expected this. Mike sat up and took her hand. Shaking, Prithi pulled it away. "Don't worry, Prithi. We're safe. Go to work."

When she left the room, Mike sat at the table in front of a cup of coffee, his head in his hands. Maybe he'd been a bit quick on the trigger; army training never left you. But you couldn't make an omelet without breaking eggs. He had a lot to do and this was no time for regrets.

Scared, Prithi showered, dressed and headed off to work. Despite being up all night, she didn't feel tired. Perhaps it was the adrenaline or maybe the fear. It would probably catch up with her later. The office was almost deserted. Being the first day of Ramadan, it would be surprising if any of the local Arabs turned up, and the rest would be late. Quietly she sat at her desk. Slowly, what had happened was sinking in. She was an accomplice to murder. Wrapped up in her thoughts, she didn't notice Rajan standing at the door until he spoke.

# Chapter Thirty Eight

# The Hunt

Ali Essa rose early, washed and prepared himself for his prayer. Having resisted the temptation to stay up late and talk like the rest of his family, he felt quite refreshed. First day of the holy month of fasting! Locally, life for the entire Muslim population would be upside down until the new moon was sighted again. Usually it was quiet on the first day, but as the ritual fasting during the day and feasting at night began in earnest, his office would get busier and busier.

Spending the day tired and not eating or drinking, it only took someone to smoke or even sneak a favorite cup of coffee for others' patience to fail, despite the religious preaching of tolerance. Although all were required to remain peaceful and serene, many failed and tempers flared. At these times it was difficult for the police.

Finishing his prayer, Ali Essa was about to have a light breakfast of dates and yoghurt when his direct line rang. Swiftly he answered it. On the other end was the duty officer who spoke excitedly and rapidly. There was trouble in the gold *souq*, some kind of raid.

Not bothering with his breakfast, he downed his last glass of water for the day and quickly dressed. Trying not to disturb his still sleeping family, he headed for the garage. He backed his white Mercedes Benz out and drove a little distance from the house before reaching over and pulling out of the glove box the portable flashing blue light. Lowering the window, he stuck it on the roof, where the powerful magnet held it in place.

As to be expected, the streets at that hour during Ramadan were nearly deserted. Choosing the route over Al Maktoum Bridge, he drove down the Creek road then swung into the maze of roads that lead to the *souq*. On the approach to the *souq*, he found the road blocked by two ambulances and several squad cars, their red and blue lights flashing randomly in the early morning light.

Ali Essa jumped from the car, quickly returned the salute of one of the policemen on guard then strode purposefully towards the centre of activity. All was in chaos. Tearful merchants surrounded the police as they tried to clear a path for the ambulance men. Spotting the duty officer, Ali Essa walked rapidly over.

" Sabah Al Khair." Wheeling around, the officer instantly recognized the captain. "*Sabah Al Noor, seedi.*" He gave a snappy salute and awaited Ali Essa's instructions. "Tell me, lieutenant, what's happened!"

Animatedly the officer launched into a report. "Some sort of a raid, *seedi*. Four people shot, three dead, including one of our men! The other was also a patrolman. He's unconscious, badly wounded."

Barely comprehending, the Major was amazed. "Bad, bad! Who was the patrolman? Married?" Struggling to remain unemotional, the duty officer's voice was choked. "Dead one is, *seedi*. The other's not." Ali Essa regained his aplomb. "The others?" Seeing his commanding officer acting professionally, the duty officer also cooled down. "Old Yemeni caretakers. Must have disturbed them. They killed both of them." Ali Essa looked at the officer quizzically. "They?" Confidently, the duty officer went on. "Yes, *seedi*, this must have been the work of a gang. Nearly twenty shops have been broken into and ransacked. Gold…they were after gold."

Without another word, Ali Essa strode over to the crashed patrol car, which wasn't that badly damaged. There was a body alongside it covered by a white, bloodstained sheet. On the other side, two ambulance men were working frantically on another, trying to give the prone figure life-saving oxygen. While he watched, they lifted the policeman onto a stretcher then hurried him through the crowd to the waiting ambulance. He shook his head sadly then pushed his way through the chattering mob and went down the road to where the other two bodies lay.

Forcing his way through the crowd that was being kept at bay by several patrolmen; he bent over and examined the bodies. Shot clean through the head or chest, they obviously died instantly. The lieutenant was right; this was the work of a gang—a highly skilled one.

On the way back to the damaged police car, he met the duty officer running toward him. "*Seedi, seedi*, you're wanted on the radio. It's Colonel Arif!" Slightly shocked, Ali Essa reacted instantly. "Colonel Arif?"

Hurriedly, he made his way to his car, reached in and pulled out the handset. Calling up the station, he was patched immediately through to Colonel Arif, the Sheik's senior and most trusted aide. After a brief greeting, the Colonel told him to report to the Sheik's *majlis* immediately.

When he reached Zabeel Palace, he drove straight to the *majlis* private entry. A sole guard saluted as he strode in. Waiting for him in the foyer was Colonel Arif, who led him without hesitation into the large almost deserted meeting room. At one end was the Sheik dressed simply in a white *dishdasha* and prayer cap.

Striding toward him as the pair entered, the Sheik extended his hand. "*Salaam Alaykum*, Ali Essa. *Tayhl*." Major Ali Essa saluted and then took the open hand of the Sheik and returned the greeting. The Sheik led him to a row of sumptuous cushions, asked him to sit then sat down alongside.

"Tell me, Ali Essa, what is the problem in the *souq*?" Briefly the Major outlined what had happened. As he gave his report, the Sheik moved his head slightly from side to side in an expression of disbelief and sorrow.

"Never, never before have we had such a raid, and on the first day of the Holy month. Why, Ali Essa? Why? Do you think it could have been the work of our own people? Surely not! All they need do is come to our *majlis* if they are in trouble. Have we ever denied anyone help? Why this?"

Colonel Arif also shook his head; he, too, was shocked and hurt. Ali Essa continued. "I don't think it was our people, Sheik. It was well-planned, possibly a professional gang. Maybe Pakistanis or Indians, even Iranians. Not our people." It was an effort for the captain to sound convincing, as he did have some doubts.

"Colonel Arif, Major Ali Essa, I want all the merchants to be compensated, along with the families of the dead. Please, I don't want news of this incident to spread. Try and keep the press away, and I want the *souq* to stay open." Both men acknowledged his wishes in unison. "And I want this gang caught and punished! On a Holy day! I still can't believe it." With that, the Sheik rose, shook their hands and left the *majlis*, his head and shoulders slumped down.

On his way back to the scene of the crime, Ali Essa struggled to work out who could have committed this vicious act. One thing was sure, it was well-planned. This was not just a simple snatch and grab done on the spur of the moment. Someone or some gang had put a lot of thought into it. To him, that didn't seem like an Indian or Pakistani gang. Perhaps it was a gang of illegals from Afghanistan; they were well-trained militants who needed the money for arms. They had been around in the neighboring Gulf countries causing trouble. Maybe they'd come to Dubai.

Arriving back at the scene, he found the ambulances gone and the police tow truck hauling the damaged patrol car from the shop window. Approaching the duty officer, Ali Essa was overcome by a sadness that weighed heavily on his shoulders. This was a part of his life as a police officer that he really hated.

"Lieutenant." The policeman snapped to attention. "*Seedi?*" Pointing to the crowd that still milled around, Ali Essa lowered his voice. "Lieutenant, I want all the merchants to be taken back to the station to give statements of what they estimate their losses to be. Don't be too long, or their imaginations will take over. And another thing, Lieutenant... is there anybody here that knew the dead patrolman?" Pointing to a policeman who was in the background, the lieutenant also kept his voice low. "*Na'am, seedi.* Constable Obaid." The captain headed for his Mercedes. "Bring him to my car."

Shortly after, the policeman, struggling to hold back his emotions, arrived at the car and saluted sharply. "*Na'am, seedi?*" Ali Essa saluted back. "You knew the dead man?" The patrolman took a deep breath. "*Na'am seedi.*" Opening the door for him, the captain's voice was soft. "And where he lived?" Hesitating for a moment, the constable started to get in the car. *"Na'am, seedi."*

Silently, Ali Essa reversed the car carefully down the alleyway. As he did, he saw a tear slowly trickle down the otherwise imperturbable face of the policeman. He, too, was struggling with his emotions and there was a heavy lump in his throat. In almost a whisper, the passenger guided his superior to a group of houses in a small compound not far from the central police station. Stopping at one with a carved wooden door in the wall, they both got out

The policeman knocked on the door and they waited until a little Arab boy opened it slightly. Upon seeing the familiar face of Obaid, he grinned, opened the door wide and welcomed them in. Ali Essa's heart was in his mouth. He'd done this several times before when he was in Traffic and it hadn't gotten any easier. Particularly now, as it was one of his men.

Entering the house, Obaid told the boy to fetch his mother. Almost immediately, a young Arab woman dressed in a black cloak but with her face uncovered, appeared. Upon seeing the face of Obaid and with a glance at the officer alongside him, she instinctively gasped, her hands going to her face, and then collapsed onto the floor. The boy scared ran to her. Already his mother was crying. "Mother, mother, what is wrong? What has happened?"

It was Ali Essa's turn to step forward. Placing his hand on the boy's shoulder, he asked him to be calm. Squatting down, he rested level with the boy's eyes that were now wide and glaring. "It is your father. He's not coming home."

Suddenly the boy bristled. "Not coming home? He has done nothing! Not coming home?"

No longer could Ali Essa control the tears that crept down his face as he looked at

the scared but proud young boy trying to defend his father's honor. "Son, your father's dead. That's why he's not coming home. He was a brave man. He died doing his duty."

Disbelief crossed the boy's face. "No, no, he's not dead! No!" Turning to his mother, he shouted at her. "Tell them it's not true, mother. He's not dead!"

Ali Essa stood and backed off. This was the worst day of his life that he could remember. Turning to the other man, who was trying to dry the tears rolling down his cheeks, his voice was husky as he whispered, "Stay with them, Constable. I must go. Let them know we will look after them."

Saluting the officer, Obaid turned his attention to the two grieving family members as Ali Essa quietly left.

Getting into the Mercedes, he muttered, "What is this? The first day of the Holy month we must be tested like this?" Feeling bad at his mild reprobation, he drove to a nearby mosque, washed, entered its cool interior and prayed. Without his belief he felt he would not be able to go on.

When he entered the police station, he found a crowd of angry merchants shoving and pushing to get into the duty officer's room. Several of the duty staff were trying to hold them back, and there were noisy scuffles. They had gotten over their initial shock and were now trying to impress with their injured dignity. Despite his sadness, Ali Essa managed to smile at the scene. Merchants will be merchants. Very quickly they were turning this to their advantage. When they heard there was compensation to be paid, each merchant would claim he had the entire contents of Ali Baba's magic cave in his shop. It would be an unenviable task to try and get an equitable agreement on the amount of money to be paid. The next two or three days would be a trial.

During the time that the compensation claims were being discussed, his men scoured the *souq* for clues. There were none. Fortunately, Ali Essa didn't have to tell the merchants not to close. The night after the raid, they were open as if nothing had happened. Keeping the press at bay was another thing. One or two reporters from the Arab newspapers had heard the rumors and rounded on the site like jackals. It took Ali Essa's wits to prevent the story from growing out of all proportion.

Not quite the rumor mongers of their Arab brothers, the English journalists were a little more circumspect but could be a lot more dangerous. Stories in English could reach the international press a lot easier than the more colorful and flamboyant Arab ones, and they had a lot more credibility.

The three dead were buried in accordance with Muslim tradition. Again, Ali Essa had to comfort the family of the dead policeman, and yet again it was a task he found hard and did not relish. Among the family were the man's old mother and father. He had been their sole surviving son, their other two sons having drowned in a fishing accident. Their grief was palpable.

Ali Essa was glad to get back to the station and the squabbling merchants with their sanctimonious howls of having been robbed of their very life's savings. They were all lies—both parties knew there were more, well hidden, smuggled gold pieces that could now see the light of day and creep onto the shelves without too much scrutiny.

The Sheik's generosity was more than adequate to cover their losses. However, to the families of the victims it would never be enough to replace their loved ones, although they were grateful for his caring offer. Meanwhile, Ali Essa was contacting the hospital at half-hourly intervals to see if the only remaining witness was conscious.

Three days later he was coherent enough, although he couldn't speak, his jaw having been smashed by Mike's bullet. To Ali Essa's dismay, he was also unable to write, as the bullet had also broken his wrist. Whatever. All this wouldn't have made any difference. He hadn't seen his assailants, nor could he have added anything to the investigation.

Four days after the raid, Ali Essa's office erupted as the duty officer stormed in, noisily snapping to attention as he threw a quick salute. "*Seedi*, we have one of the gang!" Rapidly returning the salute, Ali Essa was instantly on his feet. "Where? How?" Leading the way, the duty officer addressed the Major as he strode after him out of the room. "He's in interrogation now!"

Having even neglected his cap, Ali Essa took the steps two-by-two down into the basement, making straight for the room that held the prisoner. Nearly breathless, he arrived at the door. Inside was the pathetic figure of a pajama-clad Pakistani, crying, begging and pleading for the guard to free him. At the sight of an officer, the miserable captive threw himself at Ali Essa's feet and clung to his ankles.

"Get him off! Get him off! Who is this man?" Two policemen grabbed the skinny wretch and threw him back onto a seat in front of the table. "He is one of the gang, *seedi*!" Ali Essa looked him up and down. "This scrawny rogue is part of the gang?" Surprised at his doubt, the duty officer stepped forward. "*Seedi*, he was caught red-handed. Look, he was trying to sell this bracelet!" Stepping forward, the arresting officer opened his hand and Ali Essa saw the man was holding a piece of golden jewellery. Smiling with satisfaction, the policeman continued. "He was trying to sell it back to the merchant it was stolen from!"

Looking first at the arresting officer then back at the prisoner, Ali Essa turned on his heel. "Lieutenant, can I see you in my office?"

Slightly crestfallen, the officer followed the Major up the stairs into his room. "Lieutenant, firstly, this was a well- planned raid. Do you honestly think that dirty, scruffy Pashtun could be part of a well-planned raid?"

Shaking his head, the officer remained silent. "Secondly, if he had been, do you think he would be stupid enough to return and sell off one, just one, out of the many that have been stolen?"

Again the officer remained silent. "Sit. Tell me the whole story."

Visibly shaken, the officer sat and repeated what had happened. A merchant had recognized the bracelet when the suspect had brought it in. Pretending to have to assay it in the back room, he'd called the police and two of his neighbors. When the police had arrived, the merchant and his neighbors were sitting on the screaming, kicking, and cursing suspect, whose dignity had been severely bruised when they had leaped on him.

"Where did he get the bracelet?"

More confident now, the officer spoke up briskly. "He said he found it!"

Ali Essa leaned forward on his desk. "Where?"

Sheepishly, the officer looked at the ground. "I haven't asked him yet."

Without a word, Ali Essa rose and headed back to the interrogation room with the officer scurrying behind him. Entering the room, he marched straight up to the prisoner. "Tell me where you got the bracelet or you will be charged with murder and theft in the Sharia court." As one of the policemen translated what had been said into the man's mother tongue, the suspect's eyes grew wide and he again threw himself at Ali Essa's feet. Blubberingm he protested his innocence.

Finally, Ali Essa disentangled himself. "Answer the question!" Eventually, one of the guards managed to translate the man's hysterical story. He had found it in the rocks on the Creek bank. "Take us there now!"

Standing on the rocks looking out over the swirling tidal waters of the Creek, Ali Essa was more than convinced that this babbling idiot's story was true. What baffled him was how the bracelet got where it was found. In the hot sunlight he tried to imagine what could have happened. Across from him on the other side of the Creek were the stacks of containers in Port Rashid. Behind them, travelling to and fro, were the large yellow cranes unloading the huge container vessels that were moored alongside. Further down the Creek lay the sprawling, exotic mix of the old and new buildings of Dubai.

Perhaps that was it! The gang had arrived by ship and left with it. These container vessels had a twenty-four-hour turnaround. "I want a record of every ship that came and went that night!" Shocked at his harsh tone, the lieutenant struggled with his pen and notebook to write down the instructions as Ali Essa snarled them out. "And every fishing boat and every service vessel!"

Stepping back from the rocks, he looked around. There was nothing but parked trucks driven by illiterate Pakistanis, the same as the one his men had captured. Very unlikely they would have the brains and talent to put together a raid like the one that had just happened. The suspect's story that he'd gone to the Creek to have a shit and clean himself sounded reasonable. "Show me exactly where he found the bracelet."

Dragging the man forward, they quickly translated. Shaking, the man pointed to the rocks where the water swirled back and forth. Ali Essa peered into the water. Maybe one or more of the pieces could have been dropped in panic. "Get the divers in. I want the creek bed scoured." Scribbling frantically, the officer nodded. "Yes, *seedi*."

Some hours later as Ali Essa watched, the police diving launch arrived and two scuba divers dropped backwards into the waters just astern of the boat that had anchored near the rocks. Patiently, Ali Essa gazed at the stream of bubbles that marked where the divers below worked back and forth.

His patience was rewarded with a shout from one of the divers, who then produced a dripping rifle above his head. Ali Essa nodded and waved. The forensic report had stated that the victims had all been shot with a similar weapon, an AK 47. Still not much to go on. Unfortunately, with the Iran/Iraq war going on the other side of the Gulf, these rifles were in good supply and very difficult to trace.

A little later, the second diver surfaced with a shout and yelled instructions to the launch. Hoisting anchor, it made its way slowly to where the diver was treading water. Handing him a rope, the crew watched as he dived again. Several minutes later, he emerged, gave more instructions and the two men on the launch put the rope around a winch and hauled away. Not long afterwards, the dripping, muddy shape of a motorcycle appeared above the water. The men in the boat struggled to pull it in. Ali Essa waited for another hour, but nothing else was found.

Sitting in his office, Ali Essa pondered over the evidence to date. One rifle— useless; impossible to trace; could have belonged to anyone, even if forensic proved that it was the rifle that fired the shots. The bike? Now that was more interesting. But still, the amount of gold taken weighed nearly a couple of hundred kilos. One bike would struggle to carry that weight. Perhaps the gang rode it back and forth. Again, the noise would surely have woken the drivers asleep on their beds slung under their trucks' trailers.

Puzzled, he went out into the courtyard where the bike stood, cleaned and dried. Of course, all identification had been obscured. The engine and frame numbers had been ground off. Anyhow, it could have been any number of similar bikes stolen then stolen again by young Arab boys. Nothing unusual about it, except...he peered closely...two angle iron supports welded across the frame where the backseat had been. Each support had a bracket with two hooks attached to it. Good, solid job, done by a professional. Scratching his head, he walked around the bike. Was it possible that one bike had been used on one trip? If so, whoever rode it knew what he was doing!

Heading back upstairs to his office, he sat thinking. Ramadan was not a good time for such deep thoughts. He had fasted all day and, it being late in the afternoon, most of his thoughts were on Iftar when he would have his first meal and cup of coffee of the day. Giving up, he left the office and headed home to be with his family at sunset.

On his way to work the next morning, he mulled over the bike again. Maybe it wasn't a gang, just one person. There was a cross-country bike club in Dubai, and perhaps their records might be useful. Reaching for the radio hand piece, he called the station and instructed that they get the names and addresses from the club. It was a long shot, but it might turn up something.

Sitting down at his desk, he was about to open the file on the raid when the duty clerk arrived with several more files. "*Sabah Al Noor*, constable." The clerk put the files on the table, stepped back and saluted. "*Sabah Al Khar, seedi.*" Flipping through the files, Ali Essa looked up at the policeman, who was still stiff at attention. "Stand easy, Constable. Anything interesting?"

The duty clerk relaxed and pointed to one file. "No, *seedi*, only the same old rubbish, except this one. That wild boy from the next Emirate in trouble again. Drunk and fighting at the same nightclub where he was in trouble before."

Picking up the file, the captain opened it. "Before? I don't remember that." The clerk leaned forward and turned over a few pages in the file. "Yes, *seedi*, about eighteen months ago, an Englaisee was involved." Nodding his head, Ali Essa responded thoughtfully, "Oh, yes, that's right. Military man nearly killed the little—. If it weren't Ramadan, I'd use the word! Would have saved us this trouble."

Picking up the file, he scanned through it. Sooner or later this boy was going to get into serious trouble, or worse, get himself killed. He nearly did that night when he mixed it with the Englishman. As he browsed through the pages he came across Mike's details. Interesting...ex-SAS, service in Vietnam, still worked here with Dubai Petroleum Company. It had been a one-off thing and he'd stayed out of trouble apart from the Indian girl he lived with. No point in hauling him in over that, or he'd have to arrest half the British expatriates in Dubai. Closing the file, he sat back and reflected upon the raid again.

Later in the day, the clerk bought him the membership details of the local bike club. Idly running down the list, he felt he was wasting his time when suddenly he saw Mike Hunter's name. Sitting up, he opened the file on the Sheik's son again. Yes, it was the same man. Just a coincidence? Bike rider, ex-military, tough man and well-trained. "I think I'll call him in, just for a talk. Who knows?"

Lifting the phone, he asked the clerk to get Mr. Hunter on the line. A little later, the clerk replied that the man he wanted was out on a platform in the Fatah field. For a moment, Ali Essa thought of leaving a message for him when he got back, but it may alert Hunter if he were indeed the perpetrator. If he was out on a platform, maybe he had a good alibi. Besides, he wasn't going far from there.

# Chapter Thirty Nine

# Treachery

When Prithi left, Mike worked for a short while to put the boat and trailer away in the work shed, emptied out the ice and the fish from the cool boxes then went inside to sleep for the rest of the day. After the raid he was totally exhausted. Rising late in the afternoon, he was dressed by the time Prithi arrived back from the office.

Having to negotiate the crazy Ramadan rush-hour traffic all the way from Dubai had not left her in a good mood. Neither had the conversation with Rajan. Now he was pressuring her to leave Mike. On top of all that, she was deadly tired. With hardly a word, she went to the bedroom and slept for several hours. Awaking, she showered and emerged to be greeted with a glass of champagne—Mike's attempt to put her in better humor. Naked and without smiling, she took the glass, gulped it down while Mike watched her admiringly. "Get used to drinking it. It's what millionaires drink." As she dressed she had a couple more glasses. Now in a better frame of mind, she accepted Mike's offer to go out for dinner.

"We're going to play it cool, Prithi." The waiter had just left with their order. "I'm going to give notice next week and you can, too. Tell them we're going on a trip around Europe or something. Nothing expensive. Doing the right thing." All Prithi could do was nod in agreement. She was now an accomplice to armed robbery and murder. Whatever Mike wanted to do, she would have to go along. "I'll get the Land rover ready over the next week or so. Melt

215

down the gold and cast it into two bumpers." Listening to him, it seemed to Prithi as if he was talking to himself. "Probably another week on the platform then you and I can leave. We'll let them dock our pay in lieu of service. Don't want to hang around too long."

Bearing food, the waiter interrupted their conversation. Silently, Prithi ate her meal. It was obvious that Mike had it all planned out. Pausing in his meal, Mike continued. "We'll drive to Khor Khalba over the mountains and pick up a dhow to India. I've got enough cash to bribe the captain and crew to keep their mouths shut. Anyhow, who's going to worry about us? You've got an Indian passport and I'll have a visa. The Land rover's for touring. Nobody but us will know its bloody bumper bars are worth a king's ransom!" With that, Mike filled Prithi's glass with wine and settled back, laughing to himself.

While Prithi was back in the office, Mike set about melting down and casting the stolen jewellery into its disguise. He was oblivious to the fine and sometimes exquisite craftsmanship; it would all be smelted and cast into two bumper bars. Early in the morning, Mike made sure the coast was clear then climbed into the boat that was still on the trailer. Lifting the cushions from the bunks, he opened the cool boxes stashed inside them and gazed down on their glittering contents. Carefully lifting them out one by one, he carried them off the boat, climbed down and deposited the cool boxes into the middle of the work shed. Setting them alongside the two steel moulds he had made of the bumper bars, he started up his home-made furnace. Two lots of gas bottles were connected to two acetylene torches with wide nozzles. Above them on a frame was a fabricated ladle. Lighting the torches, he waited till the ladle was glowing bright red hot then began lowering the pieces of jewellery into it, watching as they melted slowly down into a golden puddle. When the ladle was about three-quarters full, wearing insulated gloves he carefully lifted it by the long handle and poured the molten metal into a partition in the mould. This he repeated time after time until all the gold had been melted and cast. Then, in spots where there were gaps, he melted down the lead and filled them. Grinding off the reinforcing angles he'd fitted to the mould, he now had a smooth surface for the front of the bumper. Carefully, he sheathed the back surface where the gold was exposed with sheet metal. The finished product was a steel gold sandwich. With care, he drilled the holes in each bumper for the bolts to hold the angle brackets. He meticulously caught the filings from the drill bit. Next step was to bolt the brackets to the original bumper bar supports on the vehicle. When he had finished, they looked like solid steel bumper bars. After spray-painting them a matt black, he stood back and admired his work. Even he was impressed. They almost appeared like the original steel Land rover bumpers. It would be impossible for anyone to guess what they really were. Gathering up the fine drops of spilled gold and all the filings, he melted them down and made a crude nugget pendant. This he would put on one of Prithi's chains. Although the work had taken several days, he was pleased. They could travel at a moment's notice.

Once in India, this would be the end of the adventure. Maybe he could find another. For a moment, he had a twinge of regret that it was coming to an end. Still, he had Prithi, and just her body made up for whatever he might miss. And he loved her more than any women he'd loved. Indian mysticism, that's what it had to be. He was under her spell. He laughed to himself as he locked the shed doors.

"One more week on the platform and we are away." Prithi smiled. She was weary of all this subterfuge and was pleased at the idea of leaving and getting away. "I'll ask Don to go fishing on the Friday I get back. That'll put people off the scent. Then on the Sunday, we'll leave. Head over the mountains to Khor Khalba, fix a charter boat and that's it. Bombay here we come!" That night, they downed two bottles of champagne while enjoying a long, languorous session of lovemaking before dropping off to sleep. The next morning, Mike left early for his last shift on the platform.

With Mike away, Prithi moved back to her flat in Dubai. It cut down the travelling by half. Besides, she wanted one more night with Rajan just to say goodbye. He wouldn't be happy, she knew that, but she felt she must close this chapter in her life. Rajan was all smiles when she agreed he could come around again one evening. Welcoming him in jeans and T-shirt, she tried to keep him at arm's length so it would be easier to tell him goodbye.

It wasn't easy, and after sharing a takeout meal together, she found herself drawn magnetically, once again, to bed with him. Their lovemaking was fierce and passionate. When it was over, they lay in the stillness of the night. In the darkness, Prithi gathered up all her strength.

"Rajan, I'm going away." For a moment there was silence. "On holiday with him?" Rajan's voice was tense. Prithi's response was rapid. "Away for good." The body alongside her stiffened. She could hear Rajan's breathing quicken. "For good? Why?"

Now it was her turn to stiffen slightly and breathe heavily. Almost as if she were on drugs, she heard herself talking. Try as she may, she couldn't stop herself. It was as if she were outside of her body, watching, seeing, but not in control. "Mike and I are going to India for good."

This time the silence was longer. When he finally spoke, Rajan's tense voice was full of emotion. "Why?" For a moment, Prithi didn't say a word. Rajan had raised himself onto one elbow and was staring intently into Prithi's face. In the dim light he could see her hair spread across the pillow. Beneath her black eyebrows, her eyelids were closed. Following the curve of her neck, his eyes lit upon the honey-brown skin as it swelled and covered her firm breast that rose up and down with every breath.

"We have gold we are going to sell and live in India." It had been said. Ever since the raid, inside her was a desire to tell someone, like a confession. Someone, anyone. The time had come and it was Rajan.

"Gold? You have gold? How? Has the Englishman been investing or something?" Prithi's answer was brief. "Something." Falling back on the pillow, Rajan stared in the dark at the ceiling. " 'Something' means *stolen*."

This time there was no response from Prithi.

"Stolen! He's stolen gold!"

For several minutes, all that could be heard in the half-darkened room was their breathing. Suddenly Rajan sat up. "It's true! The story in the market that there had been a big robbery. Afghan rebels, they said, but it was your Englishman!" Grabbing Prithi's arms, he pulled her up to his face. "It was him, wasn't it?" Tears rolled down

Prithi's face. For the life of her, she couldn't understand why she'd said anything. Letting her go, she slumped back onto the pillow. Rajan lay back on his.

"It won't work, Prithi. If you and your Englishman go to India, you will be killed and the gold stolen. You don't know these people. Once they think the gold is stolen or black, you will not stand a chance." There was no reply from the girl, just a sob. "And if you stay here, you will get caught. It's said that a policeman was killed. You are an accomplice. You will get the death penalty."

A sharp gasp followed Rajan's harshly spoken logic. Remaining silent, tears continued to flow down her cheeks. "You are in serious danger, Prithi. You must do one thing." Her reply was barely audible. "What?" Rajan didn't hesitate. "Show me the gold. I will take you and the gold to India. At least I know the language these people speak and I have contacts."

This time Prithi reacted. "Never, Rajan. Never! Mike will catch us and kill you! He can, you know, with his bare hands. He could kill you!" There was deathly silence. Both of them hardly dared breathe.

Then, in a soft cruel voice, Rajan spoke. "Then we must kill him."

Prithi's hands went to her face. She let out a small scream and shook her head. "Listen, Prithi. If you don't, you will die, and if you go to India with him, you will
die!" The girl sat bolt upright.

"No, no, no, Rajan! No!" Leaping from the bed, she grabbed a T-shirt and pulled
it over her naked body.

Staggering from the room, she headed for the fridge and took out a plastic bottle full of water. In almost one gulp she swallowed the contents. Slowly, she returned to the bedroom and sat on the edge of the bed. Dragging on his jeans, Rajan sat next to her. Neither of them spoke. Finally it was Rajan that broke the silence. "I'm going. Think about it, Prithi. Think about it!" With that, he kissed her on the forehead, finished dressing and left.

That night Prithi didn't sleep. Tossing and turning, she tried to think of a way out. What would happen to her? Rajan was right.

Mike had got her into this terrible state. All her dreams of happiness had evaporated and now she faced capture or, even worse, death. Was it worth it, to die? She remembered the picture in the local paper of two murderers publicly executed in Ras Al Khamaih last week. Their lifeless bodies hung from a pole with the crowd around them staring. Not her. No! Feeling sick, she leaped from the bed to throw up in the bathroom. She was sick until no more would come. In bed she hid under the sheet until the morning light crept ominously in.

Sitting at her desk the next morning, she looked terrible. Dark shadows were under her eyes that were still watery from lack of sleep and crying. Mid-morning, Rajan appeared at her desk, pretending to check the intercom system. For a while, Prithi said nothing. Then, just as Rajan was about to leave, she whispered to him to come around that evening.

When he entered her flat, he knew she had come to see the situation his way. Without spelling it out, they agreed to do what Rajan had suggested.

"On Friday he will go fishing. Come to the house in Ajman. I will give you a map. Ring me first. Come Friday. Go now."

Without saying a word, Rajan rose and left. Outside her door, a slight cruel smile crossed his face.

Catching a taxi, Rajan headed for Ajman. Why should he care for the Britisher? They had stolen from India and now it was his turn to take some back. And the girl, she would do it; he had her in his grasp. She was like all Indian women. This was his right. He was a man and he was from India.

All he carried was an overnight bag with a few clothes stuffed inside it, along with what little cash he had and his Indian passport. At the bottom of the bag was a barbarous hunting knife that he'd bought in the market. Double-edged, it was extremely sharp and longer than his forearm, a formidable weapon.

Arriving at the house in Ajman, he alighted from the taxi then paid the driver after having quickly looked around. Inside the house, Prithi was waiting. Cautiously, he entered the darkened interior. It was sparsely furnished. Mike and Prithi had only used it occasionally. Barely speaking, Rajan carefully moved around. Satisfied it wasn't some sort of trick, he suddenly turned and pulled Prithi to him. Surprisingly, her body was stiff and unrelenting.

"What's the matter? You don't like me?" Her hair swirled around her shoulders as she shook her head. "I'm scared, Rajan. Very scared." Rajan kissed her gently on the cheek. "There's nothing to be scared about. I'll take care, just you see. When is he coming back?" Prithi's mood changed slightly. She leaned into Rajan's body. "Late. When he goes fishing with his friend, it's always late." Rajan held her head in his hands and kissed her on the lips. "That's good. We can get ready for him."

They agreed that when they heard him coming, Prithi would be in the bedroom in the dark and Rajan would take up a position behind the door. When Rajan pulled the knife out, Prithi's hands went to her mouth and she let out a muffled scream. Tears began to flow down her cheeks. "Do we have to do this, Rajan?" There was terror in her voice. "You know we do, Prithi. You know it."

The afternoon shadows lengthened into nightfall, and about eight o'clock they heard Mike's four-wheel drive crunch down the driveway. Mike was in a good mood. Despite it being his last fishing trip with Don, he'd caught a lot of fish and drunk a lot of beer. So had Don. After they had sorted out the boat and trailer, they drunkenly embraced and told each other how wonderful they were and how they'd always be friends. Beer talk, but it felt good.

After parking the four-wheeler, he made his way to the house. Only the kitchen light was on. Prithi must be in bed. Probably a headache. She'd been suffering from them of late. "Prithi, I'm home. Prithi!" Going to the fridge, he reached in and pulled out another beer then snacked on some leftovers. Finishing the beer, he pushed open the door to the darkened bedroom. "Prithi?"

Had he been more sober, Mike would have been quicker to detect the slight movement behind the door and the flash of steel. But he did not. Rajan drove the knife hard into Mike. It sliced through the flesh, muscles and nerves of his right shoulder instantly paralyzing his right arm. With a scream of pain, Mike lashed out with his only good arm, but to no avail. Again the knife came down, slashing a groove in his face and hacking into his chest. This time, with a grunt, he drove his left fist in a karate blow to where he saw a face.

Connecting, it smashed into his assailant's jaw and nose. Staggering backwards, Rajan fell on the bed with Mike following. Desperately, his terrified would-be assassin drove the knife upward with all his force, almost to the hilt. The knife penetrated Mike's stomach, a mortal blow, and Mike slumped with a gasp to his knees. Leaping to his feet, Rajan drove home the advantage and plunged the knife hard into the exposed back.

A feeble scream left Mike's lips. Hoarsely, he cried "Help me, Prithi. Help!" Then he died. For a moment the room was silent. The foul smell of blood mixed with shit and piss permeated the room. In his death throes, Mike's bowels had lost control. Shrieking, Prithi ran to the bathroom and slammed the door shut. Dropping to her knees, she was violently ill into the pedestal. Throwing up again and again, she weakly reached up and flushed the contents away and slumped with her head on the bowl.

"Open the door! Prithi, open the door!" Hammering on the bathroom door, Rajan finally forced his way in. Covered in blood, he went to the basin, turned on the tap and started to gently wash his face. Mike's last fruitless blow had broken Rajan's nose, slightly dislocated his jaw and split his lips. Already his face was swollen and painful. "Shut up, Prithi! Shut up!" The girl's sobbing was getting on his nerves. After completing washing his face, he dragged her to her feet. "You must help me now! We will bury him. Now!"

Slithering and sliding in the muck, the two of them struggled to haul the inert body across the kitchen floor to the outside. Rajan found a wheelbarrow and they managed to get it over the frame. Wobbling from side to side, they pushed the bloody load to the back of the yard. Fortunately, it was mostly soft sand, and in less than half an hour, Rajan had dug a shallow grave. They unceremoniously dumped what was left of Mike into it and shoveled sand in until it was completely covered. Looking around, Rajan found several sheets of roofing steel, which he dragged over to cover the freshly disturbed ground. Finally, with great effort, he picked up a few slabs of paving stones and dropped them on the roofing sheets.

Prithi had hurried back to the house and was frantically, almost hysterically, washing away the blood with the hose from the outside garden. For three or more hours the two of them worked feverishly to destroy or clean away any evidence. Eventually, it was all done.

Remaking the bed with clean sheets, Rajan, after showering and throwing his clothes in the washing machine, collapsed on the bed. The pain in his face was beginning to throb. Finding some painkillers, he washed them down with a swig of whisky from the liquor cabinet. Dragging himself back to the bed, he again collapsed onto it and this time was fast asleep within seconds, exhausted by nerves and fatigue. Prithi sat on the edge of the bed and was still there at first light.

In the morning, Rajan painfully raised himself from the bed and went to the kitchen. In silence, Prithi made him coffee and an omelet. As he ate in front of her, she sat watching him but having nothing herself. Eating with difficulty, he paused and looked up at her. "Prithi, get over it. It was for the good. We must move. Get packed. Where is the gold?" Nodding her head, Prithi mutely beckoned Rajan to come with her.

Leaving the food barely touched, he followed her outside. In the work shed she pointed to the old Land rover. "It's in the bumper bars." Surprised, Rajan wasn't sure what she had said. "Where?" Stiffly, she walked to the vehicle and pointed to the bumpers. Rajan still couldn't understand what she was getting at. "In them? How?"

Flatly Prithi explained. "Mike melted it down and turned it into bumpers." Rajan ran his hands over the front one. "My God! Really? Truly the man was an artist. Nobody could tell." Tapping it with his fist, he then picked up a piece of steel and scratched the surface of the bumper. "Are you sure? Look, it's just steel." The girl sadly shook her head. "It's inside, Rajan. Like a sandwich. You can't see it from outside."

Opening his hands in an expression of amazement, he then gingerly touched his face. "And you were right. He could have killed me with his bare hands." For a moment, they both stood looking at the vehicle without saying a word. Rajan moved towards the house. "Come, Prithi."

Rapidly, they packed two suitcases with clothes. Gathering up their passports and money, they went through Mike's drawers and removed his money and passport. "Well, he was ready! There's about fifty thousand dollars here, Prithi. That'll get us to India." In another drawer, they found a detailed map of the route over the mountains.

Having packed, they headed back to the Land rover. Carefully stowing the cases away, they covered them with a tarpaulin. When finished, Rajan returned to the house. Minutes later he was back, clutching two bottles of whisky and a bunch of keys. "Wouldn't get far without either of these. Get in." Starting the Land rover, Rajan backed it out then headed cautiously down the road.

Ten minutes later they pulled into a petrol station, filled the tank and motored off towards the east. "We'll follow the Englishman's plan. Stop overnight in the mountains then head for Khor Khalba early in the morning. Nobody will be suspicious." Despite the pain in his face, he smiled then leaned over and pulled Prithi towards him. "Smile. Don't worry, you're safe now. We'll be in Bombay soon, and rich!" Prithi smiled wanly as the four-wheel drive vehicle rumbled steadily towards Hatta in the mid-morning sun.

## Chapter Forty

# The Chase

The more he thought about it, the more he was convinced. Ali Essa again read the file of Mike Hunter. Ex-Army, intelligent and smart. Probably he'd seen it as a challenge. It wasn't a gang of thieves from the sub-continent; it was one or maybe more British expatriates!

First thing Saturday morning, he sent the duty sergeant with a patrol car around to the address they had on file. Arriving back about an hour later, the sergeant reported that the villa was empty with no car in the garage. "Maybe he's gone out. He couldn't be on duty, not according to what Dubai Petroleum Company told me. Are you sure nobody was home, sergeant?" The sergeant was sure. With that, the major picked up his cap from the desk. "Come with me. We're going over to their offices."

Slightly shocked to see the police so early in the morning, the receptionist was flustered. "Sorry, sir, the public relations manager is not in yet. It's Ramadan."

Ali Essa scowled. "I know, Madam. I know!"

Even more flustered, the woman tried to explain, "Sorry, sir, I didn't mean—" The major waved his hand. "Don't apologize. When is he in?"

Grateful for an opportunity to please, the receptionist went on. "I'll call him at his home."

Minutes later, she put the phone down. "He's on his way. Be here in about five minutes. Would you like to sit in his office?" Calling the office boy, she told him to take the police officers to the public relation manager's office.

Ten minutes later, the out-of-breath Palestinian arrived dressed in a *dishdasha* and prayer cap. "Ramadan, *muhburak*. I'm sorry. Fasting you know. It is difficult. I've given up smoking as well. I'm sorry. Please, what can I do for you?" Fussing around, the man shook the hands of all the policemen in his room as he rambled on. They had all stood when he entered. "Sit down. Sit down, please."

Only the major spoke. "Thank you." Taking a seat in front of the desk, he waited till the company man sat. Behind the major, the sergeant and two constables remained standing.

"Trouble, er, Captain?"

Ali Essa removed his cap. "Major. For you, perhaps."

The public relations man wasn't too sure whether to smile or laugh at Ali Essa's response. "Relax, it's not you. We're looking for the man Mike Hunter."

Slightly perplexed, the man on the other side of the desk spluttered, "He's not on duty?"

Leaning forward, Ali Essa stared keenly at the red-faced Arab. "You should know. He works here!"

Now really flustered, the public relations manager reached for a tissue and wiped his sweaty brow. "Oh, yes. Oh, yes. Sorry, sorry, it's Ramadan."

The major looked annoyed. "Please, not that excuse again. We, too, are fasting." Too embarrassed to look up, the agitated man shuffled through the files on his desk. "Ah, the roster. Yes, er, no, he is not on duty. He's on local leave."

"He's not at his villa."

"You checked?"

"Yes!"

Not knowing where to look, the public relations man stared at his papers then looked up. "Sorry, but what else can I do?"

Ali Essa put his elbows on the desk. "Where is the Indian woman who lives with him?"

Confused again, the Palestinian stared blankly. "An Indian woman?"

Ali Essa peered at him. "Are you really the public relations manager or his brother- in-law?"

Laughing fitfully, the man shuffled through the papers on his desk. "Of course. Yes, the Indian woman. One moment please." Picking up the phone, he hit the pushbuttons several times, spoke rapidly in Arabic, nodded then put the phone down. "She is not in, sir."

Concern crossed the major's face. "Name?" This time the public relations man had the answer. "Singh. Prithi Singh."

Ali Essa nodded. "Yes, that's the one." Leaning still further across the desk, he

spoke harshly. "She had a friend. Where is she? She was Australian or something."

Slightly shocked by the change of tone, the manager sat erect in his chair. "Oh,

yes, sir. A Mrs. Williams from Engineering. Do you want me to get her?" The major's response was blunt. "Yes."

Jumping to his feet, the manager quickly shuffled out of the office. Ali Essa's eyes followed him then he looked at the sergeant and shrugged his shoulders. Not long after, he returned with an older woman in tow.

"Ah, Mrs. Williams." Standing, Ali Essa extended his hand in greeting. The woman took it and shook it carefully.

"Yes, officer, I'm Mrs. Williams. Janine Williams. Congratulations for Ramadan. Can I help you?"

The policeman offered her his seat. "Thank you. Please be seated. You don't remember me?"

Blushing slightly, the woman shook her head. "No. I'm sorry." The major gave a small wave of his hand as if to dismiss her apology.

"I'm Major Ali Essa of Criminal Investigation, Dubai Police. You were involved in the affair with Mr. Hunter."

Now the woman sat up in the chair and cautiously studied the policeman. After a moment's thought, she responded, "Oh, yes. But surely that's all over."

With the trace of a smile, Ali Essa continued. "It is, but I have a few questions to ask Mr. Hunter on another matter. He doesn't appear to be at home. Can you help us find him?"

The woman shrugged her shoulders. "He went fishing with his friend Don yesterday. They were up at the house in Ajman. Maybe he's still there."

Ali Essa leaned towards her. "With the Indian woman?"

Janine Williams was immediately on guard. The major could read it in her eyes. "Don't worry, we have known of their affair for a long time. It's not about that."

Relaxing slightly, the woman spoke softly. "I don't know where the house is in Ajman, but Don does." Looking at the policeman who said nothing, she went on. "Don Johnson. He's Mike's friend. He works on the rig with him." Turning to the public relations man, the major spoke rapidly. "Don Johnson...you do know where he lives?"

Shortly afterwards, the patrol car pulled up outside a villa on the same road where Mike lived. Behind the tall wall in the garden was a Pakistani gardener idly watering the grass by hand. The garden was tidily kept with brightly colored shrubs around the edges. Sounding the bell, the police waited until the gardener opened the front gate. Seeing the police, the gardener disappeared into the house and returned immediately, followed by a big man in a T-shirt, shorts and rubber thong sandals. Courteously, he showed the police into the lounge room.

"I'd offer you coffee, tea or something, but you're fasting, no doubt."

Ali Essa found the heavy American accent a bit difficult to understand. Looking around at the expensive furniture, he finally worked out what had been said. "Yes, thank you. Yes, we are fasting."

The American continued to be helpful. "Is there anything I can do for you?" Looking him straight in the eye, the major's question was terse. "We are trying to find Mr. Hunter."

The big American looked concerned. "Is he in trouble?" Ignoring the question, the policeman continued. "Do you know where he is?"

It had crossed Ali Essa's mind to take the American in for further questioning, but looking around the villa, he could see he wasn't short of money. The oil business paid Americans well and this man did not look like he could be part of a gang to raid the gold *souq*. More like the type to raid a curry house.

Careful not to alert him just in case, Ali Essa continued cautiously. "He's not in his villa."

Smiling, the big man replied lightheartedly. "No, probably still in the villa in Ajman. We went fishing yesterday. Probably still got a hangover!"

In the same vein, the policeman asked another question. "The Indian girl, she was with him?"

Leaning back in the comfortable lounge chair, Don relaxed and put his hands behind his head. "Prithi? Nice girl. Yes, I think she was there. Didn't see her. Probably in bed. We left early to go fishing and got back late. It was dark and I drove straight back here."

The major raised his eyebrows. Noticing, Don mumbled an apology. "Yes, I shouldn't have. Had too much to drink. Sorry about that."

A little impatient, Ali Essa forced the pace. "Is there a telephone there?"

Mildly surprised by the policeman's now brisk attitude, Don answered promptly, "Yes, of course."

In a formal tone the policeman went on. "Please ring and ask Mr. Hunter to come to the Police station to see me."

Don's large paw closed over the receiver. Picking it up, he dialed the number by heart. Letting it ring, he waited. When there was no answer, he rang again. Finally, he put it back on the hook. "Maybe he's on his way back here?"

Ali Essa wasn't convinced. Sharply, he asked Don the villa's location. Now worried, the big man got up and walked to the desk. "No problem. I'll draw you a map." Taking a piece of paper and a pen from the drawer, he laboriously started sketching the site. After some discussion, one of the policemen said he knew where it was.

Back in the police car, Ali Essa radioed through to the Ajman Police. One of their patrol cars met them at the border and they sped through the almost deserted small town streets to a road leading to the beach. Following the numbers, they stopped at the one given to them by the American. Ringing the bell on the gate in the high wall, they waited for several moments.

Impatiently, Ali Essa addressed the Ajman sergeant from the patrol car. "Your permission to break in?"

Holding his hands up, the policeman didn't hesitate. "Yes, *seedi*, no problem." With that, two of the Dubai policemen rattled the gate lock, and then with a kick from one of their boots, it sprang open. Wandering into the sparse garden, they looked around for any sign of life. There was none. Going around the back, they found Mike's big American four-wheel drive and a boat on a trailer. Entering the back door that was not locked, they searched around and found nothing.

Ali Essa looked perplexed. Ordering his men to keep searching, he went to the patrol car and radioed the Dubai station to send another car around again to check the villa in Dubai. Still puzzled, he was strolling around the back when he heard a shout from the work shed. Breaking into a jog, he entered the building and saw the five other policemen gathered around one spot. One of them had a very small, shiny lump in his hand. Seeing it, Ali Essa felt the hairs on the back of his arm rise.

Gold! It was a little nugget of gold! "Where was it?"

One of the policemen replied instantly, "There."

Pointing to just behind the leg of a workbench, the policeman stepped forward. Pushing him away, Ali Essa bent down. Barely visible in the dust were several more drops of gold—nowhere near what had been taken in the raid, but enough for him to deduce that the stolen jewellery had been there. "Search the house, the four-wheel drive, the boat, everywhere! And this time, carefully!"

At his command, the policemen scurried to their task. His instinct had been right. It was the ex-soldier, the Englishman with a sense of adventure and a chip on his shoulder. No further gold was found in the work shed. Moving back into the house, they searched it thoroughly for more evidence. Pushing open the bedroom, one of the policemen noticed a small, dark puddle where the door had been. Bending over, he put his finger in it. Blood! The rest of the policemen came running at his shout. Searching around the room, they found more traces of blood.

*Why the blood?* thought Ali Essa. Reading the look on his face, the sergeant spoke up. "Perhaps they fought with each other."

That could be the answer. The blood was fresh and maybe somewhere in the yard was a body. But where was the gold? Where was Hunter? "Ask around! Ask if anybody has seen somebody, a vehicle, anything, leave this house!"

Spreading out, the police went from villa to villa. Shortly after, one of them returned leading a shaking Pakistani with him. "He is a watchman. He says he saw an old jeep drive down the road this morning."

Impatiently, the major again questioned the policeman. "Did it come out of here?" Translating the question into Urdu, the policeman shook the witness to speed up the answer. "Yes. He says yes. Two Indians in the jeep. One man driving, one woman with him.

Really excited now, Ali Essa's voice was gruff. "Is he sure? Is he sure?"

There was another rapid-fire conversation in Urdu. "Yes, *seedi*, he is sure. One Indian man and one Indian woman."

Striding towards the patrol car, the major barked back, "Get a description of the vehicle! Which way did it go?" Rapidly, the police extracted the information from the still trembling little Pakistani. What had happened? Where was Hunter? Why the blood? Whatever, they needed to stop that jeep! Jumping into the patrol cars, they sped off in the direction given to them by their sole witness.

Meanwhile, Ali Essa had the police put out a bulletin in both the Emirates on the wanted vehicle. Not long after, they received a report of a similar jeep stopping for petrol some fifteen kilometres down the road. Speeding up, they made for the service station.

In the patrol car, Major Ali Essa thought through the evidence to date. Obviously, the gold had been melted down, mainly to disguise its origins but also to make it more portable. Most likely it was now in the form of ingots and hidden somewhere in the old four-wheel drive. Less obvious was why two Indians were driving the vehicle. Where was Hunter? Could he have gone ahead to arrange the sale of the gold? Where to? Most probably India, where it would be more valuable. But then, why Hunter? Why not one of the Indians? That left the question of the blood. It could be that there was more than one involved in the raid and they had an argument. Whatever, the answer was surely with the occupants of the vehicle they were chasing.

Pulling into the service station, they quickly questioned the attendants. Yes, they had filled the tank of such a vehicle. It was an old Land rover and it only had two occupants, a tall Indian man and a pretty, young Indian girl. Fortunately, they had also noted the registration number. Immediately, another bulletin was issued to the road patrols. With luck, by evening they would have captured the fugitives. It not, surely the next day.

# Chapter Forty-One

# Doubts

Driving steadily along the road towards the mountains, Rajan and Prithi remained silent. For Rajan's part, his jaw hurt badly and he thought it was broken. His nose was broken but only painful to touch. Swollen almost twice its normal size, it had also blackened both his eyes. He didn't want to talk. For her part, Prithi was still in a state of shock after the brutal killing of Mike the night before. Approaching the Hajar Mountains, they stopped at a small roadside restaurant. Although it was Ramadan and meant to be closed during the day, a side door was open for those who were not fasting.

"You hungry?" Prithi shook her head. Although she wasn't hungry she went with him into the restaurant. She watched as he painfully tried to eat a light meal of lentils and roti. Having only a Coke, she sat in silence. Leaving the restaurant, they drove a little further then pulled off into a small, hidden, rocky *wadi* and parked in the shade of a thorn bush. With the heat of the afternoon sun shimmering around them, they slept in the seats of the vehicle.

Several hours later, with the sun sinking low and the skinks that were basking in its heat on the rocks disappearing, Rajan backed the four-wheel onto the main road. All was quiet with no traffic to be seen and Prithi still slept. As they cruised along the well-made road mountain road, Rajan's mind turned to the problems ahead.

With the money they had, finding a dhow owner to take them to India wouldn't be difficult. Given enough money, an owner wouldn't ask questions and the corrupt Customs officials in Bombay could be easily bribed. His biggest concern was going to be selling the stolen gold in India. Once the message got out (and surely it would) that there was a large quantity of illegal gold on the black market, every crook, petty or otherwise would be after them. It would be tricky trying to sell the gold while staying alive!

Suddenly a thought struck him: could he trust Prithi? She was his weakest link. Captured by crooks, she could give his secrets away. Maybe she'd meet up with someone more powerful than him. Glancing at her as she slept, he realized that she was a liability, and a serious one. To take her to Bombay with him would be extremely risky, yet to leave her here could be even more so. Her beauty was her biggest danger. There would be plenty of men like him who would risk all for her favors.

Driving through Hatta, Rajan checked Mike's map then turned off onto a minor road that would lead to a large *wadi* and pools of fresh cool water. There they would stay the night. On the way, coming across another small roadside restaurant, they stopped. By this time Prithi was well awake. Ordering several parcels of Indian food, they took them to the four-wheel drive and drove off down the stony road to Wadi Hatta.

Eventually they reached the top of a steep hill, and as they climbed over it, Rajan stopped the vehicle. Darkness had fallen. In front of them lay the huge, rocky bed of an ancient river. Over thousands of years it had become an almost dry stream, flowing only whenever there was a flashflood. Surrounding the valley were tall, dark-brown mountains tinged with purple. The whole valley was dimly lit by the moon, and the pools sparkled faintly in its light.

Guiding the vehicle carefully down the steep slope, Rajan turned off the track and bumped along a pebbly *wadi* bed. Bouncing up and down, the Land rover made slow progress and they eventually arrived at a site where the water still flowed in a crystal clear stream from pool to pool. Stopping on a flat rock by one of the pools, they got out and stood quietly in the still of the night. Apart from the stream of water whispering nearby, the only other sound was the occasional croaking of frogs in the reeds by the pools. Above them, the crescent moon surrounded by twinkling stars slipped towards the dark purple mountaintops. Rajan pulled a blanket from one of the suitcases in the back and laid it carefully on a patch of soft grass near the pool.

"Sit, Prithi. We'll stay here tonight." Going back to the vehicle, he took out the parcels of food and a bottle of whisky. He placed the parcels on the ground alongside the blanket and watched as Prithi opened them and then laid out the paper plates and napkins. Needing cups for the whisky, he returned to the vehicle and bought back two paper ones and a bottle of water. Quietly, they ate some of the chicken *biryani* and rice with their hands, occasionally taking pieces of roti and pickles. Rajan drank one paper cupful of whisky then handed another to Prithi. She sipped it slowly at first then finished it in a quick gulp. Offering the empty cup to Rajan, she waited till he filled it again. In the dark night, the whites of her almond shaped eyes shone bright and shiny. "Soon we will be rich, Prithi. Rich and in India." Prithi's reply was a slight smile.

Finally she stood. "I'm going to wash in the pool." Dropping her jeans, she stood under the pale moonlight in just panties and T-shirt, her long legs smooth and dark. When she moved to the water's edge, Rajan watched as she bent and splashed the water around her face. As she did, the T-shirt became wet and clinging, outlining the shape of her firm breasts. "Maybe I'm wrong," muttered Rajan to himself. Moments later, he, too, dropped his jeans and stood in the cool water carefully washing his swollen face.

Back on the blanket, they drank another whisky in the moonlight. Rajan moved closer and took her in his arms. Gently lying her on her back, he removed her T-shirt and panties. She didn't object. Tentatively but passionately he kissed her then removed the remainder of his clothes. Under the fading moonlight, he entered her and they made love beneath the stars.

Afterwards, Rajan rolled on his back and gazed at the stars. Soon Prithi was asleep, naked, her arms and legs spread out on the blanket. Carefully, Rajan raised himself and, still naked, moved quietly to the four-wheel drive. Pulling the knife from the bag, he returned cautiously to Prithi's side. Then, in one swift movement, he raised the knife, placed his hand over the naked girl's mouth and at the same time plunged the knife into her bare chest straight through her heart. For an instant Prithi's body bucked while her hands and feet twitched helplessly. In a moment she was dead.

Rajan removed his hand from her mouth and squatted back on his haunches. Looking at her face, he saw her staring eyes with tears that trickled down each side of her face. He sat down and stared at her for a while. Naked in the moonlight, she lay perfectly still with the hilt of the knife sticking out from between her breasts.

Glancing around, Rajan stood up. Not a sound could be heard; even the frogs were silent. He bent over, removed the knife, walked to the pool and washed it clean of blood. Placing it back in the vehicle, he went back to Prithi's lifeless body. Crouching, he pulled the blanket over her, then, struggling, lifted her into his arms. Staggering bare-foot over the rocks and cursing as he stubbed his toes, he eventually found a crevice in the stony surface. Below the cracks were caves and hollows carved many thousands of years ago by the flowing waters that had now dried and disappeared with time.

He was breathing heavily from exhaustion as he eased the burden of Prithi's body out of the blanket into the crevice where it slipped down into the depths without a sound. Placing a rock into the blanket, he dropped that into the same crack where it, too, vanished. Both body and blanket would be there for years, perhaps decades, before they were found, providing nature's scavengers had not completely removed the remains.

Back at the vehicle, he squatted, still naked, in the pool and washed himself free of bloodstains. Pulling his jeans back on, he took another blanket from the back, made a pillow of a suitcase and clothes then lay back, closing his eyes. After his nerves had settled some, he sat up, reached for the whisky bottle and gulped down the remaining contents. Burning, it swept down into his stomach and it was not long before he felt fully relaxed. Even so, he could not sleep. Getting up, he found the other bottle. Half an hour later, he'd drunk about half its contents as well. The moon by this time had completely disappeared, and in the pitch dark, he fell into a drunken sleep, snoring loudly.

Early in the morning, before the light, he was awakened by the sound of goats' bells in the distance. Instinctively, he looked around for Prithi then instantly remembered what had happened. With an aching head, he climbed into the vehicle, found a bottle of water and thirstily gulped down its contents. Before the sun rose, he cleared up the campsite, carefully stowed Prithi's belongings under the back seat and then moved off.

Steadily he drove back up the *wadi* and headed for the Hatta road. Crossing it, he followed the signs to Huwaylat, the route shown on the map that would take him across the mountains down to Khor Khalba. By midday, he should be in the little port negotiating a charter to Bombay for himself and the Land rover. He thought of Prithi but had no regrets. There would be plenty of Prithis in Bombay when he had sold the gold.

# Chapter Forty-Two

# Ali Essa's Search Ends

Before sunrise, Ali Essa, after praying, had broken his fast with dates, milk, honey and bread. Staying the night at the police barracks in Hatta, he'd had an uncomfortable night's sleep in a strange bed. The night before, he'd been on the telephone to the Ajman Police Headquarters. They had sent another team around to the house in the afternoon. After a long and thorough search, they'd found the body of a European male buried in a shallow grave covered with sheets of roofing iron.

It didn't take Ali Essa long to guess it was Hunter. Obviously, it was only the Indian pair he was chasing now. Smiling grimly to himself, he thought how the British still underestimated the Indian treachery. Hunter had found out the hard way. Somewhere out there in the mountains were the Indian woman and her boyfriend with the cargo of gold.

After hearing the news about Hunter, he'd sent a team from the Dubai headquarters to question the employees of Dubai Petroleum Company. The Indian girl had been friendly with a good-looking, young Indian man, a technician working for a contractor that was installing the communications equipment. He, too, was missing from his work. To Ali Essa, it was now clear. The two had plotted to take the stolen gold from Hunter and were headed for India, where there would be a welcome black market. He had no pity for Hunter, just a sense of dissatisfaction that he'd not been able to take him alive.

Sitting in the office, he was waiting to hear the dull *whop-whop* of the police helicopter he'd asked to be sent from Dubai to help the search. Somehow or other yesterday, the pair he was chasing had given them the slip, probably pulling off into one of the numerous *wadis* that lined the road through the mountains.

While he waited, he leaned back and read through the faxed copy of Hunter's file that had been transmitted to Hatta during the night. Not that he expected to find anything new, but you never knew. Hearing the sound of the helicopter, he picked up his cap and headed outside. Watching it land, he waited until its rotor blades slowed, then, ducking his head, ran to the cockpit. Gingerly, he climbed into the back, shaking hands with the pilot and the co-pilot as he sat. Also in the back was another policeman from Dubai.

Clipping on his safety belt, he nodded to the pilot. The chopper rose gently from the square of bitumen, then, with its nose down, moved forward, gathered speed then rose higher and banked to the right. Ali Essa let out an involuntary groan. Flying by helicopter was not his favorite form of transport. Reaching cruising height, the pilot headed for the large Wadi Hatta.

Looking down, Ali Essa could see the misty purple mountains of the majestic Hajars. Stony, void of almost any greenery, they looked like the surface of the moon. In the distance were the sparkling blue waters of the Arabian Sea. He didn't hold out much hope of finding the fugitives. There were too many ways out. They could have even gone down the large *wadi* into Oman. If they had, it would be difficult. Despite the fact that relationships with the neighboring country had improved, it would not be easy to get their co-operation. Then there was the possibility that they could have doubled back through Burami and Al Ain. Maybe the service station attendants were wrong and they never came this way.

Banking again, the copter flew low over the Oman-U.A.E. border post. Lines of trucks and cars stood in the early morning light waiting for their entry visas. Ali Essa shook his head. It was like searching for a needle in a haystack.

Driving steadily down the narrow road to the village of Huwaylat, Rajan came across another of the small roadside restaurants that seemed to be open, despite it being Ramadan. Braking to a halt, he parked between two light pickup trucks whose trays were piled high with cases covered by old tarpaulins. Reaching into Prithi's bag, he pulled out her passport and methodically shredded it into tiny pieces. These, along with most of her personal belongings from her handbag, he put in the plastic bag that had previously held the whisky bottles.

Furtively he looked around, then, leaving the Land rover; he scuttled over to a nearby rubbish bin and dropped the bag inside. Next he got hold of her two suitcases and again, looking carefully around, stuffed them under the tarpaulin of one of the nearby trucks. Satisfied he'd gotten rid of all evidence of Prithi, he entered the restaurant by a side door.

Half-full of Indian drivers and laborers, it was dark and smelled strongly of food odors. Sitting at the only empty table, he ordered a plate of spicy beans and local bread. The dish came with a salad sprinkled with hot, green chilies. When the waiter put the plate down, Rajan asked for headache tablets, water and strong black coffee. Rolling a couple of chilies in the bread, he quickly ate them. When the waiter returned with the tablets, water and coffee, he swilled them down then ate a portion of his meal.

Back into the four-wheel drive, he drove through the almost deserted village and out onto the mountain road. Already his remedy for the headache was working and he felt much better, although his jaw still pained him. Following the high-voltage transmission lines suspended on spindle towers, he ground his way up the mountain trail, through a pass and over the top. Changing gear, he headed downward toward the coast.

Abdul Karim and Obaid bin Rashid stood beside their little Suzuki four-wheel drive patrol car. Colored green, it had "Police" in Arabic and English painted in white on its sides and a flashing red light on its roof. Although it was only nine o'clock in the morning, they were already feeling the pangs of their fasting. Idly chatting, Abdul Karim leaned on his service rifle while Obaid bin Rashid looked lazily up the mountain road. Upon seeing the cloud of dust rise up over the mountain pass, Obaid bin Rashid wandered out into the middle of the road. It was unlikely that any bandits would come this way, despite the bulletin they'd received on the radio earlier that morning. This was probably just another local goat herder. As the vehicle approached, he began to wave his arms for it to stop.

Upon seeing the patrol wagon, Rajan panicked. Pressing his foot hard on the accelerator, he drove straight at the policeman in the middle of the road. Although the policeman tried to jump out of the way of the speeding vehicle, the fender clipped him, sending him spinning in the air. Landing, he struck his head on a rock and his neck was broken, killing him instantly. Shocked, the other policeman raised his rifle, snapped off the safety catch and fired a shot. It hit the cab of Rajan's vehicle, went in one side and harmlessly out the other. The next shot missed completely. Speeding up, the vehicle rounded a bend and was almost out of sight when Abdul Karim fired off his third shot. This time luck was with him. Hitting the rear wheel, it burst the tire.

Rajan felt the back of the vehicle suddenly sway. Panicking further, he stomped on the brake and turned the steering wheel. It only made a bad situation worse. Sliding sideways, the four-wheel drive hit the rocks on the edge of the road, teetered for a minute, then rolled over onto the steep, rocky slope.

Yelling in fear, Rajan clung to the steering wheel as the vehicle completed its first roll. Picking up momentum, it started its second. Unable to cling on any longer, Rajan was flung out the door that had sprung open. Landing on the rocks, three of his ribs were instantly broken, along with both of his legs. Not that it mattered. With a scream, he instinctively held up his arms to save himself from the tumbling mass of metal. It was in vain. His scream was stifled as the heavy chassis of the vehicle crushed his skull then continued to roll down the slope until it stopped at the bottom in a cloud of dust.

Stunned, Abdul Karim remained motionless for a moment then ran to where the inert body of his companion lay. Kneeling down, tears began to stream down his cheeks as he saw the thin trickle of blood coming from the lifeless lips. Covering the staring eyes, he jumped to his feet and ran to the patrol wagon. "Help! Help! Send an ambulance! Help!"

Upon hearing the plea on the radio, the pilot of the helicopter came on the air, located where the patrol wagon was and headed quickly to the site. Landing on the road in a cloud of dust, Ali Essa didn't wait for the rotor blades to slow. Leaping out, he ran down the road, stopped briefly at the dead body then followed the wild instructions of the other policeman to where the crashed vehicle lay. His heart leaped. The smoking wreck at the bottom of the slope was a Land rover.

He tugged his police revolver from its holster and made his way cautiously towards the body of Rajan. As he neared it, he lowered the weapon to his side. The grey, bloody mess oozing from the man's skull clearly showed it wasn't necessary.

Picking his way through the scattered luggage and debris, he searched for the gold. It was nowhere to be seen. The policeman from the helicopter joined him. "Look for gold! Look for gold!" Bewildered by Ali Essa's sharp orders, the policeman started scratching through the crushed cab of the four-wheel drive vehicle. Both of them searched frantically but could not find a trace.

Ali Essa couldn't believe it was all for nothing. Where was the woman? There was no sign of the young Indian woman. Maybe she'd escaped with someone else and the gold. If it hadn't been for Ramadan, Ali Essa would have used his strongest curse.

Giving up the search, he was about to climb the rocky slope when the sunlight finally filtered down into the valley. For a final time, he turned and glanced back. A pale yellow gleam caught his eye. Running back, he went to the front bumper of the mangled wreck. A small part of the metal was peeled back. After blowing hard on it then dusting it with his hand, he reeled back in shocked delight. "The gold! The gold!" He'd finally found Hunter's gold.